SECRET AGENT MOM

SECRET AGENT MOM

CASE FILES OF AN URBAN WITCH™ BOOK ONE

MARTHA CARR

MICHAEL ANDERLE

DISRUPTIVE IMAGINATION

SECRET AGENT MOM TEAM

Beta Team
Kelly O'Donnell, John Ashmore

Thanks to the JIT Readers

Dorothy Lloyd
Jackey Hankard-Brodie
Dave Hicks
Angel LaVey
Wendy L Bonell
Diane L. Smith
Deb Mader

If I've missed anyone, please let me know!

Editor
Skyhunter Editing Team

DEDICATIONS

To Family, Friends and
Those Who Love
To Read.
May We All Enjoy Grace
To Live The Life We Are
Called.

— *Michael*

CHAPTER ONE

A thirty-six-inch television hurtled across the pawnshop, trailing sparks and the glitter of hastily cast magic. Lucy Heron ducked just in time to save her head, and the television crashed into the wall behind her. She often told her kids that too much TV would be bad for them, but she'd never thought this could be why.

"You won't get away with this, Haugensen," Lucy called in her northern English accent, clutching her desert willow wand as she peered across the cluttered shop. "Even if you win this one, more Silver Griffins will come for you."

A gnome skulked behind the counter. The diminutive figure carried a wand, its tip glowing with power. "What kind of a cheap accent is that? You sound like you're not sure if you're from Scotland or not."

Lucy scowled and sent sparks over the gnome's head with her wand for good measure. "Careful, you tosser. Never underestimate a tyke from Yorkshire."

The gnome returned the volley with a few sparks of his

own. "Ha!" he snorted, smiling as ash danced across Lucy's shoulder.

She quickly brushed it off, smiling. A good battle always lifted her mood. "Pretty good wand skills. Your mom was a witch, wasn't she?" yelled Lucy. "You're a rare bird."

Haugensen growled and tried to adjust the back of his pants, but without success. He wore battered old khakis that rode a little too low to hide his ass from the world and a Hawaiian shirt as garishly colorful as an explosion in a paint factory. Right now, he also wore an expression of frustrated fury. His whole face seemed to fold in on itself as he waved his wand wildly around, levitating loose pieces of stock at Lucy.

"Get the hell out of my shop!" he shouted. "You have no right to be here."

"I have a sworn duty to be here," Lucy said. "Someone has to stop you selling dangerous artifacts. Did you seriously think the Silver Griffins would ignore what you've been doing?"

For a part-gnome, part-wizard who made his living altering and selling illegal artifacts, Reidar Haugensen wasn't much of a magical. His locking spell on the door had barely worked, his levitations were clumsy, and it was taking him forever to muster the magic for his next spell. Still, if Lucy had learned anything in a decade of fighting magical crimes, it was that lousy magicals could still be dangerous opponents. That was the problem with magic: it became more deadly when it got out of hand. That was why the world needed the Silver Griffins.

"You can't have it!" Haugensen screamed, his voice high

with fear. "I paid good money for it, and I have a buyer who's doing the same. You have no right to interfere with the free market."

"I do when it's an illegal market." Lucy ducked again as a PlayStation shot through the air, missing her by several feet. "It doesn't get more illegal than this."

On a counter in the middle of the room sat the object she'd come to retrieve, an old mortar and pestle carved from green-veined stone with remnants of a sandy mixture in the bottom. It looked ordinary, but Lucy knew better than to trust appearances. The most powerful magic could be hidden in a rock or a stick.

"You have magic of your own already." Lucy crept along behind a display case full of game consoles. Her Silver Griffin amulet, showing two interlocking circles and her field agent number 485, caught the light as it hung from a chain around her neck. "You don't need an artifact that can give you an hour of magic. It's not worth risking time in Trevilsom Prison for. Hand it over, and we can pretend this never happened."

As importantly, they could finish before a passerby called the police. Lucy had a lot of love for the mundane authorities, who kept her family safe from ordinary threats like fire and theft, but the last thing she needed was for the thin blue line to get themselves turned into toads.

Haugensen flicked his wand and pressure grew in the air around Lucy. She snapped off a diversionary spell, and the gnome's magic closed in on a cabinet instead. There was a crash as the cabinet shattered in the grip of an invisible fist and showered her in shards of glass. Her amulet flashed, and a protective field shone briefly around her,

3

sheltering her skin from them. However, the charm's power was too weak to protect her clothes as well, and the fragments sliced her favorite Green Lantern t-shirt to ribbons all down one side.

"You'll pay for that," she shouted indignantly. "Literally. This cost me forty quid."

"You paid for it with squids?"

"Quid! Forty quid! English pounds! Not everything in the world comes priced in dollars."

While Lucy was distracted, Haugensen crept toward the middle of the room. He wrapped an arm around the mortar and hugged it against his chest as he backed away.

Looking up from her ruined shirt, Lucy raised her wand. Now that he wasn't hiding behind the counter, she had a perfect shot at him. Her hand was steady as she aimed.

"Stop right there."

Haugensen took a step back.

"Form to contain in bonds of chain," Lucy chanted.

Magic shot from the tip of her wand, forming steel chains as it hurtled across the pawnshop. A loose end knocked over a stand of guitars, which hit the ground with a chorus of twangs and crashes before wrapping around Haugensen. They pinned his arms to his sides, but the gnome's wand hand was still free, and he waved it as he chanted.

"Hammer blows and ancient tools, save me from these bonds of fools."

A hammer and chisel floated over from a tool rack at the side of the room and started battering at the chains. Sparks flew as metal collided.

"Seriously?" Lucy strode across the room, stepping over the broken glass and fallen guitars. She grabbed hold of the mortar and pestle, ready to wrench them from Haugensen's grip.

As she touched the mortar, a spark fell from the chains into the sandy mixture inside. Flames flashed, and she staggered back coughing as yellow smoke filled the air.

Suddenly, the whole world changed. Lucy found herself standing at the secret underground railway station for LA's Silver Griffins HQ. She faced Normandy, the station keeper gnome, who held a box of homemade cupcakes, a box that she'd left in the back of her car when she came into the pawnshop. In her hand was the mortar and pestle, cold and heavy inside a purple plastic bag, ready to be dropped off at headquarters. The station seemed completely real, every tile on the wall in place, the air full of steam. Down the platform from her, an unfamiliar wizard guarded a male Light Elf with bound hands.

"...which is really weird," she heard herself say, though she didn't exactly know why, "because now this whole moment feels like déjà vu."

She glanced at the clock on the wall and saw that an hour had passed since she confronted Haugensen in the pawnshop. It was worrying, but she didn't panic. Maybe she'd lost some memories, or perhaps something else was going on here.

Then the world shifted again, and she was back in the shop, waving away the cloud of fumes.

Haugensen lurched back, still clutching the mortar and pestle, coughing and blinking as he tried to clear the smoke from his eyes. His wand waved, directing the hammer and chisel against his chains. One of the links broke with a *crack*, and the steel lengths clattered to the floor.

Lucy pointed her wand and shot another spell. This time, the magic grabbed the back of Haugensen's oversized shirt and yanked it over his head, covering his face.

"Hey!" Haugensen yelled. "That's not fair. You can't use a man's shirt against him."

As he turned his hand to tug at the garment, the magic holding the hammer and chisel fell, and the tools dropped to the floor. Lucy cast another incantation, this time binding Haugensen's legs. He lost his balance, wobbled for a moment, then crashed down in an undignified heap.

Lucy pried the mortar and pestle from the gnome's hand. Her skin tingled from its barely contained power, and she remembered that flash-forward in time, standing on the station on her way to deliver this to the authorities. It looked like the mortar had predicted the future, and that foreseeing was about to come true.

"Do you know how dangerous this is?" She held it up to take a closer look. The green seams in the rock glowed. "To give anyone magic, even for an hour, without the training or experience to know how to handle it? I spent years training as a witch. You have generations of gnomish wisdom behind you, but if you give this to some kid fresh out of school, who knows who they might hurt?"

"Enough with the after-school special." Haugensen wriggled around onto his knees and held his hands out, pleading. "Please. I've made some promises to some very determined people. If I don't deliver that to them, I might as well break my legs right now."

"It's all right, Reidar. You'll be out of their reach for the next three to five years, depending on good behavior."

"I can't go to Trevilsom. I'm too pretty. And who will look after my children?"

"You don't have kids."

"My pets, then."

"You don't even have rats here."

"My plants! My poor plants!"

Lucy peered into a corner of the room, where a couple of unwatered ferns were dying in their pots.

"Honestly, I think your plants might be better off without you." She turned back to him. "The citizens of LA certainly will be."

"Fine," he agreed with an exaggerated sigh. "I'll come quietly. Just one more thing before we go."

"What's that?"

A moment too late, she noticed his wand glowing. It had been disguised as a talisman hanging from a leather bracelet. "Don't feel bad." He sneered. "That always gets even the best agents." There was a flash of light, and she staggered back, desperately blinking as her world turned black. Something tugged at the mortar, but she clung tight. She couldn't let this thing get out into the wild. Then the tugging stopped, and there was a rush of footsteps.

"Hold it, Haugensen," another voice said.

Eyes watering, Lucy blinked away the aftermath of the flash. As her vision returned, she saw the gnome standing in the doorway of his shop, his hands in the air. Another man stood in his way, wand inches from Haugensen's face. He was dressed in camouflage pants and a tight black t-shirt and wore wraparound shades beneath his short, dark hair.

"Ringo Fuller," Lucy said. "What brings you here?"

"Same as you, I expect, Agent 485," Fuller said. "This scumbag and his latest acquisition."

"You do know you can use my name, right? I don't go around calling you 'level three bounty hunter.'"

"Funny. Ha. Ha." Fuller took off his shades and peered into the shop, his gaze settling on the mortar. "Seems you beat me to it."

"As usual." Lucy smiled sweetly. "There was that consignment of bad wands last month, the Light Elf forger trying to make his way to Mexico, that amulet that went missing from the museum..."

"You wouldn't have found that last one without me."

"You didn't find it at all."

Fuller glared at her, then prodded Haugensen with his wand.

"This guy would have been long gone if I hadn't turned up."

"He would have come back if only to clear out the safe, and I would have been waiting."

"Maybe, maybe not. Right now, I caught him, and that makes the bounty mine." Fuller held out a hand. "Gimme the mortar."

Lucy laughed. "Nice try, sunshine, but I got the artifact without your help, and I'm taking it straight to HQ. In fact..." She looked at the shelf of antique clocks at one side of the room. "...I know for certain that I'll be there in fifty minutes." She put on her most dramatic voice. "I've had a vision!"

Fuller snorted and shook his head. "Fine, you keep the artifact, but I'm taking this guy to Trevilsom. He's earned a big enough bounty to pay my rent for months."

"As you wish. As long as he's off the streets, that's all that matters."

"Hey!" Haugensen glared at her. "You said you'd let me go if you got the artifact."

"I said I'd let you go if you handed it over." She held up the mortar and pestle. "Too late for that now."

Fuller took the wand from Haugensen's hand, then pulled out a thick plastic tie and bound his wrists.

"Come on, short stuff. We have a portal to catch."

He led Haugensen into the back of a black van with an eagle painted on the side. By comparison, Lucy's electric Rivian SUV looked deeply mundane.

"See you around, 485," Fuller called before he drove away.

"See you soon, Level Three."

CHAPTER TWO

Lucy closed the door on the clutter of the pawnshop and got in her SUV. The shop would need to be tidied up and emptied of any magical artifacts before Haugensen's lease ran out, to ensure that non-magicals didn't end up walking away with a bag of infinite oceans or some type of hypnotic gem. That mess was for someone else to deal with. She had a more urgent task: getting the mortar locked up safely.

She took a purple zip-lock bag out of the glove box, placed the mortar and pestle inside, and sealed it shut. Runes flared for a moment, silver symbols hanging in the air, before fading from view. That should keep the artifact from hurling her forward through time again or causing any other trouble before she got it to headquarters.

The Rivian started smoothly and headed out quietly into the traffic along Sixth Street. Lucy made a mental note to thank Charlie again for his choice of cars. Her husband's taste for electric cars wasn't only good for the world, it made her journeys more pleasant, and she didn't ever want him to think that she took him for granted.

A quick drive took her to a Starbucks on West Third Street. She parked the Rivian, grabbed the box of home-made cupcakes off the back seat, and picked up the mortar and pestle before heading into the coffee shop.

The place was bustling with early afternoon customers, some grabbing a coffee to go, others sitting at the tables with their laptops or notebooks out, making the most of a workspace away from home. Lucy hurried past them to the back wall near the bathrooms and paused for a moment to enjoy the lovely chocolate smell that hung in the air, tied to the magic that would hide what she was about to do. She tapped the wall with her wand. It shimmered, and she stepped through to the other side.

As the wall reformed behind her, Lucy hurried down the open metal stairs toward the platforms below. The rumble of subway trains rose to meet her, and the chatter of magicals waiting on the landings. Signs above the stairs pointed in a dozen different directions, from green local signs to Burbank and Anaheim through to red long-distance ones indicating Washington DC, Paris, and Singapore.

Halfway down the stairs, a turnstile closed off a narrower passageway to the left. Lucy tapped her wand against a sensor pad on the top.

"Agent 485 reporting with a retrieval. Open sesame." It didn't open, and she sighed. "Such a wasted opportunity. What I meant was, Agent 485 reporting with a retrieval. Doorways open and gates part, let law's agents to its heart."

The turnstile *clicked,* and Lucy walked through into a

tunnel barely wide enough for two people to pass each other. Her footsteps echoed as she set off along the tunnel, then down a winding spiral staircase at the end.

The stairs ended at the entrance to a small platform sitting next to a single track. A shiny blue train car waited on the rails, its bodywork polished and gleaming.

Lucy stepped onto the platform and held out her wand. A sensor in the ceiling above her *whirred* as magic-mechanical sensors turned their attention on her.

"Agent 485," she called to the whitewashed walls. "I have a drop-off."

"Welcome, Agent Lucy Heron," said a smooth baritone voice. "Please take a seat. Your train will depart shortly."

The door slid silently open, and Lucy walked on board. The only seats were two leather benches facing each other across the car. One was occupied, so Lucy took the other one, setting down her box of cupcakes and the purple bag holding the artifact on either side of her.

Two people sat on the opposite seat. They seemed strangely familiar although she had never seen either of them in her life. One was a wizard with blond hair and a neatly trimmed beard. He wore a charcoal suit with a narrow tie and trainers, what Americans called sneakers, in matching bright red. He was tapping a pine wand against his thigh and watching the other guy in his peripheral vision.

The other traveler was a Light Elf, his silver hair tied back in a ponytail beneath a purple bandanna that hid the tips of his ears. Despite the magical cords binding his wrists, he had a smug, leering smile, the sort of look that said he was used to owning everyone and everything around him. A list of charges hung in front of him, the black letters hovering in the air.

"Archibald," the charge sheet announced. "Current status: Arrested pending processing. Charges: Theft; Misuse of magic. Further notes: The suspect used magic to steal from mundane neighborhoods, without regard to the risk of exposure or the impact on his victims…"

The details went on, but Lucy had dealt with enough magicals like Archibald to get the idea.

"Well, hello, my lady," he said. "What a delight to see such a fair vision on this most miserable day."

"Seriously?" Lucy snorted. "Save your nonsense for the Renaissance Faire. I come from the land of posh accents. It takes more than a 'my lady' and a couple of 'fa la las' to impress me."

"Ah, an Englishwoman. You came out here for the excitement of the new world, perhaps? Let me tell you. I can give you a whole world's worth of excitement."

Lucy yawned and leaned back. "Your lines are older than this country, and even that's not very impressive. Now shut your gob and leave me in peace."

Archibald narrowed his eyes, but he was all out of witty comebacks. He tried to raise his middle finger, but his magical bonds wouldn't allow it, and his captor smiled wryly at the elf's grunt of exertion.

"Now departing," said the platform announcer's rich voice. The train's doors closed, there was a puff of steam outside the window, and they shot off along the tracks in a sudden burst of speed. Lucy instinctively placed her hands on the cake box and the magical bag, but neither moved despite the acceleration. The car's movement was smooth and even, never tilting, tipping, or juddering, a hundred times more comfortable than riding the tube back in London.

They pulled into another station a few minutes later, one that was kept secret even from most magicals. The train stopped as abruptly as it had started, and the doors opened.

"After you." The wizard gestured at the door.

"Thanks." Lucy picked up her bag and box and stepped out onto the platform. Steam billowed from the train's front, filling the air with a pale haze that matched the old-fashioned station. There were wooden waiting benches, a big round analog clock hanging from the ceiling, and a mosaic of blue and silver tiles decorating one wall. The place was deserted except for Lucy and the station keeper. It always seemed familiar after many trips here, but that feeling was particularly intense today as if every last detail from the swirls of steam to the papers on the notice board was exactly like it had been once before.

The wizard got off the train behind her, pushing Archibald ahead of him. The elf dragged his feet as if scuffing his shoes would somehow put off what was coming for him.

Lucy walked over to the station keeper's office, a small wooden booth projecting from the wall between the platform's exit tunnels. The keeper, a gnome in a navy blue uniform with gleaming brass buttons, pulled up the wooden-framed window that formed the front shutter of the booth.

"Afternoon, Normandy," Lucy said.

"Good afternoon, Agent Heron." The gnome touched

two fingers to the brim of his cap. "How are you today?"

Lucy was always impressed by the pride that Normandy brought to his job of taking care of the station. He had explained to her once that this work for the Silver Griffins was an honored position, like that of the gnomes who cared for the libraries of dangerous magic back on Oriceran. That made both his work and his uniform a sign of great prestige. Still, having met gnomes like Haugensen, she couldn't imagine that they all took their work as seriously as Normandy.

"I'm doing well, thanks," she said. "Although I still reckon they should put a lift in here."

"A lift?"

Lucy laughed. "An elevator. Guess I still haven't gone fully native, huh?"

"Nor I." Normandy wiggled his fingers and magic sparkled around the tips. "As my grandfather says, however far you travel, one foot is always planted back home."

"He sounds like a wise man, your grandfather."

"For the most part, yes, though he does like a good fart joke." Normandy chuckled. "Speaking of the young at heart, how are Charlie and the kids?"

"Lively as ever. Eddie helped me make these for you."

She put the box of cupcakes down on the counter and Normandy opened the lid.

"Mm, those smell good."

"Chocolate ganache filling and a buttercream icing on top."

"You're too kind, always bringing these treats for a simple gnome."

"You earn them, keeping this place so nice. Besides, I

love baking, and so does Eddie."

"So I see." Normandy held up a cupcake with the unmistakably clumsy icing of a three-year-old. "I shall particularly relish this one. Now tell me, what brings you here today?"

Lucy held up the mortar and pestle in their purple plastic bag.

"Retrieval mission. There was a prisoner too, but I let a bounty hunter take him. He'll end in the nick either way, so it's all good."

"What were you retrieving? Pardon my curiosity, but I grew up around library gnomes, and old habits die hard."

"It's meant to provide non-magicals with power for an hour at a time." Lucy shook her head. "I can't imagine what irresponsible sod came up with that idea. I think it must have some other effects too because there was dust inside when I first grabbed it, and that dust caught on fire in the fight. The smoke gave me a vision of coming here, which is really weird, because now this whole moment feels like déjà vu."

She glanced at the wall clock and saw that an hour had passed since she confronted Haugensen in the pawnshop, as her vision had predicted.

On the wall next to Normandy's office was a row of brass mailboxes, each one neatly numbered above the keyhole in its center. The wizard from the train, still leading the disgruntled Archibald, walked up and scanned the numbers on the mailbox doors.

"Good morning, sir," Normandy said to him. "How are you today?"

"Mighty fine, thank you," the wizard said. "And

yourself?"

"Oh, getting by. It's a quiet day today, so I might do some polishing later."

"Don't worry. I ain't gonna leave my messy paw prints all over your shiny mailboxes."

"I didn't mean to say—"

"I'm only joshing with you." The wizard winked. "I know full well how much effort you put in here, Normandy, and it's mighty good of you."

Using one long finger, he scrolled down the charge sheet hanging in the air next to Archibald, then drew a slender brass key from his pocket and turned back to the boxes.

"Whoa, whoa, whoa!" Archibald held up his bound hands. "There's no need to do that."

The wizard unlocked one of the boxes, swung the door open on well-oiled hinges, and raised his wand.

"Come on, man! Let me go. I've learned my lesson."

"Bye, Archy. Good luck with the trial."

"No, seriously, I know things, I can—"

"When law takes hold, and conscience fails, let elder winds take you to jail."

With a wave of the wizard's wand, Archibald burst into a cloud of gold dust that swirled through the air and vanished into the mailbox, as though being sucked up by an eldritch vacuum cleaner. The door slammed shut, and the wizard locked it before handing the key to Normandy.

"Thank you, sir." Normandy turned his attention back to Lucy. "Do you know which tube you need?"

"Number twenty-seven."

"Well then, feel free..." Normandy gestured down a

dark corridor to his left. "They're all in order again—janitorial cleared out the gremlins last week."

Lucy walked down the short corridor to a large wall covered in large, clear vacuum tubes. She found number twenty-seven—she had been given the number at the start of her assignment—and found a cylinder in a matching size on the rack to one side. The mortar and pestle, still wrapped in their spell-proof bag, fitted snugly inside. Once it was all closed up, Lucy inserted the cylinder into the bottom of tube twenty-seven. There was a sound like a kid slurping up the last of a milkshake through their straw, then the cylinder shot up the tube and away.

"Mission complete." Lucy smiled to herself, brushed off her hands, and headed back to the platform. The little blue train carriage was still waiting, steam trickling from the engine at the front. She stepped inside and sat where she had been a few minutes before. The blond wizard was also back in his seat, his legs stretched out in front of him, showing off the bright red trainers that seemed so out of place with his suit.

"Are you traveling far?" she asked with a smile.

"Thought I might ride the rails out east, see the wild frontier. I hear there's a gold spike somewhere on this here railroad. And you?"

"Oh, probably uptown for some shopping, catch a show, enjoy the sights of LA." She shrugged. "Or maybe I'll get off at the one stop this goes to and pick up my SUV from Starbucks."

"It's a wild and cray life in the Silver Griffins." He leaned forward and held out his hand. "I'm Ellis, Agent 399."

"Lucy Heron, 485." She shook. His handshake was firm, but not in the overly forceful way of salesmen or business executives trying to prove their fake friendliness credentials. "Is Ellis your first name or last?"

"Both."

The doors shut, there was a burst of steam, and they whizzed out of the station, down the darkened tunnels of the underground network.

"Seriously?" Lucy raised an eyebrow. "Your name is Ellis?"

"What can I say? My pa had a strange sense of humor, and my ma was too whacked out from giving birth to stop him from having his way. Some folks might have thrown away a name like that first chance they got, but me, I leaned into it. Reckon it makes me stand out."

Lucy laughed and pointed at his shoes. "You certainly don't blend in."

"Well, thank you kindly."

She looked him over with the evaluating gaze that came from years of detective work. He was in his early to mid-thirties, like her, and seemed well-kept as well as amusing. Perhaps she could find a chance to introduce him to her friend Sarah, who had a thing for quirky blonds.

"I haven't seen you around LA before," she said. "Did you just arrive in town, or have I got badly lost again?"

"I'm what you might call a traveling agent, mostly dealing in cross-border chases."

"Like a US Marshal?"

"Sure, except without the cowboy hat."

"I'm not sure they make those in red."

"Shame. I'd really stand out then."

The train suddenly stopped, and the voice of the station announcer rolled through the carriage.

"We apologize for the delay, but there are reports of gremlins on the track at your destination. Please remain seated. We will be moving again shortly."

Lucy pulled out her phone and checked the time. She was due at a PTA bake sale after school, and she didn't want to be late again. Delays tended to cause awkward questions about her work.

"I couldn't help overhearing your conversation with Normandy," Ellis said. "About that there artifact you were returning. Do you know much about it?"

"Not really. Only that it was my mission."

"I heard tell there was an ancient coven of witches who used a mortar and pestle like that. Story goes, they were mighty powerful in their day. Seemed like they always knew what their opponents were gonna do before it happened, so they always came out on top."

"Interesting. Where can I find them?"

"Nowhere anymore. They went extinct many years ago. Even their language is gone."

"How did that happen, if they could see what was coming?"

"Their power worked right up until it didn't, and by then they had a lot of enemies who were sick of losing and looking to even the score. 'Course, all of this is just stories, and the world's full of pestles and mortars, but still..."

The train started moving again, more cautiously this time.

"It looked like someone had used that artifact recently," Lucy offered. "They'd made a magical compound, and some of it was still in the bowl. That was what triggered my vision."

"Could be a descendant of that tribe, or maybe someone's found a book of their spells and decided to give it a go. A book like that went missing a while back, without any clues as to how it got lost or where it went to."

Lucy shrugged. "Nothing like that came up in my investigation."

"Funny thing is, this is the second time I've heard of spells that might be connected to that book. None of the Silver Griffins' top brass have been able to recreate the contents, any more than they could decipher those spells in that strange old language. What's gone is gone, but maybe only for us."

Lucy leaned forward, curious to hear more, but at that moment the train slid into the station. Much as she wanted to ask more questions, she was running late now, and she had to get to that PTA meeting.

"Nice meeting you," she said. "Perhaps I'll bump into you next time I'm in town."

Then she dashed off the train, waving her wand ahead of her to open the magical barrier. Taking the spiral stairs two at a time, she ascended to the station's corridors, and from there out into the Starbucks.

The smell of the coffee shop filled her with a craving for tea. She glanced at the counter and saw there was no queue. Maybe she could spare a minute or two to fuel up. It would make her faster later.

"Tea, please, to go," she said to the barista. "Make it as quick as you can. Time's been getting away from me today."

CHAPTER THREE

Lucy hopped into her Rivian and put her tea in the cup holder. Then she drove out through the afternoon traffic, one eye on the clock and the other on the road as she headed for her kids' school, fingers tapping impatiently on the wheel. It wouldn't be the first time that work made her late for a PTA meeting, but she felt the same twitch of annoyance at herself and the world that she did every time. It wouldn't have been so bad if she could explain it to all the other moms, but what was she supposed to say—sorry I'm late, but I was doing battle with a gnome? So much for her sworn duty to keep magic hidden.

Valentine Heights Elementary was bustling with kids and parents, some of them heading home after a busy day, others lingering for the promised pleasures of the bake sale. Lucy grabbed the last parking spot on the street and grabbed two more boxes of home-baked treats from the back seat, one full of brownies, the other peanut butter cookies and snickerdoodles. Just in time, she remembered the shredded side of her t-shirt, grabbed a crumpled

Wonder Woman hoodie from under the passenger seat, and pulled it on. It wasn't exactly the look most PTA members went for, but if it was good enough for the kids, it was good enough for her.

As she was getting out of the vehicle, she remembered her tea.

"Criminal waste to let a cuppa go cold," she said to no one in particular as she retrieved the cup, set it on top of the boxes of baked goods, and headed through the school's front door.

As she hurried down the hallway, she saw Ashley waving at her.

"Hi, Mom!" Ashley called with all the unfettered energy of an eight-year-old.

"Hi, sweetie." Lucy stroked her daughter's neatly tied back hair and kissed her on the forehead. "And hello to you too, Dylan."

"Hello." Lucy's oldest son towered over his sister. He had always been a serious soul, and at the grand old age of twelve, that tendency had become particularly pronounced. He watched the world with the thoughtful intensity of a saint's marble statue.

Lucy tried to straighten his dark, wavy hair, which was sticking out all over, but no matter what she did, it still looked like it needed a comb.

"Come on, you two." She held up the boxes. "We don't want to be late."

She hustled them down the crowded corridor to the room where the bake sale was taking place. Moms and dads from the PTA manned tables piled with cookies, brownies, pies, and every sort of cake that the school's parents had managed to bake between them. The place smelled like a baker's heaven, and the kids outside the doors looked like they couldn't wait to get in.

"Lucy!" Kelly Petrie was standing by the entrance, a clipboard in her hand and a bright smile on her perfectly made-up face. "So glad you made it. We were starting to worry."

Lucy glanced at the clock. Technically, the sale didn't start for two more minutes. "I got caught up with work." She glanced around in case anyone else was in earshot, but even her kids had rushed past in their eagerness to bag the tastiest treats. "Finally caught Haugensen red-handed with that artifact we'd been tracking down."

"That's super," Kelly said. "I'm sure that will go down great with the promotion board, now that they're deciding who gets the Field Supervisor job. Of course, what would also go down well would be rounding up a family of rogue trolls, explaining away the destruction to the press, and still making it here in time to run the school bake sale."

"How…" Lucy gaped at Kelly. How could anyone pull off a day like that and still turn up like this, dressed in a perfectly pressed pant suit and with hair like she'd just stepped out of a salon? It wasn't like Kelly's district was any closer than hers or that the Silver Griffins had given the other woman a magic carpet to jet around town.

"I got changed." Kelly leaned forward to share the words in an exaggerated whisper. She looked Lucy up and down. "You should try it sometime."

"I should get going." The tapping of Lucy's foot on the floor was the only visible sign of her annoyance. "There's probably a stall waiting for me to run it, right?"

"There was, but we found someone else. You can relax. You've certainly come dressed for it."

Lucy held up her boxes as if they were a shield defending her last shred of dignity. "I'll go add these to a table."

"Before you do," Kelly tapped them with her pen, "what did you bring?"

"Brownies, as I told you I would." Lucy cringed at the sharpness in her voice. Her accent got thicker as it always did when she was angry, cutting off some of the words. So much for not letting Kelly get to her again. "Also, some snickerdoodles and peanut butter biscuits."

"Mom, they're called cookies." Dylan rolled his eyes as he approached. "You're not in England anymore."

"I'm still *from* England, dear." Lucy sighed. "We invented this language, don't you know."

"England, huh? For some reason, I always hear Scotland." The corners of Kelly's mouth turned up in an imitation of a smile.

"Simple mistake. The more you finally get bigger assignments, the more you'll be able to tell the difference in dialects."

Kelly smiled harder, blinking a few times. "Isn't your mom swell?" Kelly turned her smile on Dylan, then pointed across the room. "Brownies are table number three. Thank you *so* much for helping out."

"Helping out, indeed," Lucy muttered as she walked over to the table. She'd done as much as Kelly to organize this event while equally busy with work and her kids. But of course, Kelly was here and being the face of the event, making sure that everyone knew how much effort she'd put in.

Lucy drew a deep breath. No point getting bitter about it. That wouldn't help anyone. Instead, she should focus on the moment, as her yoga instructor said. Peaceful minds, peaceful hearts, peaceful…stomachs, maybe? That didn't sound right, but with so many cakes in one place, it was all she could think of. She opened the box of brownies and looked around for a space on the table.

A whiff of something unpleasant made her gag. She set the box down and checked the bottoms of her shoes, then the floor, looking for anything that could have made that rotten egg smell. No one would buy cakes while that was all they could smell, and the school was counting on them to raise money for new athletics equipment. Still, no matter where she looked, she couldn't see anything that might be making a stink.

People were edging away from her table as though skunks populated it, the parents carefully not looking her way, the kids pulling faces and making vomiting noises. She blushed and fought the urge to hurry away, leaving someone else to deal with this. She was as responsible as anyone on the PTA, and that meant dealing with the bad things as well as the good ones.

Leaning over the table, she caught a fresh whiff of unpleasantness and realized in horror that it was coming from her brownies. She snapped the lid back on, hoping that it wasn't too late, that the stench hadn't oozed into the other baked goods on the table.

She lifted the lid of the other box a wary inch and sniffed. To her relief, all she could smell was peanuts and cinnamon, meaning that the cookies and snickerdoodles were okay.

Dylan strolled up with a cookie in his hand. "You okay, mom?" His eyes went wide, and he pinched his nose. "Eugh! What is that?"

"Nothing to worry about, honey. You go hang out with your friends for a while."

Lucy sipped her tea to calm her nerves as she stared at the offending box. What had gone wrong? She'd only made the brownies yesterday, and she'd checked on them this morning, a great excuse to eat brownies for breakfast. Then she caught a glimpse of Kelly's smug smile and remembered her pen tapping on the box lid. Of course. A wand was a good way of channeling magic, ensuring that a spell was cast with the best possible power and accuracy, but it wasn't strictly necessary. Other objects could direct it, and any pointing device would do for some simple magic—a finger, a stick, even a pen.

Lucy turned her back to Kelly, grinding her teeth in anger. Members of the Silver Griffins were supposed to only use power sensibly, responsibly, with restraint. They absolutely weren't meant to use it against each other, but there was no way for her to prove what Kelly had done. The other woman was going to get away with this.

Perhaps Lucy could undo it. All she had to do was manage a little discreet magic, as Kelly had done. How hard could it be?

Best not to answer that question, just in case.

She pressed her finger against the box and let her power flow. It was difficult to control without the aid of a wand, and with the distraction of people coming up to buy cakes and talk to her. She fought to maintain her focus while nodding, smiling, and chatting about the kids' soccer team, while her finger tingled with magic and the box trembled on the table.

"Hi Lucy, what did you bring?" asked Mary Holmes, Ashley's teacher and a staff representative on the PTA.

"Peanut butter biscuits and snickerdoodles." Lucy lifted the lid on that box while keeping her hand pressed to the other one. The magic was flowing through her, and she didn't want to risk breaking it off now in case that caused an accident. On the other hand, she didn't want Mary to look at the box and notice the sparkle of power as she unraveled Kelly's spell.

"None of your famous chocolate brownies? That's disappointing."

"Well…" Lucy tapped her finger on the lid of the closed box and winked. "Maybe if you come back in a moment. Got to give all those other brownies a chance."

"Well then, I'll be back shortly." Mary winked and walked away, leaving Lucy to finish her spell.

After a minute that felt like an hour, she picked up the box, opened the lid a crack, and nervously pressed her nose against it. She took a breath, shallow at first for fear that a rotten stink might make her throw up, then more deeply as she instead sucked in the deep, rich smell of chocolate, sweeter than when she'd taken the brownies out of the oven. She tugged off the lid and set the box down.

"Ooh wow!" a teacher said, zooming in on the box with a wide smile. "Those smell delicious."

Others crowded in around him, all wanting a taste of Lucy's brownies.

She smiled and gave Kelly a triumphant look. The other woman's smile was cold and sharp as an icicle. Lucy might have won for now, but this wasn't over.

Lucy wondered if she should report Kelly to their bosses. It would improve Lucy's chances of winning the Field Supervisor role, with a raise and an office of her own.

Then she thought better of it. One of the reasons they weren't supposed to use magic against each other was to prevent arguments among the Griffins. Better to let this one go for the good of the team. Besides, she'd won. Far more people had gathered around her table than Kelly's.

Lucy smiled and basked in the glow of a job well done.

CHAPTER FOUR

Once the baked goods were all sold and the tables cleared away, it was time to head home. Lucy, Dylan, and Ashley piled into the SUV, where Ashley pulled an old calculator out of her bag and started disassembling it for parts, while Dylan took out a book on history.

"Did you know that the Vikings came to America before Columbus?" he asked as they pulled away from the school.

Lucy smiled. Dylan took after her in more than his gift for magic. He had also absorbed her fascination with history and all things ancient.

"Did you know that the medieval Basques fished off Newfoundland," she said, "and no one in Europe could work out where their cod came from?"

"Guess it shows how we're all connected." Dylan looked thoughtfully out the window.

"Yes, it does, sweetheart."

They stopped at the nursery to pick up Eddie on the way home. He immediately started chattering away about his day, with the disjointed but delightful rambling stream of consciousness that came from being three years old. He and Ashley chatted while she connected bits of calculator into something new.

"Last stop, Heron residence," Lucy said as they reached the driveway of their pale pink rancher. "Please have your tickets ready for inspection and try not to block the pavement while neighbors are passing."

"It's called a sidewalk." Ashley shook her head.

"Really?" Lucy said in mock surprise while she released Eddie from his safety seat. "We walk on our feet, not our sides."

Ashley was first out of the car, walking up to the house with her backpack over her shoulder and a circuit board in her hand. She opened the front door, and there was a burst of yapping, followed by the rapid patter of paws as Buddy dashed out, wagging his tail. The dachshund hurried past Dylan, giving him a wary look as he went, and Dylan stared down at his feet, cheeks turning crimson. Lucy was happy for Dylan to feel guilty a little longer about what he'd done to the dog. It might encourage him to learn more control when it came to wielding his magic. If Buddy hadn't quite got used to his little dachshund legs yet, at least his old confidence was returning. He nudged Lucy's leg, and she paused to pat his head before taking Eddie out of his seat.

"Little Buddy!" Eddie exclaimed, and wrapped his arms around the dog's neck, then laughed as the canine thoroughly licked his face.

"Come on." Lucy smiled at the adorable sight. "Everybody inside."

"Hey there, Lucy," a voice called out from across the fence.

"Hey, Al." She ushered Eddie through the front door, then went over to where her neighbor was leaning, a rake in one hand and a baseball cap in the other. His gray hair stuck out in a wild halo, like dandelion seeds about to blow off in the wind. "How are you doing?"

"Not bad, not bad at all." Al pointed at Lucy's house. "I see your guttering's come loose again. They have a new fixing for that down at the hardware store. Josie reckons it'll hold up better in heavy rain."

"Thanks, Al. I should get going now, but I'll check it out later."

Lucy knew better than to ignore Al's advice. As it took expert witches to keep magic under control, it took expert builders to keep a house in good condition, and Al had decades of experience in the trade. She suspected that part of the reason he gave her so much advice was that he missed his job, and she was happy to give him a chance to feel useful.

"While you're down at the store, keep an eye out for Jimmy Sanchez." Al winked. "Seems he's been spending a lot of time around Josie."

"No!" Lucy laughed. "Jimmy's my age, and Josie must be, what, forty now?"

"Eight years ain't that big a gap. Question is, can he sober up long enough to impress her?"

The sound of Buddy yapping drew Lucy's attention.

"I should get going," she said again, taking a step back.

"Sure. Oh, hey, whatever happened to your old bloodhound?"

"The other Buddy?" Lucy glanced down at the dachshund. "He, uh, went to stay with family."

"Oh, I'm so sorry!" Al put a hand over his mouth, and Lucy realized a moment too late how much that sounded like the old "went to live on a farm" line.

"No, he's actually with family!" She patted Buddy's head. "This one needs dinner, so I should head in. Catch you later, Al."

She stepped away from the fence before he could find some other angle of conversation.

"Catch you later, Lucy."

Inside the house, the kids were already at the table while Charlie pulled a big dish of mac and cheese from the oven. He looked particularly cute wearing a "Kiss the Cook" apron over his shirt and slacks, with his blond hair as disheveled as Dylan's.

"Hey, handsome." Lucy kissed him on the cheek. "How's my installation wizard?"

"Wishing I'd never heard about the latest Windows update." Charlie shook his head. "Everyone I've dealt with today has been to fix a problem this release caused. Well, except for one case of gremlins." He set the dish down on the table, then wiggled his fingers, making sparks of magic fly. "And I soon dealt with them."

"No magic at the dinner table!" Dylan declared. "If I'm not allowed, neither are you."

Charlie glanced at Lucy, and they both laughed.

"Caught by my own rules." He rummaged in his pocket, produced a dollar, and dropped it in a jar on the counter. It was mostly full of slips of paper, where the kids had promised to do extra chores to make up for breaking the household magic rules, but when Lucy and Charlie transgressed, only a donation toward the Halloween candy fund would do.

"This all looks delicious." Lucy took a seat. She spooned some broccoli and kale onto her plate, then passed the bowl to Ashley, who reluctantly extracted a single piece of each. "You know greens will help you grow up big and strong."

"I don't need to be strong," Ashley said in the flattest of deadpan tones. With one hand, she picked up a fork to prod suspiciously at the greens. "I don't need muscles. I have technology."

"Big and strong like trolls can go?" Eddie peered at the greens.

"Sure," Charlie said. "Or like Superman."

"Except that trolls are real." Dylan spooned a huge helping onto his plate. For a skinny kid, he could put a lot of food away.

"Superman! Superman! Superman!" Eddie chanted, beating his spoon against the table.

"You can watch cartoons later," Lucy said. "First, you eat."

For a few contented moments, there was only the clatter of cutlery and sounds of chewing.

"Quiz time," Charlie said. "What's the world's tallest mountain?"

"Everest!" Dylan exclaimed.

"Well done, one point to you. What continent is Ethiopia in?"

"Africa!" Ashley announced.

"Point to Ashley. Okay, a trickier one. What's the capital of Peru?"

Dylan frowned. "Timbuktu?"

"Nope."

"Santiago?"

"Closer."

"Jakarta?"

"Definitely not. Let's throw this one open. Eddie, what do you think?"

"Superman!"

"Close, but no. Mom?"

Lucy frowned as though thinking hard, then shrugged her shoulders. "Search me."

"Ooh, no, wait, I remember!" Dylan's hand shot up. "It's Lima!"

"Well done!" Charlie's smile widened, and Lucy's heart skipped a beat. He had a way of bringing joy into the room, no matter what happened. She squeezed his hand, and he squeezed back.

Eddie, his hands covered in cheese sauce, made as if to wipe them on his shirt.

"Stop right there!" Lucy pointed at him. "Not on your shirt. Go wash your hands instead."

Eddie sighed and got down from his seat.

"Quick now," Lucy urged. "I don't want you holding everyone's dinner up."

"I can't go faster," Eddie said. He bent over. The air shimmered, and where the small boy had stood there was now a sloth, crawling with slow, cheese-covered steps toward the bathroom. "See?"

Dylan and Ashley laughed. Lucy and Charlie exchanged

a look, both stifling their grins. Just because Eddie was adorable didn't mean he should be encouraged.

"You know the rules against using magic," Lucy said. "I want you human again, hands washed, and a note in the magic jar on your way back."

"But mom…"

"Unless you want us to eat apple pie and ice cream without you." Charlie pointed at a pie that sat steaming on the counter.

Suddenly Eddie was human again and hurrying to the bathroom. This time Lucy and Charlie joined in the laughter.

After dinner, Lucy left the kids to help Charlie wash up while she headed into the garage. Instead of storage space for a vehicle, magical devices disguised as ordinary home appliances filled the place. By the door were a shower and a washing machine, both discreetly fitted with anti-magic filters for cleaning off magical residue after a mission. Next to them were shelves of boxes with labels like "screws" and "emergency pasta," with hidden spell supplies and secure boxes to store artifacts and evidence inside them.

A patter of footsteps announced Buddy's arrival from inside the house, his tail wagging eagerly.

"Hey, boy," Lucy said. "You want out in the front yard?"

Buddy *yipped* and hurried across the garage. Lucy opened the main door, letting Buddy out and sunlight in then turned back to what she was doing.

She reached behind the supply shelf and found a lump in the wall. There was a *hiss* when she pressed it, and a panel in the wall in front of her slid open, revealing her weapons rack. This was the "just in case" supply, an assortment of items for if a problem needed urgent attention and she couldn't pick things up from headquarters. There was an enchanted sword, a net of holding, two backup wands, a bag of dispelling dust, and various other items designed to deal with specific magical creatures. The taser and the pepper spray weren't magical but could still come in handy when trouble turned up.

Lucy pulled up a list on her phone and started running through her weekly check of supplies. A couple of new additions went onto the list, including a one-shot levitation bracelet in case she had to chase someone across rooftops or along cliff edges. Heights didn't bother her too much, but it was better to be safe than sorry.

"Hey there, neighbor!" a voice called from the driveway.

Lucy hastily closed the panel and turned to face Esther Romano as she walked up to the garage, dyed blonde curls bouncing above her baggy pink tracksuit. Esther's corgi, Duke, strained at his lead as he tried to get away from her and go hang out with Buddy.

"Hello, Esther." Lucy smiled and leaned against the wall. "How are you doing?"

"Nice setup you have in here." Esther peered around. "Did I see you closing some sort of cabinet there?"

"No, just popping some things on the shelves." Lucy patted a tub. Fortunately, the rattling of wand parts matched its label of "spare tools."

"Well, I was out walking Duke, and I saw your door open. Thought I'd say hi." Esther looked around the room as if she was doing an inspection. "You should make sure a place like this is locked up properly at night. I heard that

Jimmy Sanchez left his car unlocked the other night, thieves went through it, took the radio and that tool kit he keeps in the trunk."

"I'll be sure to lock up once you're gone."

"You know who I saw outside Josie's the other day?"

"No, but I have to be getting on with—"

"Paul Rudd. I swear it was him. He had a baseball cap on and big sunglasses, and he'd grown a beard to hide his face, but it was him all right. Paul Rudd, out buying hardware."

"If you say so, but I really should—"

"You know who else I've seen around Echo Park?"

"Am I going to care?"

"Of course you're going to care! Why, do you not have Paul Rudd in England?"

"I'm pretty sure they have Paul Rudd everywhere now, but—"

"Well then, you'll want to know about—"

"Hey, Lucy!"

Sarah and Jackie, Lucy's best friends, strolled up the driveway. Both of them grinned at the sight of her trapped between the shelves and Esther's latest gossip.

"Hi there, Esther," Jackie continued. "Are you joining us for our run?"

"Oh no, I don't run." Esther backed reluctantly away, taking Duke with her. "I mean, I could, but it's Duke. His legs just aren't up to it."

"Of course. Duke should probably stick with walking then."

The three of them waved Esther goodbye. Once she was out of sight, they burst out laughing.

"She's a sweet lady," Jackie blew stray strands from her blonde bob out of her eyes, "but she sure is nosy."

"I like to think of it as caring," Sarah said. "She wants to know that everyone's okay."

"That's why you'd never make it as a Silver Griffin. You're far too generous. We have to be suspicious of people's motives."

"Well, I'm glad she's not a Silver Griffin," Lucy said. "We need someone to patch us up when we get hurt, and I'd hate to go explaining troll bites to a non-magical doctor."

She checked the latch on the hidden compartment, then closed the garage door. No sense in tempting another inquisitive neighbor to come in.

"Do we have plans to run today?" she asked, remembering what Jackie had said.

"I hope not." Jackie let out an exaggerated sigh. "I spent all morning chasing down an escaped gargoyle near Silver Lake, and my feet are killing me."

"So how about a cuppa and some apple pie instead?"

"Now you're talking!"

They went into the kitchen, where the leftover pie was still cooling on the counter.

"When you say 'a cuppa,'" Sarah began, "does that mean you're going to make us drink tea again?" She pulled a face, then turned her pleading gaze toward the coffee pot.

Lucy laughed. "Don't worry. I wouldn't make a medical professional get by without a proper hit of caffeine."

She poured coffee for the other two and made tea for herself, then served them each a thick slice of pie. "I do have a question for you, though. Have either of you heard of an ancient tribe of witches who had a mortar and pestle for their symbol?"

"You know me." Sarah shook her head. "I flunked every history class I ever took. If I can't slice it open or treat it with antibiotics, it slides straight out of my brain."

"I've heard of a tribe like that," Jackie offered. "All myths, but sometimes there's truth in folklore. Apparently, they were originally from Oriceran and migrated here the last time the magical gates opened."

"You're saying they were on Earth for thousands of years?"

"For sure. They came from the Dark Forest on Oriceran, and they looked for places like that to live, dense woodland or places with really impressive trees. That's why a lot of them ended up in western America. The redwoods made it feel like home."

"I get it. They were nature types, like the Wood Elves."

"Kind of, yeah. They lived as close to nature as witches can, and they didn't use wands but channeled their power using whatever wildlife was around them. They could blend into the undergrowth, just vanish from sight. As long as they were among plants, they were safe."

"What happened to them?"

Jackie shrugged and chewed on a mouthful of pie while she tried to recall a half-forgotten history lesson.

"Killed off in one of the wars on Oriceran, I think. No one's seen or heard from them in hundreds of years. I know that much."

"If they moved here, how did they die on Oriceran?"

"Huh." Jackie's brow wrinkled in thought. "Good question. That's the thing with myths and legends. They don't have to add up because they're mostly not true. Maybe there was a tribe like that once, and now we're misremembering their story, or perhaps it's a jumble of different stories that all got mixed in together."

"That's a shame. I like the idea of living in the woods, getting closer to nature."

"Are you telling me you'd give up tea and apple pie so you could pretend to be a tree?" Sarah looked appalled. "Yoga classes, games night, hot showers, Netflix…"

"When you put it like that, maybe I'll stay here and make another cuppa instead."

CHAPTER FIVE

Nathaniel sat on a bench at the edge of the picnic area, a tuna sandwich and a can of Coke laid out next to him. It wasn't much of a picnic, but then he wasn't hungry. He merely needed something to make it look like he belonged here, to avoid raising any questions. It was the same reason why his wand was hidden in his bag and not sitting next to him, ready for action. Not that most people would be bothered by one more tourist sitting in Angeles National Forest, but he wasn't worried about most people.

He sipped the Coke and immediately wished he'd brought something without caffeine. His foot was tapping away like a woodpecker trying to peck its way into the dirt. With a deep breath and a couple of moments focused on the forest noises, he managed to calm himself down, but by the time he'd taken a couple of bites of the sandwich, his foot was at it again.

A northern flicker came in for a landing near Nathaniel, a brief flash of red showing through the black and brown that made up most of its feathers. It looked at him quizzically, took a couple of hopping steps closer, and tilted its head on one side.

"That's right." Nathaniel nodded at the bird. "I belong here as much as you. Well, nearly as much. The important thing is, there's no need to worry."

The flicker, apparently reassured, peered at the ground, then started pecking for bugs.

"Must be nice, living out here. No traffic, no salesmen, no advertising boards screaming at you to buy more stuff. No TV constantly blaring away in the background."

He closed his eyes and listened to the sounds of distant songbirds and the wind blowing through the branches above. His foot slowed its tapping until it stilled, and a smile spread across his face.

"Perfect."

The growl of an engine disturbed the peace. He looked up to see a midnight black Harley Davidson Deluxe stop at the far side of the picnic area, well off the tracks where people were supposed to drive. Birds fluttered away, and even the trees seemed to lean away disapprovingly from the mechanical growl and the billow of smoke from its exhaust. The engine switched off, and a short man hopped off the adapted seat, hung his helmet over the handlebars, and looked around. He pulled a phone from his pocket, glanced at the screen, glanced at Nathaniel, and nodded in a satisfied way. Then he unfastened a canvas bag from the Harley's back and walked determinedly in Nathaniel's direction.

"Sorry, buddy," Nathaniel said as the flicker looked around in alarm. "I think this one's my fault. If it's any comfort, I'm planning on making the world a much better place."

The flicker took to the air as the biker approached. He was four feet tall, broad-shouldered, and well enough groomed that he could pass as a diminutive human, although his dwarven ancestors would have been appalled to see how short he had cut his beard. He climbed up onto the bench next to Nathaniel, smelling of motor oil and old leather, set the canvas package down next to him, and pulled out a cigar.

"Delivery from Mister Zero." The dwarf slid the package over to Nathaniel. Then he pulled out a chunky metal lighter and lit his cigar, adding a cloud of smoke to the air around him. Nathaniel tried to wave the smoke away, drawing a derisive snort from the dwarf, then gave up and focused his attention on the package.

The canvas was old and stained, greasy to the touch. Nathaniel opened it carefully, revealing a selection of glowing crystals and a cheap reporter's notebook.

"I was expecting something more tome-like. You know, ancient power, long-lost spells, Indiana Jones meets J. R. R. Tolkien."

"Mister Zero always keeps his word," the dwarf said. "Look inside the book."

Nathaniel flicked open the notebook. Inside, detailed scrawling filled every page, some of its instructions in English, other parts written in ancient sigils or classical Latin. Oriceran runes and alchemical equations filled several sheets. The penultimate page was a diagram of a magic circle.

"That's not just the spell itself. It's all the theory underneath it," the dwarf said. "In case you wanted to look under the hood before you accept Mister Zero's generous terms."

Nathaniel scrutinized the pages, pretending that he understood what he was looking at. He knew enough theory to follow the spell and to understand that the power in the crystals would be able to carry it off. In the end, that was all he needed.

"Here." The dwarf held out a tablet. "Sign to show that you agree to the terms. Interest rate is in the third paragraph."

Reluctantly, Nathaniel accepted the tablet. If this was what it took to bring his people back, he would pay whatever price it took. He scribbled his signature across the screen with the tip of his finger, and there was a *click* as the camera took a photo of him while he signed.

"That'll do." The dwarf pocketed the tablet. "I'm curious. What do you want all this for anyway?"

"I'm going to resurrect my people." Nathaniel was happy to talk to anyone who took an interest.

"Your people?"

"My mother was descended from a long line of woodland witches who came here from Oriceran a thousand years ago, to escape the wars after the gates closed. The original ones are extinct now, and all that's left is a few of us with fragments of their power, tied to our connection to nature."

"Nice origin story, I guess, but how does that matter now?"

"The more countryside is lost beneath cities and freeways, the more our power fades. Our magic is dying, one felled tree or polluted river at a time, and no amount of carbon offset can bring back the dead. If I can revive our ancestors, I can save my people from losing our magic."

"Couldn't you do that yourself?"

Nathaniel shook his head. "Magic's like money—the more you lose, the harder it is to get it back. I need a boost to get me going. Besides..." He peered at the contents of the notebook, the spiky symbols and harsh, assertive words of the spell. "This isn't nature magic."

"No shit, Sherlock." The dwarf jumped down off the bench, ditched the end of his cigar, and ground it out beneath the heel of a sturdy old army boot. "Just remember, the first repayment is due in a month, and Mister Zero doesn't make exceptions, no matter how many trees you've lost."

He stomped away across the picnic ground. A minute later, the Harley roared into life, dirt spraying from its tires as it turned and headed away.

"Talk about making a deal with the devil." Nathaniel rubbed his eyes. "Still, what else am I going to do?"

The northern flicker, which had reappeared the moment the dwarf was gone, tilted its head to look at Nathaniel, then got back to pecking for food.

Nathaniel put the crystals and the notebook in his backpack, finished off his sandwich and Coke, and put the packaging into the bag too, so he could take it home to recycle. Then he headed into the forest. His route took him along a well-worn track, following the lower slopes of a steep, wooded hill until he was an hour away from the nearest road. Then he headed off the track and deeper into the wild, nodding respectfully to the trees as he passed and pausing to greet the animals that came out to watch him.

The flicker kept him company along the way, sometimes fluttering ahead to spy the way, other times perching on his shoulder for a rest.

At last, they reached a bowl in the earth, sheltered by a steep rise on one side and angular rocks on the other. The plants grew more densely around its edges, but the interior was barren ground, featureless except for the stones of what had once been a house, reduced to rubble by the centuries. On one large stone, an engraving of a mortar and pestle was still visible, despite years of erosion and a spattering of lichen.

The flicker stopped at the edge of the empty ground, but Nathaniel kept going. It was a warm day, and the walk had made him sweat, but the moment he entered that ground, an icy chill clawed at his flesh.

"I brought you an offering." He pulled a raw, plucked chicken from his bag. He knew that he should have caught the sacrifice, but he'd never had the stomach for hunting. Instead, he'd picked up something from an organic butcher at the Farmers Market on West Third Street. He figured that organic was practically as good as catching it himself.

He placed the chicken in the middle of the ruins, then pointed his wand at it.

"Inferno."

The chicken burst into flames, and for a moment hungry faces appeared in the air, cast orange by the fiercely blazing fire. Then the chicken was nothing but ashes, even the bones crumbling into black dust. The spirits pulled back to watch Nathaniel, their hunger briefly sated, and the bitter cold let him go.

He took out the notebook and started preparing the

spell. It was an order of magnitude greater than anything he had ever tried before, and he struggled to keep his hand from trembling at the thought of what might happen if it went wrong.

First, he scratched a circle in the dirt, then marked the symbols from the book at twelve points around its circumference. Then he laid the crystals at those points, power glowing from them. Although he couldn't see the spirits, he could sense them gathering around one of the crystals, drawn by the power it held.

"I don't understand you." Nathaniel looked at the empty air where the spirits were. "If I'd been killed here, I'd want to get as far away as I could, not hang around like the last guest at the dead end of a party."

This time, the cold was a swift, stabbing shock, like icicles piercing his skin. His ancestors hadn't liked that question.

"Okay, okay, I'll get on with it."

Nathaniel walked around the inside of the circle, tapping each crystal in turn with his wand. As he did so, the crystals cracked and the power flowed out, filling the air around him. As the last one released its load, he stepped back into the center, wand in one hand and notebook in the other, and started chanting the spell.

The words felt strange in his mouth, angular and ugly, leaving a taste like dust on his tongue. Whatever they meant, they were doing the job. The power swirled and spiraled around him, then formed into pillars, which rippled and twisted until they took on the form of long-dead witches and wizards, dressed in outfits made from animal hides, their hair decorated with feathers and wooden beads. Each one had the mortar and pestle symbol somewhere, whether stitched onto their clothing or tattooed on their skin. None of them carried wands. Slowly, as the words kept spilling out of Nathaniel, the spirits became more solid until he could barely see through them anymore.

It was working! The stories were true. His ancestors were here in all their power, and with a little more effort, he would have them at his side, restoring his magic, returning the strength of nature.

He flipped the notebook page, expecting to find more words for the spell, but he was at the end. This was it. He had done everything, but his ancestors were still only half present. One of them reached out for him, but her fingers felt like nothing more than a brush of wind. Nathaniel kept chanting the last lines of the incantation, his voice growing louder and more shrill. He drew in all the power he could, desperately trying to make the spell stronger, to bring his ancestors past this final point and into the world.

One of the crystals shattered as the last of the magic in it was used up, jagged fragments flying across the circle. Then the next one exploded, and the next, and the next. With each broken stone, the ancestors grew fainter until the last crystal shattered, and the final figure drifted away like smoke on the wind.

Nathaniel sagged and let out a deep sigh. The power was gone. The spell had failed.

Automatically, he started clearing up after himself, wiping out the circle in the dirt and bundling up the broken crystals. They wouldn't be worth anything now, but it was important to leave any space at least as good as when you had arrived there.

The flicker landed on his shoulder. It brushed the side of his head with one wing as if it was trying to reassure him.

"What do I do now?" Nathaniel looked at the bird. "How am I ever going to repay my debt to Zero without my ancestors' power?" He swallowed. "What's Zero going to do to me if I can't pay?"

CHAPTER SIX

Lucy knelt on all fours on her yoga mat, clenching her stomach muscles as she moved her spine up and down in time with the teacher's instructions. The faint rumble of traffic on Glendale Boulevard seeped into the room, but it wasn't enough to disrupt the sense of peace and calm that filled the studio.

"Now send your legs back," the instructor said, her voice serene, "and lower yourself onto the floor for a moment."

"That's more like it," Jackie whispered from the mat next to Lucy. "Time for a quick nap."

"Sometimes, I don't think you take this seriously at all." Lucy smiled at her friend's expression.

"Sometimes, I don't take life seriously at all. It's a lot easier that way."

"You have to start taking life seriously once you have kids—they won't do it for themselves."

"One more reason not to have kids. My life is serious

enough hunting down rogue magic. I don't need to deal with rogue diapers as well."

"Hands on the floor," the instructor said, "push your shoulders up and raise your head into upward-facing dog."

There was a rustle of movement as the whole class shifted pose.

"You're missing out." Lucy arched her back, feeling satisfaction at a stretch that was growing deeper with practice. "Those first words, the cheery smiles, the Mother's Day cards…"

"The laundry. The tantrums. The bugs they pick up. And did I mention nappies already?"

"It's the first thing you say every time we have this conversation."

"Rightly so. I don't want to deal with someone else's poop."

They went quiet as the instructor came around, checking their poses and making small adjustments. She shifted Lucy's shoulders a few inches, and something fell into place, making the stretch feel like less of a strain and more like her body easing into itself.

"Now bring your feet forward a little at a time," the instructor said as she came back to the front of the class, "and slowly raise yourself into downward facing dog."

Lucy glanced at Sarah, who had the mat to her other side. She was already in the new pose, body forming a steep inverted V, her ponytail falling past her face as she faced the floor. She was beaming with happiness.

"How do you do that so easily?" Lucy asked as she raised herself into something neither as steep nor as effortless as her friend's pose. "It's all I can do just to get my bum into the air."

"I just sort of do it," Sarah said. "You guys are doing great, though."

Lucy brought her feet forward a little more, steepening her pose. She might not have Sarah's natural flexibility, but she was determined to do as well as possible. As with everything, practice made perfect or at least made you a bit better than you had been the day before. That was how she faced life, improving by tiny increments one day at a time —a better cookie recipe here, a sharper summoning spell there. The best she could do in life was to keep doing better than her past self.

"You're ridiculous." Jackie looked at Sarah with a mocking scowl. "I swear, there's snake somewhere in your DNA, giving your spine that unnatural curve."

"Walk the feet back," the instructor said, "and into cat cow again."

There was a fresh wave of collective movement as the class got down to hands and knees and started raising and lowering their spines.

"Who comes up with these names, do you think?" Lucy asked. "Like, I can see that we look a bit like cats, but cows? They're not exactly supple. And it doesn't feel like much of a compliment."

"I don't know." Sarah smiled thoughtfully. "Have you watched cows in a field? They're usually so relaxed, standing there without any worries. I'd love to be like that."

"They don't have worries because they're stupid," Jackie said. "They don't know that they're going to end up as burgers."

"Aren't they better off not knowing? They're happier that way."

"I'd rather know," Lucy said. "If someone's coming for me, then I'm going to stop them, no matter the odds."

Jackie laughed. "How would you fight back as a cow?"

"Slowly, and with a lot of mooing."

"Okay, we're nearly done," the instructor said. "Now onto your backs, eyes closed, and relax. Take some deep, soothing breaths, and be mindful of your body."

Lucy could practically hear Jackie rolling her eyes. Her fellow Silver Griffin kept coming to yoga for the flexibility it gave her. However, she'd made her opinions on the spiritual side of it clear more than once, occasionally in earshot of the instructor. Lucy, on the other hand, found it helpful to take this time to shape her emotional state. Concentrating on her breath, the world and all its worries seemed to fade away. There was only her, at peace. So peaceful, she had occasionally fallen asleep on the mat back when the kids were younger, and she struggled to get a proper night's sleep.

"In your own time, eyes open," the instructor said in her usual soft, soothing tone. "That's it for today. I hope to see you all here again next week."

They got to their feet, rolled up their mats, and got ready to leave. As they were fastening their shoes, Lucy looked at the ordinary women and men walking past her, most of them oblivious to the presence of magic in the world.

"Isn't it amazing?" she whispered to Jackie. "The way people can go about their lives with no idea of half the things that happen. What would the world be like if everyone knew what we see?"

"It would be a mess," Jackie replied. "Most people can't be trusted to drive a car safely. Imagine what they'd do with a grimoire."

The three friends walked out of the studio together and down to the parking lot.

"Anyone up for a coffee?" Sarah asked.

"I'd kill for a cuppa," Lucy said.

"Sure, why not?" Jackie glanced at her phone. "Just a quick one, though. I have a date this evening."

They crossed the boulevard and the parking lot of the coffee shop on the corner of Aaron Street. People were hurrying in and out, getting their caffeine fix, but it didn't take long to get served, and soon they were sitting by the window, sipping from steaming mugs.

"Who's this date then?" Lucy asked.

"No one you know," Jackie said.

"Mysterious. How did you meet this elusive stranger?"

"Same way anyone meets anyone these days." Jackie waved her phone. "A dating app."

"Doesn't that take some of the romance out of it?" Lucy made a face. "It makes it look like online shopping, browsing for features until you find one that fits."

"That's the beauty of it. No random encounters. No trying to guess whether someone's interested or if they're even single. If I'm going to do this, I'm going to do it efficiently."

"That doesn't sound very romantic."

"How romantic was your first meeting with Charlie? You guys have been together since you were eighteen, so

I'm assuming an awkward encounter at a party or a drunken fumble after a prom."

"Actually, it was really sweet. I was staying in London for a few days, seeing the sights, and I found this picture in the National Gallery, a big oil painting of the execution of Lady Jane Grey. It was so sad, seeing this young woman's last moments, and so beautifully done, I kept going back to it every day. Then one afternoon, there was this cute blond guy there before me, as entranced by that painting as I was. We were there for ten minutes, not talking, just enjoying the art together before I even spoke to him. It turned out he didn't know the history behind the painting, so I told him about it. He bought me a cuppa to say thank you, we kept talking until the museum closed, then we went to dinner, and it all took off from there."

"Let's get this straight, you bored some poor guy to death with a history lecture, and he still liked you enough to buy you a coffee? That's not romantic. That's a damning judgment on what counts for dating in England."

"I think it's sweet," Sarah said. "A chance encounter, a shared passion, a moment of connection."

Jackie stuck two fingers in her mouth and made a barfing sound. "Think I'll stick with the app. The last thing I need is some dreamy art lover."

Lucy smiled to herself, as she always did when she thought back to that first meeting, and to everything that had come after. More than a decade later, she still felt that she was the luckiest woman in the world.

In the parking lot outside, a kid was standing by one of the cars. An oversized hoodie hid his face, and his hands were somewhere up his sleeve, but there was something about him that didn't seem quite right. She watched as he turned on the spot, examining the cars.

"Wait a minute." Jackie gestured at Lucy. "You said it was a painting of an execution. Are you telling me that your lifelong romance hinges around some chick getting her head chopped off?"

"You don't see her being killed. It's about the moment beforehand, about grief and dignity and lost innocence."

"And that's what counts as a turn-on in Britain, is it?"

"Says the woman who judges all her dates by their shoes."

"Man or woman, you can tell a lot by the way someone takes care of their feet."

"So is tonight's date a man or a woman?"

"That would be telling."

"What's their footwear like?"

"Once I know that, I'll know whether they're getting a second date."

A car pulled into the parking lot and the driver climbed out. As he did so, the strange kid walked up to him. The man frowned for a moment, then his eyes glazed over, and he reached into his pocket.

Lucy grabbed the wand from her bag, slid it up her sleeve, and headed for the door.

"Jackie, I need you to back me up just in case," she said. "Sarah, can you keep an eye on the bags, please?"

"Why, what's happening?" Sarah looked around, bemused, as her friends strode out the door. Jackie hung back a few feet behind Lucy, who walked up to where the man was about to hand the kid his keys.

"Hi there," she said. "Is everything all right?"

"Everything... is... good..." the man said, his face and voice equally expressionless.

"Sure it is." Lucy turned to the shorter figure. Up close like this, she could see who was hidden in the shadowy depths of his hood, not a human child but a face like a shaved stoat, the visage of a Willen.

"You don't need to worry." The Willen's pupils started to rotate. "Just stand back and let me take the nice car, yes?"

As the hypnotic power of those eyes bored into Lucy, she felt a haze settling over her mind. With one hand, she grabbed the slender Silver Griffin amulet that hung around her neck, merely another piece of jewelry to most humans, but to her, a protective lifeline. Its defensive spells kicked in, and the power of the Willen's gaze faltered while she slid her wand discreetly into her hand, revealing it to the Willen but not the inhabitants of the coffee shop.

"Silver Griffins," she said. "Do you want to do this the easy way, or do you want my colleague to whack a restraining spell on you?"

The Willen glanced at Jackie, who responded with a malicious grin.

"They taught us how to be gentle," she said. "I prefer to play rough."

The Willen raised his hands, paws still hidden by his baggy sleeves.

"I just wanted to try driving," he said. "I've never done it before."

Lucy imagined the untrained Willen, barely able to see over the dashboard, trying to steer through the busy city traffic and the absolute carnage he would have caused.

"That doesn't make things any better." She glanced at Jackie. "If I take him to the station, can you deal with this bloke, then drop my bag at home before your big date?"

"Sure thing."

"Come on then, sunshine." Lucy pocketed her wand, laid a hand on the Willen's shoulder, and led him away.

Behind her, the hypnotized driver blinked, then looked in confusion at his outstretched hand, his keys dangling from one finger.

"That's weird," he said. "I was parking, and then..."

"You look dazed," Jackie said. "Probably sunstroke. We should get you in and find you a glass of water."

"Sunstroke? But I've been indoors all day."

"Indoor sunstroke. Big new problem. Not enough people know about it. Come inside, and my doctor friend can explain."

CHAPTER SEVEN

Telaven stood facing La Brea's Lake Pit. At the far end, a model of an ancient elephant was sinking into the lake, its tusks and trunk waving in the air. Telaven felt like he was that elephant, drowning not beneath a thick layer of tar but under the stench of it, something dense and acrid that clawed at his throat. The humans walking by seemed almost oblivious, none of them bothered by the unbreathable air, but to a Light Elf, that chemical stink was as dreadful as the city's traffic or the loaded garbage trucks headed for the dump. Urban humans claimed to be so civilized, yet they lived in a cesspool of their own making, and the ones in this city had turned one of the worst smells in nature into a tourist attraction.

He pulled a scarf up across his nose and mouth, trying to blot out the scent. It was hot in Los Angeles, but not as hot as the Sahara, and he regularly dressed more heavily there to shelter him from the sun and the dust storms. In only a few days, he would be back there, amid the silence of the sands, that miraculous country he had left Oriceran to explore. First, he needed to get this out of the way.

A few humans were roaming the park, talking, drinking coffee, taking photos of themselves and each other. When they came near, Telaven reached for his long silver hair, making sure it still covered the pointed tips of his ears. He waited until none of them were nearby, then turned away from the pits, ducked into a low concrete structure, and touched a magical sigil hidden in the rough surface of the concrete. The floor at his feet opened into a staircase heading into the ground. He hurried down them, while above him the sigil shimmered and the ground sealed shut.

The staircase was made of concrete, as were the walls to either side and the ceiling holding back the earth above. It had probably been ugly even before decades of dirt had been trampled in, as magicals went down to beg for help from Zero. Old electric lights only added to the feeling of somewhere rundown, creating pits of gloom that alternated with brightly lit patches of grime.

Despite it all, Telaven felt energized. No amount of industrial architecture could suppress the power of the kemana. Magic flowed through the air, tingled across his skin, made him feel like he could take on the whole world. The kemanas of the deep desert were beautiful but hard to find. It felt good to set foot in somewhere like this again.

At the bottom of the stairs was a cave, with others leading off from it in the distance. It looked as though it had bubbled up through the ground, a cavernous space lined with a thick, shiny layer of tar. Drips hung from the ceiling, having hardened a moment before they fell.

"You're here to see Mister Zero?" A gnome looked up at

Telaven. There were dozens of gnomes around the cavern, all dressed in suits and fedoras. This one had a skinny purple tie and a set of rings with matching purple gems. Some of the others had gold bracelets, ostentatious watch chains, or jewels glittering on their ears.

"That's right. I am Telaven of the—"

"You're number twenty-seven, and we're currently serving number twenty-three." The gnome pulled a numbered ticket from a device on the wall and handed it to the Light Elf. "Go join the line."

Telaven clutched the tiny fragment of paper as he went to stand in line behind two winged Arpaks and a brutish Kilomea. The gnomes bustled around them, running in and out of side chambers, fetching and carrying.

Near the back of the kemana stood a single black crystal, as tall as Telaven and a foot wide. It was a perfect example of its type, not a single crack or imperfection visible. The power of the place radiated out from it.

"What you here for?" the Kilomea asked.

"Excuse me?" Telaven stared into the creature's face, which looked like it had been crumpled up, scarred, and given an extra beating with the ugly stick.

"I said what are you here for? What you trying to get from Zero?"

Telaven frowned. If he liked talking to strangers, he wouldn't have moved to a desert. However, those desert wanderings and the few encounters with people they brought taught him the importance of being polite and gracious when company became unavoidable.

"I'm looking for a spell that can protect travel routes in shifting ground," he said. "The weather is changing where I come from. As the desert expands and the winds shift, it's becoming harder for the nomads whose paths I share. Nothing lasts forever, but if we can preserve those paths, the land will live a while longer, and the desert will be held back."

"Desert's bad then, yeah?"

"I love the desert, but if we let it take over, people will die. Life on the sand is not for everyone."

"Like wasabi peas."

"Like what?"

"Wasabi peas." The Kilomea made a small circle with one finger. "Tiny. Green. Taste like your mouth's on fire."

"Sounds horrible."

"Exactly. Not for everyone."

A Light Elf emerged from a cave mouth beyond the crystal, clutching something in a velvet bag, and rushed away up the stairs. A moment later, a gnome scurried past with a clipboard.

"Number twenty-four," she called out.

One of the Arpaks disappeared into the cave the elf had emerged from.

"What about you?" Telaven asked, remembering that questions both ways were important to such interactions.

"Gonna get myself buffed up." The Kilomea flexed his already bulging muscles. "Be the strongest there is."

"With the price this man asks, is it worth it for something so mundane when you could simply exercise instead?"

"When I'm winning all the challenges of strength, when I'm being hired by every rich magical with a score to settle, when I'm the most respected of all Kilomea, yeah, it'll be worth it."

The Arpak scurried out from behind the crystal, shaking his head.

"Monsters," he snapped at the gnomes. "You're all monsters."

Then he vanished up the stairs.

"Number twenty-five."

The other Arpak hesitated, then shook her head. "I've changed my mind." She too hurried away.

The gnome with the clipboard shrugged. "Number twenty-six."

"About time." The Kilomea grinned and headed off around the crystal.

Telaven stood alone in the cavern, watching the gnomes scurry around. They moved swiftly and nervously as if they were constantly being chased.

After a few minutes, the Kilomea appeared. His whole body had swollen up except for his head, which now looked strangely small, as if someone had stuck a doll's head on a giant. He grinned and winked at Telaven.

"Worth it," he said, "even at that price."

"Number twenty-seven," the gnome with the clipboard called.

Telaven followed her around the crystal and into a deeper cave beyond. It was finely decorated, with thick rugs, antique furniture, and walls decorated with oil paintings, signed movie posters, and a row of framed platinum disks.

In a massive, plastic bucket seat in the middle of the room sat one of the strangest creatures Telaven had ever seen. He was huge and orange, the folds of his flesh spilling out from beneath a sheet-sized Hawaiian shirt and over his tiny shorts. His eyes bulged, and flaps of fat hung from the undersides of his arms. The only small thing about him was his feet, from which a pair of cheap plastic flip flops hung. For a moment, Telaven thought that the creature must be eating his gnome servants, to have ended up this bloated. With those tiny feet and that huge body, he couldn't imagine how the creature would even get around.

"What are you?" Telaven asked. He had been away from other magicals for so long that he couldn't remember if that was a polite question. He didn't care. He had never heard of a creature like this.

A dwarf stood behind Zero, dressed in biker leathers and with his beard cut short. At Telaven's exclamation, he took a step forward and pulled out a shotgun with an ax blade fitted on one side. He pointed both barrels at Telaven.

Zero chuckled, and the sound came out like the gurgling of a half-blocked drain. He held up a hand, and the dwarf stepped back, lowering his gun but still glowering.

"Now, now, Gruffbar," Zero said. "I don't mind an inquisitive soul."

He leaned forward, and the seat creaked beneath him. Black liquid oozed out around his belly, ran down the legs of the chair, and through a grate in the floor. A musty smell billowed across the room, and Telaven was glad that he still had his scarf up.

"I'm unique, is what I am," Zero said. "Unprecedented. Ancient. Spawned so far back that no one remembers where I came from, or how, or why."

"Don't you know?"

"Maybe. That would be a secret, and secrets are valuable. I don't give them away, and something tells me that's not what you've come here to barter for."

Telaven watched the thick, black liquid oozing from orange flesh. "The tar. It comes from you, doesn't it?"

"Aren't you a clever boy?" Zero said. "But really clever people don't waste my time. So, what do you want?"

For the second time that day, Telaven told his story about the spreading of the desert, the changing climate, the ancient routes at risk of being lost, and the people whose lives depended upon them. The story of the place he had called home for centuries and for whose future he now feared.

"That is sad." Zero nodded. "However, I don't deal in emotions. I deal in power, in favors, in secrets. You understand that, yes?"

"I understand." Telaven nodded. "I need a spell to make those ways through the desert endure, and I'll pay almost any price for it."

"Almost, eh? Well, that should be good enough. As it happens, I have the spell for you. It'll mean that those ways are kept alive by travelers. Rains of fire could fall, and there would still be a route across your desert because the people will keep walking it, and the magic will come from their walking. Is that what you want?"

"Yes."

"Then let's talk price." Zero held out a hand and Gruffbar the dwarf passed him a tablet. Zero tapped on the screen for a few minutes, then held the device out for

Telaven. "Normally, I ask for repayment in either power or hard cash. I accept Euros, Yuan, or US dollars, but I prefer magic, and you'll get a better rate that way."

Telaven accepted the tablet. Trying to ignore the oily film where Zero's fingers had touched it, he stared at the screen. There were figures written on it, three in the currencies Zero had mentioned. The fourth was a number of days in magical service, during which Telaven's power would be drained for the loan shark to use. Those days were most easily counted in years, each one of them seeing Telaven's essence siphoned painfully away. It was a price he could muster, but a crippling one, and the longer he took to sacrifice his power, the more Zero would demand as interest piled up.

"You said this is how you normally get repayment," Telaven said. "Is there some other way?"

"Clever enough to see the loophole," Zero said. "I like that, and I like you, so I'll give you the other option because what I really like is secrets. I've got lots of the best ones—who killed JFK, where Jimmy Hoffa is buried, what happened to Anastasia Romanov, and which state she settled in. If you have a secret worth as much as my spell, we can swap. No debt, no ties between you and me. You go back to your desert free and clear. The question is, do you know anything that matters?"

Telaven swallowed. There only one thing that might even start to match Zero's needs, and he wasn't keen to share it with the monstrous loan shark. But the desert needed him, its people needed him, and if the alternative was years of servitude, of having his life's power drained from him every day, then it was better to take this risk.

"I know where there's an artifact you can use to clone yourself," he said. "It would take too much power for most people to use, but with everything you have here, everything you take from other people…" He tapped the screen of the tablet. "With this, you could do it. You said that there's only one of you. That must bring a special sort of loneliness. Wouldn't you like there to be more?"

"Like it?" Zero's face rippled as he grinned. "I've been counting on it. All right, elf, you've got yourself a deal. You give me the information to find that artifact, and you can have your spell. If your information turns out to be untrue, your debt comes due in raw power, and I start adding interest. How does that sound?"

Telaven drew a deep breath, steeling himself for what he had to do.

"Very well." He held out the tablet. "Adjust the contract accordingly. We have a deal."

It only took moments for Gruffbar to alter the terms. Telaven read them carefully, then signed on the screen. The tablet's camera caught his image, and the deal was sealed.

Once finished, he opened a new document and typed in a location before handing the tablet to Zero.

"Who would have thought it," the loan shark said as he read the secret. "Gruffbar, give the man his spell."

Gruffbar stepped around his employer, pulled a reporter's notebook from his pocket, and handed it to Telaven. The elf flicked through the yellowed pages full of decades-old text, his eyes widening as he saw that everything he needed was there.

"How did you know that I would want this?" he asked.

"Same way I knew that you would bring me this secret," Zero said. "I made a deal with a soothsayer many years ago, and she told me this deal was coming. I've been waiting for your secret and to hand you that spell in return."

Telaven put the notebook in his pocket, then bowed to Zero.

"Thank you, Master Zero," he said. "You have done a good thing for my people today."

With that, he departed, leaving Zero and Gruffbar alone in the room.

"I've done an even better thing for me." Zero stared at the tablet. "Gruffbar, gather the gnomes. It's time to put my plan into action."

CHAPTER EIGHT

Lucy stepped off the small underground train and onto the elegantly old-fashioned platform. She walked through the drifting steam, past the wooden benches and the pristine mosaics, toward the exit next to Normandy's booth. The station was relatively busy this morning, half a dozen other witches and wizards getting off the train with her and a couple more waiting to board when it was empty. Most hurried past, eager to get to work, but Lucy stopped at Normandy's office and knocked on the wood. The window shot up, and the gnome smiled out at her.

"Good morning, Agent Heron." He touched two fingers to the brim of his cap. "How are you doing today?"

"Wishing I hadn't drawn the late shift, but everyone has to take a turn sometime, right?"

"How's the family?"

"Eddie decided to turn into a chameleon this morning. It took us twenty minutes to work out where he was. It's a good thing Charlie's boss is understanding about parents turning up late. How about you?"

"Very well, thank you. Those cupcakes were delicious." Normandy handed her the empty box, spotlessly clean. "Please tell Eddie I appreciated his contribution."

"I will. Here…" Lucy rummaged in her Batman backpack and pulled out a paper bag, which she passed to Normandy.

"Chocolate cookies." He took a deep, appreciative sniff of the contents. "Thank you, Agent Heron."

"Thank you for keeping this place so neat."

The gnome blushed. "Just doing my job. Now, are you here for a drop-off today?"

"No, I have an appointment with Jenkins."

"Special Equipment and Weaponry, huh? You getting anything exciting?"

"I hope so."

"Well, I'm sure you know the way by now." Normandy touched the brim of his hat again. "Have a nice day."

"You too."

Lucy headed down a tunnel and up a flight of metal stairs that spiraled through the hillside above the station. At the top, a tap of her wand opened a door, and she emerged into a clean but dimly lit corridor. A voice emerged from a doorway a few feet away, talking about the stars and planets. When Lucy peered around the door, she saw an eager audience listening to an astronomer talk. At the same time, a spectacular show played out overhead across the interior of the Griffith Observatory Planetarium.

Sadly, she didn't have time to stop and take in the show today. Instead, she hurried out to the central rotunda. There, visitors watched the Foucault Pendulum swing back and forth, demonstrating the motion of the Earth while also storing up the magical power that came from an expectant crowd. Some kids watched with curiosity and adults with fascination, while others looked eager to move on. Lucy knew those divided feelings from her family's trips to museums and galleries. While she loved to take her time, and Dylan would happily spend hours on anything historical, Ashley got bored if there wasn't something technological to play with, and Eddie was too young not to want to keep running around. She loved her kids, and she wanted these days of childhood wonder to last, but a small part of her looked forward to when she could take her time again.

She hurried along the exhibit hall, past models of planets and illuminated images of outer space, approached a small door hidden in the wall and tapped it with the tip of her wand. The door swung open, while a haze of discreet magic distracted tourists from even noticing that it was there, and Lucy slipped through into a reception room.

A young wizard smiled from behind a mahogany desk. "ID, please."

"Like you don't know who I am by now." Lucy held up her wand.

"Rules are there for a reason." The receptionist scanned her wand with his. "Remember that business with the Changeling last year?"

"As if I could forget it." She cringed at the thought of how close a single magically disguised creature had brought them to disaster. "I promise, I won't complain about this ever again."

A light blinked green on the desk, and the receptionist nodded.

"Sorry for the delay. You're free to continue."

She headed left down a stairwell and into the heart of the Silver Griffins' LA headquarters. Griffins were hurrying back and forth, some of them holding tablets or documents, others with wands in hand. An occasional administrative gnome bustled past, pushing a catering cart, clutching a heap of files, or carrying a toolbox. From time to time, a pigeon fluttered past overhead, conveying instructions to an agent.

"Hi Jim, how are you doing?" Lucy asked as she passed a junior wizard standing in the doorway of a conference room. He held what looked like an old radio, but with crystals down one side and magic sparking from the aerial.

"Hi, Lucy." He held up the device. "Trying to get this working. Don't suppose you know much about interdimensional transmissions?"

Lucy shook her head. "You'd need my daughter for that."

She carried on down the corridor, then through an open-plan office. Kelly Petrie was leaning over a desk, peering at the screen of a nervous-looking witch.

"Kelly." Lucy nodded and forced a smile.

"Agent 485." Kelly nodded back. She was impeccably dressed as always, her smart suit a sharp contrast to Lucy's jeans and loose sweater. "I see that you're lowering the bar for work wear again."

"It's more practical in the field."

"Really? I've never had any problems running in a suit, but maybe it takes practice." Kelly turned her attention back to the screen and Lucy, relieved of the need to talk to her, hurried on.

Jackie was at the far end of the room, leafing through a file. She looked at Lucy as she approached, then past her at Kelly.

"Is the queen bee still acting like a B?" she asked.

"I'm sure she's a nice person at heart," Lucy said.

"I'm sure Nixon loved his mother, but that didn't stop him from being a crook."

"How did your date go?" Lucy liked that Jackie always had her back, but she didn't want to waste time thinking about Kelly.

Jackie blew a raspberry and gave a two-handed thumbs down. "Who picks a pottery class as a surprise way to spend the evening?"

"Sounds fun to me, and a great way to find out if your date is creative."

Jackie groaned. "This is LA. Everyone thinks they're creative. Next time it's a tequila bar or nothing."

"What if your date doesn't like tequila?"

"Call it a trial by fire. If they can't pass the tequila test, they're not ready for me."

Lucy laughed. "I'd love to hear more about your pottery date."

"You never will. Now scoot, I've got work to pretend to do."

From the end of the office, another set of stairs carried Lucy down through a thick layer of concrete into the realm of the Special Equipment and Weaponry department. There, the security measures were less about keeping intruders out than keeping the equipment in. Armored doors thick enough to stop a tank slid apart at a wave of Lucy's wand, to reveal a magical net hanging across the short corridor beyond. A pair of small red creatures with glowing wings were frantically flapping as they tried to escape the tangling strands.

The doors clanged shut behind Lucy.

"If you're coming in, could you bring the fire imps with you?" a man's voice called from around the soot-stained and hex-riddled corner of the corridor.

Lucy waved her wand, summoning forcefields around the imps, then dispelled the net. The creatures fell to the floor, both of them cursing in high-pitched voices and battering their hands futilely against the magical fields. Lucy scooped them up and walked down the corridor while the net sprang back into place.

Around the corner, she emerged into the echoing chamber that the Silver Griffins referred to as the range. The experimental space of Toliver Jenkins and the rest of the Special Equipment and Weapons Team was scarred and stained by the impact of their tools, from a wall covered in bullet holes to another that rippled with living purple tentacles, which no amount of counter-magic had resolved.

Jenkins whirled around, his lab coat flapping and his close-cropped ginger hair shining in the neon light. He took the imps from Lucy, then handed her a pair of ear protectors. "Put these on."

Lucy did as instructed. She had long ago learned the futility of asking "why?" inside Jenkins' lair.

A lab assistant surrounded by a magical field stood in the middle of the room. Six-foot-high speakers bracketed him on either side. Cables ran from them into a single jack, which connected to a laptop on a stand.

Jenkins grinned and gave the lab assistant a big thumbs-up. The assistant returned a far more nervous look and held up a trembling thumb. Jenkins tapped a key, and suddenly the room was full of noise, a grinding of guitars and drums so loud that Lucy's teeth rattled in her head. She winced at the volume despite her ear coverings. The assistant stood, apparently oblivious to the noise, while tiny green balls appeared from the forcefield around him, piling up around his feet, then his legs and on, until the peas buried him.

Jenkins switched off the music, and they both removed their ear protectors.

"Nothing like a good bit of music, eh?" Jenkins said.

"That was nothing like a good bit of music." Lucy rubbed her ears in hopes that they might stop ringing.

Jenkins made an exasperated sound. "Swedish death metal is an underrated art form."

He led her to the middle of the room, where the peas behind the magical field appeared to be wriggling. At a tap of his wand, the barrier vanished, and the peas rolled out across the floor, revealing an uncomfortably twitching assistant.

"You've got one up your nose again," Jenkins remarked.

"What is this?" Lucy looked at the results in bewilderment.

"Pixy-dust-powered anti-noise field. The idea is that however much noise is around you, the magic keeps you in peace."

"Peace?" Lucy looked at the peas littering the floor as realization dawned. "You mean that—"

"I may have made a small spelling mistake, in both meanings of that phrase." Jenkins waved his assistant away. "All right Nigel, you can have ten minutes off while I deal with this agent." Jenkins headed toward a doorway at the side of the room, and Lucy followed him. "What can I do for you today?"

"I'm here for my annual equipment upgrades," she said. "A new wand and a recharge on my amulet."

Jenkins sighed. "How dull. Still, this is what keeps my department funded."

They walked into another room, where rows of wands sat in racks on one wall, and Silver Griffin amulets hung from hooks on the other. There was a tingle of magic in the air, the feeling that came when a lot of power was crammed in close together. It was like the fizzing produced by combining pop rocks and cola, except it was happening in Lucy's brain instead of her mouth. The sensation was exhilarating but also distracting, and it took her a moment to realize that Jenkins had asked a question.

"Sorry, what was that?" She blinked at him.

"I asked what you're packing at the moment."

"This old thing." Lucy drew her wand and handed it over.

"Ah, the Westwell 95." Jenkins gave the wand an experimental wave. "Still a decent choice, reliable for low-level spells and accurate up to two hundred yards." He held it against his ear and tapped one end with his finger. "Sounds like the core's shaken loose, though. Have you had many miscasts recently?"

"A few, but I wasn't sure if that was me or the wand."

"Hm. This one's probably repairable, but you should have something new. Let's set your amulet to charge first, though."

Lucy put her amulet down inside one of the charging boxes at the end of the room, wooden chests edged in ancient iron and dotted with colored crystals. With a tap of Jenkins' wand, the charger lit up and started humming as it refilled the protective wards on her amulet.

"Right then." Jenkins rubbed his hands together and led her to the wall of wands. "What are you after this time? Discreet or flashy? Portability or stopping power? What sorts of spells do you cast most often? That makes a huge difference to what will suit you."

A wand near the bottom of the rack drew Lucy's eyes, a short one made from dark, unevenly shaped wood with narrow gold bands around the handle. She had no idea why it seemed so compelling, but she felt like a magnet dragged into pointing north.

"What's this one?" she asked.

"The Mark Three Tidda? Really? I know Australian wands are popular in California, but so are surfing and quinoa, neither of which will help with your magic."

"It has a good feel to it." Lucy felt the weight of the Tidda, then gave it an experimental wave. It didn't only let her channel magic, it practically called out for it, and as she levitated a wrapper from the waste bin in the corner, she could feel it amplify her power.

"It's not a bad little wand," Jenkins conceded. "Light-weight, good channeling, and it has an affinity for nature and dream magic. Wouldn't you prefer something with a bit more oomph? We got the new Rattleblaster 2200 in last week, and that's a proper fighting wand."

"I try not to get into too many fights."

"Sometimes a good offense is the best defense."

"If we're going to settle this one with cliches, I could say that the customer is always right."

Jenkins shrugged. "Each to their own. If you want it, that Tidda's yours." He glanced at the charger. "Do you want to see something cool while your amulet is finishing?"

"Always."

Jenkins took a pack of mints out of his pocket, ate one, and offered another to Lucy.

"What are you saying about my breath?"

"Just eat it," he said. "Trust me."

Lucy popped the mint into her mouth. It seemed perfectly ordinary, perhaps a little heavy on the artificial sweeteners, but nothing to get excited about.

Then she felt a lightness in her feet as if the floor was falling away. Her mouth hung open as she realized that she floated six inches in the air, and so did Jenkins.

"Flying pills," he said with an enormous grin. "No more carting a broom around or trying to steer with one hand while using your wand as a rocket. Pop one of these and you're into the air."

Lucy flapped her arms, propelling herself across the room. It was like being a bird, but with minty fresh breath.

"That's fantastic." She settled back onto solid ground. "How soon will these be available?"

"We're still in the test phase, too many accidents to

make them standard issue yet. But here…" he handed her the packet, "…just don't tell anyone I gave you them, yeah?"

As if it wouldn't be obvious where something like this came from. Lucy wasn't going to complain. She stuffed the mints in her pocket and picked up her bag as a bell on the charger chimed.

"Here you go." Jenkins handed her the amulet. "All ready for another year's service."

"Thanks."

They went out across the range, where the imps were throwing peas at Nigel while he tried to sweep the test zone clean.

"Take care out there," Jenkins said as Lucy headed for the door.

"You take care in here," she replied. "As far as I can see, it's a lot more dangerous."

As she headed back through the office, there was a flutter of wings, and a pigeon landed on Lucy's shoulder. She unfastened the message from its ankle and read it:

"Magic car suspected near John Wayne Airport. Investigate and resolve."

A stamped symbol after the words authenticated an order from the Silver Griffin command.

As soon as Lucy had finished reading, the paper disintegrated, turning into a wriggling, slippery handful of worms. The pigeon hopped down onto her wrist and gobbled up the worms as she strode through the office. She let it go before stepping out into the halls of the Observatory, leaving the bird to finish off its tip.

She hurried past the tourists to the corridor outside the

planetarium and tapped on the wall with her wand. The door opened, and she went through.

The sound of pistons echoed up the stairs, telling Lucy that the train had arrived. She dashed down, her backpack bouncing against her back, and reached the platform as the doors were about to close. She leapt on board beside a cheerful-looking gnome and a wizard with a magic carpet hanging over his arm. The train doors shut, there was a hiss of steam, and they headed off down the tunnel.

Lucy pulled out her phone and glanced at the time. Five minutes by train to the Starbucks where she'd parked. Pick up the car, drive out to the airport, by then it would be… Well, hopefully not too late to stop whatever was going on.

She gripped her new wand, enjoying the way it perfectly fit her hand. This was turning into another good day.

CHAPTER NINE

Mickey Totman's hands were sweating as he clutched the wheel of the bright red Mustang. He wanted to pretend that it was the heat making him sweat, but he knew that was a lie. He had plenty of reasons to be nervous, and now they'd piled so high they were practically pressing the sweat out of him. He was lucky that the excitement of the moment was enough to hold his fears in check.

For now, at least.

He turned off the road, through a gap in a section of temporary fencing, and onto the unused runway outside John Wayne Airport. Nearby, a plane took off from the airport itself, but this strip was strangely empty, except for three other cars and the small crowd of teenagers gathered around them.

Mickey pulled up next to those cars and enjoyed the admiring looks from the other teens. As he got out from behind the wheel, Tiffany walked over, wearing tight jeans and a cropped shirt. It was all Mickey could do to keep himself from drooling.

"I didn't believe you'd manage this." She ran a hand across the Mustang's hood. "Hell, I'm not sure I believe it now. Are you sure you're only fourteen?"

Mickey wished he wasn't. Two years was a huge age gap to a teenager, a vast generational gulf between him and Tiffany's clique, this gang of cool kids with their even cooler cars. That was why he'd needed the Mustang. Nothing else would do to establish his credibility, to show that he wasn't a kid.

"I'm old for my years." He couldn't remember where he'd heard that line, and he hoped that it was a new one on Tiffany.

"Where did you get it?" she asked. "I'm guessing it's your stepdad's, and this is your way of getting back at him."

She said it softly, but there was an edge to her voice, something Mickey didn't quite understand that made him even more excited and nervous. Too nervous to come up with a convincing lie.

"It's my brother's," he said.

"He let you borrow this? You have a very generous brother."

Mickey swallowed. "Borrow" would have been a kind way to describe it. Tony didn't know that he'd made off with the Mustang, and with any luck, he never would. The slightest scratch could cause a breakdown in their relationship that would last years. Still, as Tiffany leaned closer and smiled at Mickey, it was totally worth it.

"All right," she said. "You can relax for a few minutes. Clint and Sonique are up first."

Two of the other cars, a Dodge and a Nissan, drew up next to each other. A quarter-mile off down the runway, two teens held a ribbon stretched out to mark the finish line. The cars' engines revved, and the drivers exchanged competitive grins.

"Eat my dust, math boy," one of them said.

"See you in the rearview," her opponent replied.

Tiffany raised a flag. "Ready, set, drive!"

She swept the flag down, and the cars roared into action. Down the length of the route, teenagers cheered and clapped. From back at the start, Mickey couldn't see who was ahead, but he could see the speed at which they were racing and the way they clung to the track, driving straight as a ruler right to the end. The ribbon parted, the crowd cheered louder, and the cars halted. When the drivers stepped out, Sonique was waving her hands in the air.

"All right, kiddo." Tiffany laid a hand on Mickey's shoulder. "Let's see what you've got."

To his surprise, she climbed into the driver's seat of the other car, a blue Mustang a lot like Tony's.

Mickey touched his hand to the ignition. He didn't have the keys, but a jolt of magic bypassed any need for that. As he rolled around to the start line, he wondered how best to approach this. Was it better to put Tiffany in a good mood by making sure she won or was it better to dazzle her with his superior racing skills?

Better to go for the win. These guys took their racing seriously, and he wanted them to take him seriously. There was more at stake here than Tiffany.

He reached under his seat and touched the wand hidden there before chanting the spell he'd prepared:

"Elements gather in my hour of need, give me the power to fly forth with speed."

Energy surged from his hand, through the wheel, and down into the engine. The Mustang growled like a hungry beast. Tiffany looked at him and nodded. Was it his imagination, or did she look impressed?

"Ready!" A guy with floppy hair and a flannel shirt held up the flag. "Set! Go!"

The flag swept down.

Mickey released the handbrake and floored the gas. The Mustang leapt from its starting spot, jolting him back in his seat as he raced down the airstrip.

Tiffany had been quicker off the mark, and for the first few seconds, she was ahead of him. Then the magic kicked in, and Mickey picked up speed. After a moment, he was level with her, and then he pulled ahead.

The feeling was incredible. The rush of speed. The thrill of the race. The pulsing of magic through his body and his car. He shot forward so smoothly that it was as if his wheels didn't touch the ground. He seemed to look down on the hood of Tiffany's car as he pulled ahead.

The guys at the finishing line dropped their ribbon as they stared at his approach. It didn't matter. Everyone could see who was winning. He shot across the line, then hit the brakes. The roar of the engine died as he stopped.

The others gathered around, staring at him and the Mustang. He'd expected cheering and clapping, but instead they stood silent, stunned. Drag racing was new to him—had he been that impressive?

Grinning as if he'd won the lottery, Mickey opened the

door, stepped out of the car, and fell to earth. His first reaction was embarrassment, then surprise. It hadn't been a long drop, but it was definitely further than it should have been.

"Shit," he whispered as he looked at the Mustang.

It was floating a foot up in the air.

He'd been so sure of that spell, which he'd copied from one of his mom's grimoires. The description had said that it was about speed, so surely the "flight" part was just a metaphor.

Apparently not.

"What. The. Hell." Tiffany stared from the car to Mickey and back at the car. It wasn't his imagination, was it? She did look genuinely impressed.

He really hoped it wasn't his imagination.

"I can explain," he said.

He just wasn't sure how.

Lucy turned off the road, through a gap that shouldn't have been there in a section of temporary fencing, and onto the unused runway outside John Wayne Airport. Vehicles stood idle by this end of the runway, waiting to complete renovation work that had gone on hold when the funds for it ran dry. Not far away, planes taxied into the airport, but this strip had a different type of traffic. At the far end of the runway, a crowd of teenagers gathered around a group of cars.

As Lucy got closer, the teens turned to look at her. In doing so, they parted, revealing the bright red Mustang in their midst. A Mustang that was levitating a foot above the ground.

Lucy sighed. So much for containing this before anyone saw something they shouldn't. At least she had got here while this lot were still together.

She pulled up near the other cars, drew her wand from her bag, and stepped out onto the concrete. Dusk was falling, washing the colors out of the world, but the Mustang stood out as bright as ever.

"How are you all doing?" Lucy asked, starting the conversation with something non-confrontational. Her family hadn't quite hit their teens yet, but she had already seen how much easier it was to deal with young people if you didn't push too hard.

The other teens all turned to look at a blonde girl in tight jeans and a cropped shirt standing close to the car. Like most of the rest, she looked approximately sixteen, but the kid at her feet looked closer to Dylan's age. He was out of place here, like the car, and Lucy bet herself that there was a connection.

"How are we doing?" Tiffany gave a shrill laugh and pointed at the Mustang. "Can you not see this shit? This, this is how we're doing!"

"Uh-huh." Lucy nodded and met Mickey's eyes. "Is that your car?"

Mickey caught sight of Lucy's wand and her Silver Griffin amulet as it caught the last light of the setting sun. He rubbed his hands on his jeans, trying to wipe away the nervous sweat, but he couldn't keep from trembling at the thought of the punishment he might face.

"It's my brother's." He figured that there were some people you really shouldn't lie to.

"You're the one who…" Lucy gestured toward the vehicle, which was still hanging in thin air.

Mickey nodded and bit his lip.

"Has anyone taken pictures?" Lucy asked. "I'd love to see them."

"No phones." Tiffany shook her head. "No one's allowed to bring them when we…"

She stopped talking as reality hit her, cutting through the daze from seeing a flying car. She and her friends weren't supposed to be here at the airport, and they certainly weren't allowed to be drag racing. If she acknowledged that she knew they were doing something wrong, that could make it harder to worm her way out of the consequences.

Except that this woman didn't seem like a cop, she wasn't wearing the tacky uniform of airport security, and she didn't talk like she was someone's mother here to drag them home. Did that mean that maybe they could ignore her?

Lucy raised her wand. "Never was, never will be."

Tiffany went still, her eyes vacant and mouth hanging open, along with the rest of her gang.

"Up you get," Lucy said.

Reluctantly, Mickey got to his feet. He looked at the other teens, and every one of them lost to the world.

"Let me guess, you didn't mean to fly," Lucy said. "You wanted to drive fast so you could win the race, maybe impress the other kids."

Mickey nodded.

"This is why you've got to be more careful with your magic," Lucy said. "I have a twelve-year-old, and it's the same with him. He wants to use his magic, but sometimes it gets out of hand."

"I'm fourteen! I can handle my magic!"

"Of course you can. These things happen. Now I'm taking you home to have a chat with your parents."

"You're not sending me to Trevilsom Prison?" Mickey sagged in relief.

Lucy bit back a laugh at his exaggerated sense of what was at stake. She felt sorry for the boy, whose exaggerated fears would probably provide a punishment of their own.

"Not for a first offense," she said. "Now get in my vehicle—passenger seat this time—and wait for me."

His head hanging, Mickey did as instructed.

Lucy stepped between the slack-jawed teens and up to the Mustang. As Mickey walked away, it had started to rise. Without him bringing it down to earth, the magic was getting out of control. She grabbed at the car, but it was already out of reach.

Thinking fast, she pulled a packet out of her pocket, the mints Jenkins had given her. She popped one in her mouth and immediately felt lighter on her feet as if nothing held her to the ground. She kicked off and floated up, following the levitating car. As soon as it was within reach, she pulled herself into the driver's seat.

Once behind the wheel, Lucy could feel the magic Mickey had cast. The spell was almost a sentient thing, and it was looking for guidance. Creepers of magic touched her mind, and she responded with thoughts of the ground. Slowly, the car sank until it was only a couple of feet up.

She touched the dashboard with her wand.

"Insubvolo," she said.

The car fell to earth with a *thud*. Mickey, watching from the passenger seat of the Rivian, winced at the sound. If that had damaged the suspension, Tony would kill him.

Lucy retrieved Mickey's wand from under the passenger seat, then touched her wand to the steering wheel. "Sequi me." She cast a spell of her own on the car. It wasn't her sort of vehicle, but she could see the appeal, and she certainly wasn't abandoning someone else's car here.

The Mustang's engine rumbled to life, and its headlights came on.

Lucy got out of the Mustang and back into the Rivian, where she put both wands in the glove compartment. "Type your address into the satnav," she directed. As Mickey obeyed, she started the engine and drove off down the empty runway. "We're going to have a chat with your parents."

"What about them?" Mickey gestured at Tiffany and her friends.

"By the time they recover, we'll be long gone, as will their memories of what happened."

"Oh." Mickey slumped in his seat, disappointed. So much for impressing anyone. "And Tony's car?"

By way of answer, Lucy waved over her shoulder to where the Mustang was following them home.

CHAPTER TEN

In the cave beneath the tar pits, Zero sat reading through contracts on a laptop. The laptop rested on a shelf in front of his chair, with the platform held up by a pair of gnomes. Neither of those gnomes had moved so much as an inch in two hours. That was how Zero liked his minions—utterly obedient.

"It's been a good month, Gruffbar," he observed, taking note of all the deals they had made. "And it's not even over yet."

"Yes, Mister Zero." Gruffbar sat in a seat at the side of the room. He too had a laptop open although unlike his employer, he was using a desk. His computer was more compact, equally covered with anti-hacking runes and security wards, and similarly full of valuable information. There was very little of his employer's business that Gruffbar didn't concern himself with.

"This wizard." Zero left an oily sheen as he tapped an image on the screen. "Nathaniel Oakmantle. He must have been pretty desperate to agree to these terms. Can we put the squeeze on him anymore?"

Gruffbar called up the contract on his screen and glanced through the contents. When he saw the photo next to the signature at the end, he almost smiled.

"Maybe." He stroked his beard. "This kid's got that frantic feeling to him. He wants to bring back a lost wizard tribe before the power of his line dies, or some such heroic saga crap. If what we gave him had worked, the Silver Griffins would have jumped on it with both feet, and every magical from here to DC would have felt the earthquake. No ripples means he didn't get his way yet, and I'd be surprised if he wasn't willing to double down."

Gruffbar looked at his employer. There was a look Zero sometimes got when a new plan was stirring in his brain. His pupils would go wide, and his eyes would water, little trickles of brine running down through the creases of his cheeks. Gruffbar set his computer aside and waited expectantly.

"This lost wizard tribe, how sure are we that they're all gone?" Zero asked.

"I'm a lawyer, not a genealogist." Gruffbar shrugged. "I don't have the skills to follow the kid's line back and work out if he's really alone. If there's one thing I learned working inheritance cases, it's that there's always some forgotten family member, waiting around to mess with the will."

"What do you know about this tribe?"

"Not much." Gruffbar had done a little research when he got back, mostly out of idle curiosity. Sometimes, their clients' tragic histories were even funnier than the latest

YouTube videos of cats gone wrong. This time, he'd been disappointed by how little there was. "Woodland types. Symbol's a mortar and a pestle. Apparently, they were wiped out hundreds of years ago."

Now Zero was grinning.

"Wiped out, you say?" He rubbed his hands together. "This is what my old friend Herod didn't understand. Someone always slips through the cracks. Even when I've done it myself, someone would always get away, and you just hope they're smart enough not to come back. Right now, identifying that someone could be worth a lot to our friend Nathaniel, or to anyone who wants to stop him."

Zero reached into a pocket of his brightly patterned shirt and pulled out a whistle. He set it to his lips and blew. The gnomes dropped the plank and clapped their hands to their ears, grimacing in pain, but Gruffbar couldn't hear anything.

A wave ran across the blackness of the ceiling. Where there had been an oily blackness, deep darkness gleaming with reflected light, now there was total oblivion, a blackness so complete that it swallowed all light. Instead of looking at the contours of a cave, Gruffbar felt like he was staring at a hole in reality, a flat emptiness beyond which there was nothing.

The utter blackness fell from the ceiling to form a swirling cloud around Zero, a shifting haze made up of tiny points of true black.

Gruffbar shuddered. He'd done a lot of shady things in his time: brokered deals with dark powers and worse people, committed enough crimes to fill a book, and covered up enough to fill two more. Even he was made uncomfortable by the sight of Zero's shadow mites.

"Hello, my little whispers." Zero held out his hand, and some of the mites settled onto it. The hand vanished into the darkness up to the wrist, becoming an absence on the end of that garish orange arm.

It wasn't only the blackness of the shadow mites that unnerved Gruffbar. It was the way they could disappear into the folds of the world. If he stopped looking for them, they would vanish from view. To him, and to anyone else who wasn't consciously seeking them out, they wouldn't be there. After finding himself watched by them one time too often, he'd started looking for them before he got into the shower, before he went to bed at night and before he took a trip to the john. Because any time he didn't see the mites was a time they might be there.

"I have a mission for you." Zero ran a finger through the pooled darkness. "A lost tribe to be hunted down, if they're clinging to this wretched world…"

In a croaking whisper, he told the shadow mites about the lost tribe, about the wizard longing for them, and about what he hoped to learn. At the end, the mites swirled back into the air, spun into a vortex like an ink-black whirlpool, and vanished through a crack in the ceiling.

Zero leaned back, smiling smugly. "Now we wait."

The shadow mites emerged from a hole in the ground, hidden between the roots of trees at the edge of the tar pits.

A film finance manager, brain buzzing from one too many cocktails at the end of a bad day, magic senses alerted by her forgotten witching ancestry, watched what looked like a stream of smoke rising between the trees. For a moment, it seemed to drift east with the prevailing wind, but then the smoke parted, particles floating away in a dozen different directions. She stared, slack-jawed, then grabbed a notebook from her bag and started scribbling notes for a screenplay about sentient weather.

A stray dog, sniffing hopefully around the bins behind a burger bar, looked up as a streamer of darkness floated past. He'd spent a week once running wild with a band of mischievous trolls, and in that time he'd learned to see what other dogs didn't. However, a strange cloud wasn't half as interesting as discarded burger meat, so he turned away and got back to the bins.

The mites passed a million other people as they spread out across the city, but no one else saw them. They flew over an automotive museum and a public park, past a studio tour and the Hollywood Walk of Fame. Spreading in an ever wider net, they crossed Beverly Hills and Bunker Hill, Downtown, China Town, and Downey.

As they went, they watched for magicals. The mites didn't have eyes or ears, but they soaked in all the information passing them—the sights, the sounds, the smells. They sensed the presence of power and swirled close around it whenever they drew near.

On Skid Row, a homeless wizard was doing card tricks for a cluster of his companions. No real magic, he knew better than to do that here, but he enjoyed the challenge of making the illusion of impossibility from something mundane. As he flipped over a grubby queen of hearts, a voice from nowhere whispered in his ear.

"Mortar and pestle, ancient wizards. Do you know them?"

The wizard waved a hand past his ear as if he was trying to bat away a fly, but the voice was insistent.

"A strange wizard. An ancient witch. A magical of the woods. Do you know one?"

"Don't know nothin' 'bout that," the wizard said.

His companions ignored his words and focused on the cards. Half the people they knew talked to themselves.

"That's amazing," one of them said. "You should be on the stage."

"Mister Zero will reward you well," the mites said. "Whatever you want. A shower, three hot meals, enough whiskey to drink all this away."

"I don't know nothin'," the wizard insisted, waving more frantically around his head.

"You're smart. You're on the streets. If there's something to see, you'll know."

"Told you, I don't know nothin'!" In his agitation, he kicked the battered card table over. His small crowd scattered.

"Then keep watching," the mites said. "We will return."

In Evergreen Cemetery, a dwarf was watering the plants. He liked working there. Tending graves let him connect to the earth, and he was helping humans remember their ancestors, something they could be very bad at. The work was simple and satisfying, from cutting the grass to cleaning the gravestones to maintaining the jogging track. After nearly two decades, some of those joggers felt like familiar friends, as did the inhabitants of some of the graves, even though he only knew their names.

"Good to see you again." He patted one of the gravestones.

"And to see you," a voice replied.

The dwarf stopped and stared for a moment at the stone. Then he narrowed his eyes and looked around.

"All right, I know you're here," he said. "What do you want this time?"

"Information, of course," the mites hissed. "Have you seen a mortar and pestle sign anywhere among the tombs?"

The dwarf considered it for a minute, then shook his head. "Not that I recall."

"Have you met a wizard or witch bearing that symbol, or one connected to nature?"

The dwarf straightened his back.

"I don't know how you think this works," he said, "but I had a deal with Mister Zero, and I've paid my side. I don't owe you my work."

"Do you want your employers to hear a whisper about your qualifications, about whether you really went to those human schools? Do you want them to pay closer attention to the shortest man they employ?"

The dwarf gritted his teeth.

"You shit. We had a deal."

"Now you have a new one. Listen. Watch. Ask questions. We will be back to find out what you learn."

For a Light Elf posing beneath the Hollywood sign, the mites announced themselves as a tingling in the tips of her ears, points that were hidden by magic while she posed for the photographer. She had never been profiled in a magazine before, but her small part in a television show had grown, and she was starting to gain attention. There were few things she loved more than that.

"Can I take five, Sal?" she called.

"Sure, babe." The photographer set aside his camera and pulled out a pack of smokes.

The elf turned her back to him, pulled a mirror from her purse, and pretended to fix her makeup.

"It's good to see you," she said. "Well, maybe not see…"

"So beautiful," the shadow mites hissed. "So precious."

The elf's skin crawled, but she kept her smile natural, as she had on so many stages and film sets, in so many interview rooms.

"Is there something I can do for you?" she asked.

"Do you know of an ancient tribe of wizards, their symbol a pestle and mortar, their obsession the woods?"

Her eyes narrowed. "I saw a script like that last week, for a low budget flick they're filming outside the city. It's not real, of course, but maybe there's a connection."

"Yes," the mites whispered. "Good. You follow this. You listen for more. You tell us."

"Of course." The elf fluttered her eyelashes. "Anything for Mister Zero."

Then she put her mirror away and turned back to the camera.

All across the city, magicals heard the shadow mites' demands, remembered their debts to Zero, and promised to keep their eyes open. His was a net from which no one was ever set free.

CHAPTER ELEVEN

Dylan sat on a bench at the edge of the school yard, a sandwich in his hand and a book open on his knees. It was an illustrated history of the Spanish treasure fleets, showing storm-tossed oceans, wooden ships driven along by the power of sail, and heaps of gold doubloons. This page was about an attack by Dutch privateers, and it had a big illustration of the ships fighting, with fire blazing from the cannons and smoke billowing across the crowded decks. It was the coolest thing he had read all week, maybe all month, and he'd read a lot of books. His sandwich was forgotten, his mind far away in a world of pirates, ocean chases, and lost treasure.

"What you got today?" Sofia asked as she sat down beside him. As the first of their small gang to reach the bench, Dylan had the prized middle spot, while she sat to his right.

"Pirates." He grinned. "And you?"

Sofia held up a bundle of comic books. "Miss Marvel and Spiderman. But I was asking about your sandwich."

"Oh..." Dylan peeled back a layer of bread. "Ham and lettuce."

"No swaps today, then." Sofia tucked her dark hair back behind her ears, then took a lunchbox out of her bag. "I ain't trading mama's chicken burritos for no ham."

Lance approached, dragging his backpack through the dust behind him, and flung himself down on the bench. Despite being the oldest of their group by a whole month, he was the shortest by two inches. That didn't stop him filling more space than either of his friends as he flung his arms back and let out a dramatic sigh.

"Didn't get the part in the school play?" Dylan asked.

"Worse!" Lance declared. "I got it, but Ruth Jones got the other lead. Now I've got to hang out with her every evening for two months, and she's the worst."

"Every evening?" Dylan asked.

"Are they gonna make you miss band practice?" Sofia asked. "Because Miss Miller will kick Mister Fullstrom's ass if she loses her lead guitarist."

"I can still do band practice. We won't rehearse on weekends until next month."

"When you say every evening..."

"This is my tragedy, okay? Let me wallow in it."

Dylan opened a plastic tub and held it out to Lance.

"Here, medicinal cookies."

"Oh wow." Lance grabbed one and took a big bite. "Mom watched a documentary about the sugar industry last week, so we're not allowed cookies or cakes at home. Next month, it'll probably be dairy again, or she'll be mad about nuclear power, but a month's a long time to go without cookies."

"Gracias," Sofia said as she took a cookie. "Your mom makes the best cookies, Dylan."

He had to agree. The cookies were crumbly around the edge and moist in the middle, with just the right proportion of chocolate chips. Cookies, friends, and a good book, this was what made life worth living.

"Hey, Heron." Jeff Barr stood in front of them, cracking the knuckles of one hand as he stared at the tub in Dylan's lap. Jeff was wider across the shoulders than most teachers and his face went red when he was angry, or frustrated, or bored. His face was red now. "What you got there?"

"Cookies." Dylan looked at the dozen or so of Jeff's friends who were standing around them.

"You should give them to me."

Dylan hesitated. He wanted to put the lid back on the tub, to save the cookies for later. He wanted to tell Barr to go bother someone else. He also didn't want bruises.

"Please, have one." He held out the cookies.

Jeff snatched the tub from Dylan's hands, stuffed a cookie in his mouth, then grabbed another before passing the tub on to his friends. Dylan watched with a sinking heart as people he didn't even like ate the snack he'd been saving for after band practice.

"Not bad," Jeff said, spraying crumbs over Dylan. "I want cinnamon next time."

"Those were mine," Dylan protested, trying not to let Jeff see how upset he was.

"Now they're ours. That's how life works. Winners get cookies. Losers get crumbs." Jeff tossed the empty tub at Dylan, who fumbled the catch. It clattered onto the ground.

"You're the loser." Sofia leapt to her feet. She had the same look on her face that she'd worn right before she broke Sammy Lee's violin over his head for saying she played flute like a girl. This time, the anger was more justified. Unlike Sammy, Jeff was trying to be unpleasant.

"Look at this." Jeff grinned maliciously. "Dylan Heron's girlfriend is standing up for him."

"I'm not his girlfriend."

"What then, his bodyguard? You're ugly enough."

"That's it, you little—"

"Whoa, whoa, whoa!" Dylan jumped up, putting himself between Sofia and Jeff before she could swing a punch.

"Aw, now you're protecting her," Jeff said with a sneer. "How cute."

Behind him, his friends laughed. It was a cruel, spiteful sort of laughter.

Dylan looked down at Jeff. It didn't matter that he was a whole head taller than the bully, taller than almost anyone in their year. Height and strength weren't the same thing, and his extra inches didn't come with Jeff's unflinching willingness to hurt others, or to lie about it afterward. If the teachers knew that Jeff started all the fights he got into, they couldn't prove it.

"What's your problem, Jeff?" Dylan asked.

"Me? I don't have a problem. I've had cookies, and now I'm going to have your sandwich. My life is sweet."

Jeff took the sandwich out of Dylan's hand and sniffed at it.

"Ham and lettuce? Urgh, no thanks." Jeff dropped the sandwich, then stamped on it. "Now, what have the rest of you band nerds got for me?"

Dylan looked down sadly at the flattened bread and dirty ham. His stomach grumbled.

There was a rustle as Lance pulled out a bag of corn chips and handed them to one of Jeff's gang.

"That's more like it." Jeff rubbed his hands together.

Lance hung his head. His unhappiness didn't look like a big show anymore.

"Enough." Dylan grabbed the bag of corn chips and handed it back to Lance. "We're not putting up with this any longer."

"Yeah!" Sofia grinned and rolled her shoulders.

"Yeah." Lance stood beside them, striking his best action hero pose. Only a flicker of his eyes gave away how scared he really was.

"Oh yeah?" Jeff leaned in, scowling. "You gonna fight me, Heron? 'Cause I'll snap you like a twig."

"I don't need to fight you," Dylan snapped. "I can do magic."

Jeff made a snorting sound. It took a long moment for anyone to realize that it was laughter.

"You've been playing too much *Dungeons and Dragons*, dork." Jeff prodded Dylan in the chest with a finger as pink and swollen as a cheap hot dog. "Your level twelve warlock might have an ass full of fireballs, but this is real life, and I'm gonna kick the snot out of you."

"I really can do magic," Dylan said. "Right, guys?"

Lance and Sofia looked at each other. They knew about Dylan's unusual abilities, and they knew that they weren't supposed to know. Neither of them thought that this seemed like a good idea.

Dylan was starting to have doubts of his own. His mom

would be mad enough if she found out that he'd told his closest friends that he was a wizard. Announcing the news to half his class was a sure way to land him in trouble if mom ever found out. After all, it was her job to keep magic hidden, and here he was blurting it out to the world. It would take more than a note in the magic jar to make up for this.

Still, he'd gone too far to turn back now. If he gave up on his claim, he would convince Jeff that he was a liar, a little kid with an overactive imagination. Worst of all, he would show Jeff that he was weak, and the other boy would bully him even more mercilessly.

He was committed.

"Come on, then," Jeff said. "Pull a rabbit out of your sleeve. Summon Stephen Strange. Show us what a magical you are."

He waved his hands in the air and made mock spooky sounds. His friends laughed. In Dylan's experience, they would laugh at anything Jeff said.

Dylan drew a deep breath. He needed to do something that the others couldn't explain another way, but something small, something that the teachers wouldn't notice. Something he could explain away to everyone except Jeff.

He knelt and splayed one hand across the concrete of the schoolyard.

"Crescent plantae," he whispered.

Magic flowed through him. He never had trouble finding it. There was so much in the world, bubbling away beneath the surface like the tar pits they'd visited on a school trip. The challenge was channeling it, especially without his wand, which he wasn't allowed to bring to school.

This time, the power went where he wanted. He kept a tight grip on it as the magic ran from his head, through his heart, down his arm, and out the palm of his hand into the concrete and through to the dirt below. There it found a seed, small and withered and forgotten, but still a tiny scrap of life, a thing of tightly contained potential.

As the magic touched it, the seed sprouted. Slender roots dug into the earth, feeling their way to water and nutrients, while a shoot rose through the soil, then pressed against the concrete above. Months of growth passed in the space of a second, and the shoot hit the concrete with enough force to crack it open.

A tiny crater appeared in the playground's surface. Then a miniature green thread uncurled from its center, reaching into the light.

"See?" Dylan said. "Magic."

Jeff made a face. "A tiny plant. That doesn't prove anything."

"Fine."

Dylan closed his eyes and let more of the magic through. The shoot grew taller, turning into a pale beech sapling.

"Dylan," Lance muttered, "are you sure this is a good idea?"

Dylan squeezed tight on the flow of magic, trying to stop the plant's rise. The magic was coming faster now, tendrils of power squirming free of his grasp. Another shoot burst from the ground, and another, flinging dirt and fragments of concrete through the air. The original tree kept rising, faster and faster, branches bursting out covered in bright green leaves.

Dylan stumbled back, and his friends with him.

"I told you this wasn't a good idea," Lance said.

"With great power comes great responsibility," Sofia added, then spun as a palm tree shot up behind her.

"What does that mean?"

"I don't know. It's something Spiderman says!"

"Dylan isn't Spiderman!"

"You think I don't know that?"

Dylan waved his arms in the air.

"Nolite crescente!" he shouted at the trees, desperately trying to stop their growth. "Nolite crescente!"

Still the plants kept coming, not only trees but undergrowth too, practically a jungle, a vast mass of greens and browns and brightly colored flowers that sprawled across the schoolyard, tearing up paving slabs and knocking down basketball hoops. Some kids ran away screaming. Others stood and stared. Some of the older ones pulled out phones and took photos or started streaming.

Finally, the local pool of background magic ran out, and the plants stopped their accelerated growth spurt. Dylan sighed and looked around.

He'd definitely proved that he had magic.

Jeff was lying in a patch of ferns, eyes wide and face blank, his skin pale. Dylan grabbed his arm and pulled him to his feet.

"I… You… It…" Jeff turned his head, slowly taking it all in. Then his mouth slammed shut, and a familiar look of malice filled his eyes.

"Now do you believe me?" Dylan challenged.

"I'm gonna get a teacher," Jeff said. "I'm gonna get a teacher, and I'm gonna tell them what you did. You are in so much trouble, Heron. So much trouble."

He ran off as fast as his legs could carry him.

Dylan ran his hands through his dark, wavy hair.

"Is this bad?" he asked. "This is bad, right?"

Sofia put a hand on his shoulder.

"On the upside, there's probably no rule against growing a magical jungle in the schoolyard," she said. "On the downside, I think they might add that rule now just for us."

Lance reached down behind the bench, which the rising trees had knocked over, and picked up his packet of corn chips. He opened the bag and offered them around. Most of them were broken, some crushed to dust, but they were still tasty.

"At least Jeff didn't get these."

"I don't think Jeff's our biggest problem anymore," Sofia countered.

A cluster of teachers had appeared on the far side of the schoolyard. Some of them looked amazed, some looked confused, and several looked mad.

The angry ones were all pointing their way.

CHAPTER TWELVE

"What am I doing?" Lucy muttered to herself as she pulled the drain cover into place above her head. The metal ladder was cold under her hands, rust and old paint flaking away from its surface. When she looked down, the torch strapped to her forehead illuminated a long climb and a dirty tunnel at the bottom. That wasn't why she was having doubts.

She drew a deep breath and started her descent. Technically, she was doing her job. As a Silver Griffin, it was her duty to follow up on magical issues, and that was what she was doing.

The problem was that, in practice, her assignments normally came to her by pigeon post and involved following up on concerns identified by the Griffins' intelligence network. Whereas today, she was following a hunch concerning a long-dead tribe of witches, and in her experience, dead people weren't the ones who caused trouble.

She jumped down the last few feet, her sturdy boots hitting the tunnel floor with a *thud*. Trainers would have been more comfortable, but the boots were better for protecting her feet in tunnels full of wreckage and rats. She figured that Jackie would forgive her style-free footwear just this once.

With her hands freed from the ladder, she pulled out her new wand and gave it an experimental wave. It had worked well while dealing with the kid in the Mustang. Its magic was responsive, its grip comfortable, and something about it made her feel easier in herself. It even made her feel better about following her hunch—she couldn't imagine chasing this non-lead with her old desert willow wand.

"Lucem venite ad me," she chanted.

Glowing points of light appeared in the air around Lucy, expanded into gently glowing orbs, and settled on her, so that she seemed to shine with an inner light.

She switched off the headlamp and stuffed it into her bag. That was why she'd chosen the Batman backpack. Out of all the available options at the store, it was as close as she could get to a utility belt.

She set off down the tunnel. The air here was heavy and humid, without a hint of a breeze. Water seeped down the walls and trickled along one side of the tunnel.

As she made her way through the maze of interconnected underground spaces, Lucy examined their architecture, trying to work out what each one had originally been. Storm drain or subway, illegal speakeasy, or part of the civic network that connected government buildings? She was pretty sure that some of them hadn't fitted the uses described in history books, even before magicals had started making these tunnels their own. Now, there was a network that no city authority could have mapped or navigated.

Fortunately, the Silver Griffins didn't work for the city.

At a fork in the tunnel, someone had chalked red and green sigils on the wall. Lucy read them carefully, then turned left, pushing back against her instincts this one time. The chalk spell created the urge to go right, designed to misdirect non-magical wanderers. Within a few paces, the feeling had passed.

After a few more turns and a twisting downward ramp, Lucy found herself in a cavernous tunnel that echoed with sounds of life. Fifty yards away stood the beginning of a shantytown, rows of shelters built from wooden pallets, plastic sheeting, and even an old transport crate. Fires flickered in metal barrels, but that wasn't the only source of light. There were electric bulbs strung together along lengths of mismatched cable, and in other places, the soft glow of magical illumination.

Lucy stamped hard on the floor, then stood waiting. After a few minutes, a voice called from the darkness.

"All right, you can come closer, but don't try anything funny."

Teenagers emerged from the improvised shelters, watching as Lucy approached. Even having been invited in, she walked slowly and made no sudden moves, not wanting to startle them. She stopped by the first barrel, put her backpack on the ground, and took out the groceries she'd packed into every spare space. There were tins of beans and stewed beef, a bag of rice and another of noodles, aspirin, and bandages. She topped off the heap with a tub of her homemade brownies. Everyone deserved a few impractical treats. Then she took a few steps back.

"I brought these for you. I also want to ask some questions. Not about you, but something you can help with."

One by one, the teenagers approached. There was an Arpak with a crippled wing, a Wood Elf whose natural camouflage kept flickering on and off so that her skin looked like tree bark one moment and pale ashes the next. A troll kept shrinking and growing, unable to hold himself in one single size, and a young witch whose eyes blazed with unquenchable pools of magic. Others huddled behind, misplaced and malformed, a whole community of runaway teens whose magic refused to work right.

"I've seen you before." The Arpak sniffed at the tub of brownies. "You paid us to tell you what we knew about that pyromaniac wizard."

"That was Jackie. Agent 782. You're right that I was here with her, and I hoped you could help me out this time, as you've helped the Silver Griffins with other small assignments in the past."

The teens' need for supplies had finally overcome their nervousness. They gathered up the food Lucy had brought and rushed it away as if they were scared that she might change her mind. The Arpak passed the plastic tub around, and each kid took a fragment of a brownie, making sure to leave enough for the rest. There was none of the feral greed that some people ascribed to those down on their luck. These kids looked after each other.

"I'm looking for someone who's lost like you," Lucy said. "If they even exist."

"That's a big if," the Arpak said.

"I know. If anybody can help me with this, it's you guys."

"We don't have to help you. Not if we don't want to."

"Leontine!" the witch with the glowing eyes said. "Stop that."

The Arpak glared at her. "The Griffins aren't your friends, Twylan," he said. "They're someone else who wants something from us. If the authorities tell them to move us on, they'll be down here with wands swinging, as sure as the cops would be."

"Maybe," Twylan replied. She looked at Lucy, and the magic seemed to dance from her eyes out across her cheeks, leaving black traces like an inversion of lightning. "But they pay, right?"

Lucy pulled a small bundle of twenties from her pocket and held them up for the outcasts to see. Normally, she would have gotten the money from the Griffins' accountants, but she hadn't known how to explain this one, so instead, it came from her funds.

"Half now," she said, peeling off five notes and holding them out to Leontine. "Half after we've talked."

The Arpak snatched the money, counted it, and stuffed it into a pocket of his frayed cargo pants. Then he nodded.

"All right, ask your questions."

Lucy sat down with her backpack beside her. The concrete wasn't comfortable, but the muggy air down here kept it from being cold, and she felt too confrontational standing opposite these kids. They were so young. It broke her heart to see them living like this. The least she could do was to make this as easy as possible.

Some of the outcasts came to sit in a circle with her.

Leontine stood back, arms folded, watching through narrowed eyes.

"I'm looking for any survivors of an ancient tribe of witches," Lucy said. "They used to live out in the forest, connecting to nature, but cities have overrun a lot of their territory since then. If any of them are still around, if there are ghosts or only traces of their presence, I hope you might have seen them. Their tribe was wiped out, so if there are survivors, they'll be outcasts, living in hiding like you."

"How can we tell who these witches are?" Twylan asked.

"They'd be interested in plants and nature. They might have magic that gives them visions of the future." Lucy remembered what she had seen in the smoke from the mortar and the unsettling feeling of déjà vu when that vision played out an hour later. "They have a symbol, a mortar and a pestle."

"Sounds rude." The troll giggled, his body shrinking and growing in time with his laughter. "Pestle. Hehehe."

"A mortar and pestle are alchemists' tools," Leontine said. "A bowl and a heavy rod for grinding ingredients."

"That's right." Lucy smiled at him, but he didn't smile back. "They're used to grind spices for cooking as well. You might have seen them in a kitchen. Here."

She held up her phone, showing a picture of a pestle and mortar on eBay, then a photo of the artifact she had retrieved from the pawnshop.

"I haven't seen anything like that," Twylan said. "Anyone?"

They shook their heads.

"Ah, well." Lucy sighed. "It was a long shot." She passed the remains of the cash to Twylan. "Thanks for hearing me out."

Twylan looked down at the money. It was hard to read her expression, with her eyes replaced by the flickering of magic, but she seemed thoughtful.

"These witches were from a long time ago, right?" she said. "If they've survived unseen, it's because their powers didn't show."

"You're right." Lucy leaned forward. "Does that tell you something?"

"You might find them among the duds."

"Duds?"

"People who've lost their power. They're not really magicals anymore, not human either. They live off by themselves. They're hard to find, but they like hidden places, so sometimes we bump into them." Twylan looked up at Lucy, and her tone grew very serious. "I shouldn't call them duds. It's not a nice word. I don't know another one."

"If I wanted to talk to them, how could I do that?"

"I don't know, sorry. If anyone works out who they are, they move on. No one wants to be looked at with that sort of pity, knowing that you've lost all your power."

"Well, perhaps the Silver Griffins can—"

"Willum Grast." The Wood Elf with the flickering skin spoke a name like it was a spell. "He knows about your witches. He knows all sorts of things."

"Old Willum?" Twylan asked in a tone of surprise.

The Wood Elf nodded.

"Drunk Willum, more like," Leontine growled.

"Who's this Willum?" Lucy asked.

"He's a gnome," Twylan said. "Not a very friendly one. He lives a few miles west of Disneyland, in the tunnels around the old, abandoned missile silos."

"What makes you think that he knows about these witches?"

The Wood Elf bit her lip and looked nervously over at Twylan.

"It's okay," Twylan said. "We can talk to the Silver Griffins."

Leontine snorted, but everyone else ignored him.

"I promise," Lucy said. "Willum will never know where I got his name."

"Promise?"

"Cross my heart." Lucy gestured with her wand, which left a trail of soft sparks across her chest.

"All right," the Wood Elf said. "Willum's kind of crazy. He's got this still that he practically sleeps with and that he uses to make liquor. Not good alcohol, but the grossest, most burn-your-throat stuff you've ever tasted. He drinks most of it himself, and when he gets drunk, he throws magic around, spells that should be way beyond him. He blows stuff up, sometimes on purpose, sometimes by accident. One time I was there doing a trade, and he almost blew up his still. Then he cried for, like, an hour and kept saying sorry to the still. It was so weird.

"Anyway, when he's done blowing things up, he talks. And I mean, like, talks and talks and talks. I thought my dad was bad, but Willum..." The Wood Elf shook her head. "The time he nearly blew up the still, I didn't dare leave because we hadn't made our trade yet and he was proper crazy. He started talking about people like me, people connected to the woods. Except they weren't like me because they weren't Elves. I figured maybe he was talking about a bunch of hippies he'd run into or some dud Elves, which was why I thought of it now. But the things he said..."

Lucy leaned forward again, eager to hear more. "Go on."

"He said these people had magic. He said they were dead, but they weren't, which was when I decided it was all nonsense. Then he drew this symbol, and I think maybe it's what you're looking for."

She picked up a piece of charcoal from the ashes beside the oil drum and sketched a symbol on the concrete floor: the bowl and base of a mortar, with the handle of a pestle leaning out of the top.

Excitement rose in Lucy as she took a photo of the symbol. This was it, the lead she had been looking for. Her instincts were right. This was something worth pursuing.

"Here." She pulled another twenty from her pocket and handed it to the Wood Elf. "Thank you." She pulled out a business card with her work number and her email address from one of her backpack pockets. "In case you hear anything else."

Twylan handed her the empty brownie tub, which went back into the bag. Then Lucy got up and dusted herself off.

"Thanks for your help," she said. "It's really appreciated."

Footsteps followed her as she walked away, Leontine coming to make sure that she was gone. He stopped at the point where the wide tunnel turned into a twisting ramp.

"These kids," he said, and though he was no older than

Twylan or the Wood Elf, there was something protective in his tone, "they can look after themselves, but they need people to listen to them, people who don't interrupt or try to fit their stories into the shape outsiders want. It's good you did that."

"I'm glad," Lucy said. "I'll be back. Maybe next time I'll bring cookies."

"That might be okay." Leontine gave the smallest of smiles, then turned and walked back to the fire.

CHAPTER THIRTEEN

Charlie picked up the wastepaper bin from under his workstation, held it at the edge of the desk, and swept in a heap of candy wrappers and soda cans. He could live with other people's mess, that was one of the realities of life and especially of parenting, but he drew the line when the trash spilled off his colleagues' desks and into his workspace.

"Looks like office dad's cleaning up after us again," said Steve. He laughed. "Are you gonna tell us to make our beds next?"

"If you start sleeping here, I might." Charlie tossed one of the wrappers at Steve's head, then caught it in the bin as it bounced off. "Five points to me!"

"If that's worth five points, this has to be a ten!" Gail screwed up her Doritos bag and lobbed it across the room, landing it squarely in with the other waste.

"Not bad," Charlie said. "I bet you can't do it again."

"You're on, sucker." Gail balled up another wrapper and chucked it in. Determined not to be outdone, Steve rolled his chair back next to hers and joined the game, throwing whatever trash he could grab.

Charlie smiled to himself as he turned his attention back to work. With his younger colleagues, just like the kids at home, turning a chore into a game was the best way of getting it done. Within the IT support department of their particular cloud computing company, all his colleagues were younger than him. It felt weird to be the toughened veteran when he was only in his mid-thirties, the longest-serving team member as well as the oldest, but he didn't mind. It was a fun place to be.

"I am the champion!" Steve punched the air.

"Oh yeah? Can you do this?" Gail bounced a rolled-up M&Ms packet off the wall, then the edge of a monitor, and from there into the trash. "Double bounces quadruple your score. Square law in action."

"Who are you calling square?"

"I don't make the laws. I simply enforce them."

"Hey, guys." Charlie looked around from his screen. "Maybe you should do some work, in case someone from management comes by."

"It's not like they're going to catch us unaware." Steve pointed at the door, which was shut and locked, with a peephole so the support team could see who rang their doorbell.

"Do you think management knew what they were doing when they put that in?" Gail asked.

"Probably not," Charlie said. "Most managers I've met like to keep a close eye on things. Still, you know what the CEO's like—he understands that security trumps everything in our work."

Speaking of which, he had patches to install. He opened the files, checked the settings and where there was anything that would mess with their clients' needs, then started the installations.

From across the desk, gentle snoring sounds interrupted Charlie's work. Kieran was sitting with his mouth hanging open and his eyes closed, hands lying limp across his keyboard.

"Kieran," Charlie said quietly.

There was no response.

"Kieran." A little louder this time.

The snoring turned to snuffles, then back to what it had been.

"Kieran." Charlie stretched out and kicked his youngest colleague under the desk.

"What?" Kieran sat bolt upright, floppy hair hanging across his face, and blinked as he looked around in surprise.

"You're here to work, remember?" Charlie said. "The tickets are piling up, buddy."

"Right, yes, totally." Kieran rubbed his eyes, then leaned forward over the keyboard, peering at one of his monitors.

"Big night last night?" Charlie asked.

"I was on a raid, but our demon hunter blew our approach. The whole thing turned into a disaster."

Charlie stared across the desk in surprise. He'd had no idea that Kieran was connected to the magical world, never mind that he was moonlighting as some sort of operative.

"Shouldn't you be a little more discreet?" he whispered, nodding over Kieran's shoulder to the other two, who were making half-hearted imitations of work.

"No need, they don't do WoW, so it's not like I'm going to give away any spoilers."

"Don't do what, now?"

"WoW. World of Warcraft. You know, warriors and mages and quests and all that cool stuff. Escaping to a world that has a little magic in it."

"Oh, of course!"

Charlie laughed at himself. That would teach him not to make assumptions. Kieran's life had as much to do with real magic as an Instagram selfie had to do with high art. He was relieved to discover that he hadn't been sitting here for months not noticing a fellow magical on his team.

"I thought that late nights in your twenties were meant to be about hitting bars and clubs," he said, "not hitting dragons over the head with digital swords."

"That's never really been my thing." Charlie reached for a fresh can of soda. "I'll take Mountain Dew and a cool instance over beer and a dance floor any day."

"People like you give us programmers a bad name." Steve shook his head.

"People claiming that this work is programming give programmers a bad name," Gail retorted. "We're glorified admins. It's no wonder Charlie's constantly running side projects alongside the tickets."

"He is?"

They all looked at Charlie, who shifted in his seat. He was glad that he had the corner desk, where no one else could see his monitors. It had never occurred to him that someone might notice what he was up to.

"I get the job done, and that's what matters," he said.

"Hey, I'm not judging." Gail held her hands in the air. "Everyone has a side hustle these days. Makes sense that you'd be programming something of your own."

"Speaking of hustling..." Charlie pointed at the board on the wall, where a count of their active tickets had started flashing red. "You guys need to get on top of that before we breach our SLA."

"What about you, old man?"

"I'm on installations today. You're on tickets." He hunched over and put on a croaky old man's voice. "Now get to it, you young whippersnappers."

Gail's eyes lit up. "Bet I can clear more tickets in the next hour than either of you two."

"Oh, it's on," Steve said.

As his colleagues finally focused on their jobs, Charlie turned back to the patches. Everything was running smoothly, and some people would have left the updates to run on their own. That was fine ninety-nine percent of the time, but that other one percent was what the people they worked for would remember. You could be competent three hundred and sixty-four days of the year, but if you crashed a company-wide system on day three-sixty-five, you were going to get yourself fired. Rather than let things go unchecked, Charlie left the updates running on one monitor and opened his side project on another.

Charlie suspected that his "side hustle" wasn't what most people would consider a hustle. If Gail ever learned what he was up to, he suspected that she would be disappointed as well as surprised. He wasn't developing a new app, carrying out white hat hacks, or programming a piece of software that would get him out of the day job. He was merely monitoring the internet.

What made it interesting, the part that would leave Gail surprised and disappointed was that this wasn't any ordinary internet. Charlie monitored the magical side of cloud computing using a separate computer drive from his normal work one—a drive bound up in security runes and concealment spells.

On his screen was a sprawling diagram of interconnected lines, with colored disks at the nexuses where those threads came together. He was proud of the program he'd written to produce it, and prouder still of the results, a living map of the place where his interests connected, where the magical world made use of cloud computing to run the hidden parts of the internet.

As he watched, something flashed red at the side of the diagram. He zoomed in on it, and the lines in that area fractured, breaking down into their component strands. At this level, it looked a lot like the big picture he'd started with, only with smaller details highlighted. He zoomed in again and again until he could see what had triggered the alert. It wasn't merely one alert but dozens, a scattering of flashing red letters to point out that something abnormal was going on.

Someone was building a network within the magical cloud. They were working fast, setting up databases, discussion boards, websites, and links into social media. They seemed to half-know what they were doing, which meant that the work was fast but ugly. As Charlie watched, this dispersed network expanded, swelling out to eat up territory inside and alongside other sites. It was spread across the world, both in terms of the data centers it used and the audiences it was targeting. Like a virulent disease, its spread was accelerating, as each connection led to a dozen more.

All of that was interesting, but it wasn't enough to set off Charlie's alarms. What had done that was the way it bled over into regular networks. That was a feature of the careless work, a side effect of rushing such a big job. The person behind it was using bots and software spells so that they didn't have to do all the work themselves. While the programmers were competent enough to make it work, they weren't excellent, and they weren't running quality checks.

Charlie glanced at the updates, which were still installing fine, then brought up a diagram of his company's cloud platform on his third screen. This new magical network was creeping onto their servers, and he didn't like it. He didn't know what the new network was supposed to do, whether it was data gathering, misinformation, or something more malicious, but he didn't want to take any chances. Typing rapidly, pulling up pieces of code he had created for such an occasion, he started flinging up his magical software, wards cast using digital spells. He couldn't stop this thing from expanding everywhere, but he could at least protect the place where he worked.

As he typed away, he made a note to himself to mention this to Lucy later. It sure seemed like Silver Griffin territory.

"Thirty tickets!" Gail shouted, punching the air. "I'm still on a roll. I don't see either of you losers catching up."

"I'm on twenty-three," Keiran replied. "Some of them

are tricky problems. That's got to count for something, right Charlie?"

Fingers still flying across the keyboard, Charlie looked up with a distracted smile. "Buddy, as long as you stay awake, that's good enough for me."

CHAPTER FOURTEEN

Lucy's phone started buzzing in her pocket as she was climbing the rusted metal steps out of the tunnels. It kept on buzzing as she pushed aside the manhole cover, glanced around in case anyone was watching, and climbed out into a quiet back alley. She slid the heavy metal plate back into place, took off her headlamp, and stowed it away in the Batman bag before finally checking what was driving her phone nuts.

Nine alerts appeared on her screen. Three were text messages from Dylan's school, three attempts by the school to call her, two from her answering service telling her that people had left messages, and the last one a missed call from Charlie.

She called Charlie back first.

"Is Dylan okay?" she asked the moment he answered. "I've got all these messages from the school, and they wouldn't be doing that if it wasn't an emergency."

"He's fine," Charlie said. "Or at least he's not hurt. Apparently, something weird has happened though. The admin I spoke with said that it would be easier to show us than to explain."

Lucy's stomach sank. "He's done something magical, hasn't he?"

"Let's not jump to conclusions."

"Charlie, I'm a Silver Griffin. It's my job to jump to conclusions and to be right about it."

Charlie sighed. "Yeah, sorry, I'm just trying to avoid a panic."

"I'm not panicking. I'm preparing myself."

"You're way better at that than me. It's possible, just possible that I'm panicking a little."

"Are you on your way there?" She couldn't hear a car's engine, but Charlie had chosen one of the quietest hybrid vehicles he could find to cut down on noise pollution as well as the carbon kind.

"Nearly at the gates."

"I'll be there in ten. Meet you outside?"

"Good idea. That way we can present a united front."

She hung up and got into the Rivian, which she'd parked near the end of the alley, and glanced through the texts in case they said something that Charlie hadn't. All she learned was that the school had called her before getting hold of him.

She started the SUV and headed out into the mid-afternoon traffic. Even at its quieter times of day, LA was a busy city, but she had plenty of practice negotiating the roads.

As she approached the school, her eye was caught by a burst of bright green foliage rising over the buildings. Although she couldn't see the trees' bases, it looked suspiciously like they were growing in the playground.

She pulled to the side of the street, behind where Charlie's Prius was parked. As she exited the vehicle, she was hit by a faint but unmistakable aura of magic, like a charcoal smell lingering around the kitchen hours after someone burned the toast. The sinking feeling she'd had on seeing those unfamiliar treetops grew deeper.

Charlie was standing by his car. A laptop rested on the hood, and he was tapping away at something.

"Hey there, mister installation wizard." Lucy kissed him on the cheek. "What are you working on?"

"Something for you," he said.

Lucy looked at the screen. It was a mass of blobs and lines, with some angry red symbols at one side. Wherever Charlie put his cursor, blocks of text sprang out of the incomprehensible digital tangle.

"As romantic gestures go, I'd rather have flowers," she said.

"Sorry, I meant plural you, as in the Silver Griffins. I like your colleagues, but I don't feel terribly romantic about them."

She wrapped her arm around his waist and leaned into him, peering at the mess on the screen.

"So what is it?"

"A magical is building something new on the internet. Something big. Something I don't understand yet."

"Does that mean it's something bad?"

Charlie held a hand out palm down, wobbling it back and forth, and made a non-committal noise.

"Not by definition. But something big and unexplained makes me suspicious, especially when it's on the magical side. This here…" he zoomed out, then pointed at the red part of the screen "…that's an exposure risk for the magical world, whether it's deliberate or not. Part of the magical internet is crowding out the mundane, and that'll draw attention we don't want. Seems like something you guys should be interested in."

However hard Lucy stared at the data, it didn't make any more sense to her.

"I don't know who would deal with this. I mean, we have tech people, but it's not like the Griffins have a cyber crime department."

"Maybe you should. The future's not only software and spells. It's those things coming together."

"You're so smart." She kissed him on the cheek again. "You're also easily distracted, and the principal is waiting for us."

Charlie put the laptop away in his satchel and followed her across the road to the school. Inside, an administrator was pacing back and forth, twisting a pen between her fingers.

"Are you Dylan Heron's parents?" she asked.

"That depends," Charlie said. "Are Dylan's parents going to get detention?"

"I don't think that's how—"

"My husband's just trying to be funny," Lucy said. "I think this might not be the time. Yes, we're Dylan's parents."

"Oh, yeah, haha." The administrator's expression was half-grin, half-grimace. "Come this way, please. Principal Wallace is waiting for you."

She led them down a corridor, away from the sprawling mass of classrooms.

"I'm getting flashbacks," Charlie whispered. "Just hearing the word 'principal' sends a chill down my spine."

"I refuse to believe that you were a troublemaker. Your mum's shown me those childhood pictures, and no one that nerdy could possibly have been bad news."

"You'd be surprised at how much trouble you can get in for wanting to know what makes the school calculators work."

"You mean dismantling them?"

"You say tomato…"

"Well, at least we know where Ashley gets it from."

They walked into the principal's office, and the door closed behind them. Wallace, a round woman in a sharp suit, was sitting behind her desk, and she smiled as they came in. The space would have been well-lit thanks to the large window behind her, except that a row of towering trees partially blotted out the light.

"Thanks for coming in," Wallace said. "I really appreciate it when parents make an effort."

"You're the ones doing the hard work," Lucy said as she took a seat. "I'm sorry if Dylan's been causing trouble."

She tried to keep her attention on Wallace, but it was hard to do with a jungle swaying in her view, especially when she suspected that her son had something to do with the trees.

"As you can see, we've been having quite a day." Wallace leaned back in her chair and waved out the window. "Believe it or not, none of those plants were there yesterday."

"Really? That's amazing." Lucy tried to sound shocked, but this was nothing compared with some of the things she dealt with at work. At least jungles were supposed to exist on Earth.

"As far as we can tell, it all sprouted over the lunch break, just seemed to come out of nowhere. While our very own rain forest could be a great educational tool, it's caused something of a fuss."

"I bet."

"Unfortunately, a lot of that fuss centers on Dylan."

Lucy reached out for Charlie's hand and squeezed it. She didn't know how they would deal with this one, but she was glad she had backup.

"Really?" she asked. "What does Dylan have to do with it?"

"He was there when the plants appeared, and some of the other kids say he did it. Unfortunately, Dylan is playing into that story. I know it's crazy, trees don't just spring up because a twelve-year-old tells them to, but I think he's enjoying the attention.

"Normally, I'm in favor of guerrilla gardening—we all know this world could do with more greenery. Still, whoever did this, I don't think they've thought through what it means for our staff and kids or what it will cost the education department. That's money we won't have for new gym equipment."

Wallace sighed.

"Perhaps we can help?" Lucy said. "Organize a fundraiser, maybe? I'm on the PTA at our other kid's school. I've got form when it comes to bake sales."

"That's good of you, but I don't want to do anything that would further link this to Dylan. He doesn't need some wild story following him for the rest of his school career. In fact, I think it's important to have an honest conversation with him now, to put this story to rest."

"Of course. Can he join us?"

"Sure." Wallace pressed a button on her intercom. "Tammy, can you send Dylan in, please?"

The door opened, and Dylan shuffled into the room. He looked nervously at his parents, then down at his feet.

"Hi there, Dylan," Wallace said. "We were talking about all those trees out there."

"Sorry," Dylan mumbled. "I shouldn't have done that."

"Dylan, you're not in trouble, but your parents and I are curious—why do you keep saying that you did this?"

"Because I did it." Dylan looked at Lucy. "Sorry, mom. Looks like I'll have to put a really big note in the jar."

"Could we talk with Dylan alone?" Lucy asked. "It might be easier to get to the bottom of it that way."

"Of course." Wallace got out of her seat and walked across the room. "Take all the time you need."

Once the three of them were alone, Lucy gestured Dylan to the seat beside her.

"What were you thinking, Dylan?" she asked. "You know you're not allowed to do magic without supervision."

"I had to do something," Dylan said. "Jeff Barr was pushing me around again, he took your cookies, and then he took Lance's chips, and he just keeps taking things and being mean and... and... and... I didn't know what else to do, but at least now he'll leave me alone, right?"

Lucy frowned. She wasn't convinced that showing unusual abilities would shut down a bully, but that was a conversation for later.

"Sweetheart, I'm really sorry that happened to you, but

it doesn't matter what Jeff was doing, you can't respond with magic."

"What else was I going to do? You've told me not to get into fights!"

Lucy drew a deep breath, trying to center herself. There was a clear logic to everything Dylan said. The problem was that there were other things to consider.

"I get it, buddy," Charlie said. "But remember, magic is a big, powerful secret. We're really lucky to be part of it, but that brings responsibilities. Those responsibilities include keeping the secret, not only for us but for other people, because if it got into the wrong hands, magic could be really dangerous. You understand that, right?"

Dylan nodded. "Sorry."

"Now, I know we normally tell you not to lie, but today is different. Keeping magic secret is more important even than honesty. Can you tell the principal that you didn't do this?"

"You want me to lie to Ms. Wallace?" Dylan looked shocked.

"Just this once."

"Okay."

"You know this school better than we do. Can you think of a way to say it that she'll believe?"

"Sure." A spark of excitement lit up Dylan's face. "I can do that."

Lucy opened the door, and the principal came back in.

"How are we doing now?" she asked.

"Dylan has something he wants to say," Charlie said. "Right, buddy?"

Dylan nodded.

"It wasn't me," he said, staring down at the ground. "I said that because I thought the other kids would be impressed. It was wrong to lie to them, and you, and to the other teachers. I see that now."

"Thank you, Dylan." Wallace gave him a stern look. "It's good that you've been honest with us, but I wish you'd done that earlier."

"Sorry, Principal Wallace." Dylan was trying to look contrite, but Lucy wasn't sure how long he could keep a straight face. She hoped this would be over soon.

"All things considered, I think you should go home for the rest of the day. I don't want your classmates getting any more distracted by this than they already are." Wallace glanced at Lucy and Charlie. "Is there someone who can look after him?"

"I'll take him to work," Charlie said. "He can help clean up my office, to make up for what he did."

Wallace didn't need to know that "what he did" meant unauthorized magic, not telling tall tales.

"Well then, I think we're ready to put this behind us." Wallace shook Lucy and Charlie's hands. "Thank you for coming in. Dylan, I'll see you tomorrow."

Together, the family walked out of the school. The smell of jungle trees and exotic flowers followed them.

"I can't believe I got to lie to the principal!" Dylan was grinning as they approached the cars.

"Dylan," Lucy said in a tone chosen to wipe away that grin. "A lot of people are going to have to do extra work because of this. Silver Griffins will have to cover it up. School staff will have to rearrange their teaching. That whole playground will have to be rebuilt."

"Can't they fix it with magic?"

"And draw even more attention?"

"Oh."

"Yes, oh." She crouched so that they were eye to eye. "I'm proud of you for standing up to that bully and proud of what a great wizard you're turning into, but you really, really need to be more careful with your magic."

"Sorry, mom."

Dylan got into the passenger seat of the Prius.

"He takes after you," Charlie whispered proudly in Lucy's ear. "All that raw power and talent. He's going to be an amazing wizard someday."

"You're right," she whispered back. "Whatever you do, don't tell him that today."

Charlie fixed a stern look on his face. "Don't worry. I've got this covered."

He kissed her goodbye, then joined Dylan in the car and drove away.

Behind the school, birds were fluttering over the trees. At least someone was enjoying Dylan's work.

CHAPTER FIFTEEN

Eddie sat on the living room floor, pushing a wooden train around its track. Wheels rattled over the bumps where sections joined, making a satisfying sound. He stopped at the building block station, loaded three plastic dinosaurs into the back of the train, and pushed it on to the next stop.

"I found us some more passengers." Emily, his babysitter, held out a pair of inch-high aliens that she'd found in the bottom of one of the toy boxes. "Do you think there's space for them, or will they have to wait until the dinosaurs are done?"

"They wait."

Eddie took the aliens and stood them together on the platform. This was why he liked it when Emily looked after him. She took his imaginative games every bit as seriously as he did. Plus, she had all that curly gray hair, like a cloud hanging around her head. It made him want to stand up taller, to see if he could reach the clouds.

He got to his feet.

"I'm a giraffe," he announced.

"Really?" Emily asked. "Interesting. Does that mean you eat leaves for lunch?"

Eddie thought back to the cheese sandwiches and bowl of grapes that he'd eaten an hour before. He shook his head. "Giraffes eat cheese." He didn't want anyone to get ideas about not feeding him cheese, which was one of the best things in the world.

"So why do you want to be a giraffe?"

"Not want to. I am."

Eddie drew a deep breath, closed his eyes, and pictured a young giraffe he'd seen on the television. His body tingled as magic flowed through him, and he started to stretch. A moment later, he was standing on four hooves and a set of thin, wobbly legs, with his head nearly touching the ceiling.

"I can't argue with that." Emily looked up at him with a smile. She'd lived as a witch for over fifty years and raised two magical kids of her own, both of them now living out of state. It took a lot more than a giraffe in the living room to throw her. "But we already had your changing time for today. You were a bear cub, remember?"

Eddie's giraffe lips lifted, revealing rows of teeth adapted to chewing up lots of leaves. He had enjoyed being a bear, with all that warm fur, and Emily had helped him build a den like a bear might sleep in. As a giraffe, he had an interesting view. He could see the dusty tops of cupboards, the things people had hidden up there and forgotten, the uneven rows of books on the top shelves, and even the thin spot in the middle of Emily's hair. This was really interesting.

Another thought crossed his mind. With a clip-clop of

hooves, he walked into the kitchen and over to the high shelf where the cookie jar lived. He could easily reach it now. The problem was that he didn't have hands to open it.

He stuck out his tongue. It was long and dark and pointy, flexible enough to lick his face. He could even stick it up his nose, which was a promising prospect to explore later. For now, he wanted to see if it could work the lid off a jar. Cookies would taste far better than leaves.

"Eddie Heron, you know you aren't allowed a cookie yet." Emily planted her hands on her hips. "Please turn back into a little boy, so we can carry on playing."

Eddie wrapped his tongue around the lid. He was getting a pretty good grip.

"Eddie, what do you think your mom would say if she saw you now?"

That made Eddie hesitate. He liked Emily, and he didn't want to make her mad, but that wasn't enough to counter the appeal of cookies. His mom's disapproval, on the other hand, could make him reconsider almost anything, at least once he'd given it a try.

He uncurled his tongue from around the cookie jar, closed his eyes, and pictured his normal shape. His skin tingled, the air shimmered, and he sank back down to normal height.

"Shall we see who else could go on the train?" Emily rattled a toy box.

That gave Eddie another idea. He walked over to the wooden tracks, then closed his eyes again.

This time he thought small, imagining the brown fur and black eyes of a mouse. There was a familiar tingle, his legs shot up, and he fell into the back of one of the wagons, a passenger alongside his dinosaurs.

Emily sighed. It was important to know when you should let a little kid win. Keeping him out of the cookie jar was one thing, but keeping him from spending the whole day changing shape was becoming an impossible task. He was growing more confident in his ability and the bodies it gave him. He wanted to explore that, even if he didn't understand why. An hour a day might not be enough anymore. She certainly wasn't going to get into a row with him when he'd turned into something so small and harmless.

"Okay, little mouse," she said. "Shall we take you for a ride?"

She took hold of the front of the train and pushed it around the track. Eddie the mouse squeaked in delight as he bumped around in the carriage with his dinosaurs.

"Did you know that dinosaurs evolved into birds?" Emily asked as she crawled along the floor, keeping the train in motion. "That means there are still dinosaurs out there in the world, feathered and flying around."

Eddie poked his nose over the edge of the carriage and twitched his whiskers. A world full of dinosaurs, that was an idea he could get behind. Sure, birds didn't look a lot like dinosaurs to him, but he didn't normally look like a sloth, and that was a shape he could take on any time he wanted to.

He closed his eyes and gathered his magic. This time, instead of turning back into a little boy, he went straight from mouse to canary. The little yellow bird perched on the edge of the train, chirping and testing his wings.

"Aren't you the cutest?" Emily smiled at him.

No, thought Eddie. *Not the cutest. The most terrifying.* Because he was a dinosaur now, and even if he wasn't as muscled and scaly as the ones he'd seen on television, even if he didn't have big claws and pointy teeth, he was determined to be treated with the dignity that a dinosaur deserved.

He flexed his feathers, then fluttered into the air, away from Emily and toward the open window.

"Look at you fluttering around," she said, admiring the speed with which he'd gotten used to his new body. Then she realized where he was going. "Wait, come back here!"

It was too late. Eddie was out the window and into the back yard, flying back and forth in excitable loops.

Emily rushed out the back door, calling after him.

"Eddie, you're not supposed to be out here right now. Come back in. Eddie, what would your mom say?"

Eddie was too excited about his wings to care what anybody said, even his mom. He fluttered into the air, as high as the head of a full-grown giraffe, higher even. However, he wasn't used to flying, and his wings were getting tired already. He glided back down, moving in a spiral to keep him over the yard, and settled in the upper branches of a lemon tree.

"Eddie," Emily called up to him, "this is impressive, but wouldn't you like to be back inside, playing with your train? Or maybe we could get more building blocks out and make you another castle?"

Castles were a fantastic way to spend an afternoon, and Eddie was awfully tempted. But he was a dinosaur now, and dinosaurs didn't let the babysitter trick them into going inside. Besides, he was enjoying the sunshine and the way the breeze gently ruffled his feathers.

"Come on, Eddie, before some bigger bird tries to make you into its lunch."

Eddie took one foot off the branch and held out his claws. They weren't long, but they were sharp enough. Dinosaurs fought off their enemies. They didn't run from them.

"All right, then." Emily pulled out her phone. "I'm calling your mom."

She'd hoped the threat would be enough to bring him back down, but Eddie was in a particularly willful mood. Reluctantly, Emily brought up Lucy's number and hit the call button.

Lucy was driving southeast along the Santa Ana Freeway when her phone rang. After all the messages from Dylan's school earlier in the afternoon, she had made sure to put the phone in its cradle on the dashboard so she could answer any more calls that came in. She half-expected to be summoned back to the school when they realized that guerrilla gardeners couldn't possibly have achieved what her son had done.

Instead, Emily Sanders' name flashed up, and Lucy tapped the screen to accept.

"Hi, Emily," she said. "Eddie hasn't summoned a jungle in the living room, has he?"

"No jungle," Emily said. "He's turned into a bird and

escaped into the back yard. Now he refuses to come back in."

Lucy groaned. She had work to do, tracking down this gnome Willum Grast and anything he knew about the mysterious tribe of witches. She was already more than halfway to the Army Reserve base built over the old missile silos where he supposedly lived. Normally, she would have called Charlie and asked him to deal with Eddie, but he already had his hands full looking after Dylan, and she didn't want to put the boys together when they were both in a willful mood.

"Keep an eye on him," she said. "I'm on my way home."

She took the next off-ramp, circled, and drove back onto the freeway, heading northwest. Driving back and forth like this was no kind of fun, but at least the traffic was moving quickly. She stuck with the I-5 up past the heart of LA and Elysian Park, then turned off before the Glendale Freeway. Not long after, she pulled up into her driveway and parked the SUV.

Emily was waiting for her in the back yard, watching a little yellow bird as it hopped from branch to branch of a lemon tree.

"That's him?" Lucy asked.

"That's him."

She could have guessed even without being told. The canary had all the over-excited energy of a small boy and the slightly droopy head that said he was starting to get tired but determined to keep going. The toddler paradox, she and Charlie had called it when Dylan first started to walk. That infuriating period when kids first hit the limits of their abilities but refused to accept them.

"Hey, Eddie," she called. "What are you doing up there?"

Eddie raised one foot, then stamped it on the branch. A canary stamping was not an impressive thing. There was no trembling in the ground, no shaking of leaves, no sign of smaller creatures quaking in fear. There was barely even a tapping sound.

"He's a dinosaur," Emily explained.

"Oh." Lucy took a moment to put the pieces together. It all made a special, small child sort of sense. "Of course."

If it had taken small child logic to put Eddie up a tree, then small child logic would be the best way to get him back down. She walked into the house, retrieved the plastic dinosaurs from the wooden train carriages, and carried them back out into the yard, where she lined them up at the edge of the lawn. From his branch, Eddie watched her with his head tipped on one side.

"Okay, Emily," Lucy said. "I've got the *Diplodocus*. Do you want to be the *Stegosaurus* or the *Triceratops*?"

"*Triceratops*, please." Emily winked as she crouched next to Lucy. "My horns make me scary, so I'm in charge of this valley. You other dinosaurs had better do what I say."

They started moving the toys around, setting them up to walk through the grass in a long column.

"You're only in charge until someone tougher comes along," Lucy countered. "I wonder if there's anyone like that around? A *T-rex* maybe, or a *Velociraptor*. Something on two legs."

With a small flutter of wings, Eddie flew from his tree down to the ground and settled in front of them, staring at the plastic *Triceratops*.

"Oh no, what a mighty beast!" Emily exclaimed. "Who will triumph in this battle of the greatest dinosaurs?"

Eddie spread his wings, making himself look as big as he could, then took a step forward and pecked at the *Triceratops*. The toy wobbled for a moment, then fell, and the conquering canary hopped on top of it, head held high with pride. As far as he was concerned, it was a victory for the ages.

"Well done." Lucy put on a low, booming voice to suit the *Diplodocus*. "You are the king of the dinosaurs, my yellow friend. What would you have us do?"

Eddie hopped off the *Triceratops* and over to where his mom was moving other dinosaurs around. He looked at them for a moment, then opened his beak wide in a yawn and leaned his feathered body against Lucy's hand.

"It's hard work being king, huh?" She stroked his feathers with one finger, then opened her hand for him to hop on. While Emily scooped up the dinosaurs, Lucy carried their ruler into the house and laid him gently down on the sofa.

"Time for some juice and maybe a nap?" she asked quietly.

The air shimmered around Eddie, and he changed, reverting to the form of a three-year-old boy.

"Not nap," he said with a huge yawn. "Cartoons."

"Maybe," Lucy said. "Let's get the juice first."

By the time she was back with a drink, the former king of the dinosaurs was sound asleep, curled up against the arm of the sofa.

"They're adorable when they're unconscious," Lucy whispered.

"Make the most of it," Emily replied. "Things get very different once you reach the teens."

Lucy glanced at the time. It was probably too late to go back to work, and it wasn't as if she had anything urgent on her plate. Besides, there was a risk that Eddie might still be in a stubborn mood when he woke up.

"Would you like a cuppa before you go?" she asked.

"Go on then," Emily said. "You can tell me how the other kids are doing."

Lucy laughed. "You think Eddie's dinosaur rampage was trouble? Wait until you hear about Dylan's guerrilla gardening."

CHAPTER SIXTEEN

For the second time in as many days, Lucy found herself walking through a network of hidden tunnels under LA. She'd had to be more cautious this time, as suspicious behavior around an Army Reserve base could lead to all sorts of trouble. Fortunately, the nature of the tunnels meant that she had been able to head underground a few streets over, then find a way through the tunnels to the old missile silos.

Magic illuminated her way as she headed down a narrow tunnel in a crouch, then she straightened and stretched her spine as it opened into something larger. She wondered how long it would take to cross LA using this underground network. Many of the city's magical inhabitants used these ways regularly as a way to stay out of sight, but it was slow going, winding back and forth along passages that were never designed to get a person from A to B.

These tunnels hadn't been set up with any kind of public use in mind. Rough holes knocked through concrete walls showed where the city's hidden inhabitants had moved in after the Cold War ended and the missiles moved out. Down here, a little work with a sledgehammer could have the same effect as building an extension up above.

Smashing sounds and echoing laughter from up ahead told her that she was nearing her destination. The laughter was hollowed out and distorted by bouncing off multiple walls, becoming more menacing than mirthful, but that was fine. She hadn't come down here for the fun times she could have with the inhabitants.

The tunnels ended at an opening that had once been sealed with heavy steel blast doors. Those were open now, and judging by the dirt and rust accumulated along their edges, they hadn't moved in at least twenty years. Beyond the doors, that low, warped laughter and the accompanying crashes echoed up to her from the depths of a missile silo.

The abandoned structure was thirty feet across and perhaps a hundred deep, with walls of bare concrete. Someone had drilled holes in them to hold a series of metal girders, then built platforms on them, some in wood, others in metal. Each of the platforms partially filled a level of the silo, with empty space to one side and ladders running down.

Lucy stepped onto the topmost platform, her boots *clunking* against the metal. This one seemed to be a bedroom. There was an iron bed frame with a lumpy mattress and disordered sheets. A heap of laundry was piled up in the corner. The place smelled like it was home to a dozen teenagers or a single unhygienic troll.

She grabbed the ladder and climbed down. Her backpack shifted with a *clicking* noise as the contents knocked against each other, then protruded into her back. Fortunately, she wouldn't have to worry about that on the way back up.

As she descended, she noticed the way that the beams stuck into the walls. The holes hadn't been drilled, as she first thought, but instead had a melted appearance, almost certainly the result of construction magic.

"Who's there?" a voice shouted from the bottom of the silo.

"I've come to trade with Willum Grast," Lucy called out. "I heard that he's good for that kind of thing."

"That ain't no answer," the voice called back, gruff with hostility.

"Trust me. I've brought the good stuff. Pickard dinnerware. They told me that's your favorite."

She was halfway down now, and as she looked past the makeshift floors below, a gnome peered back up at her, his face creased with suspicion.

"Who told you that?" he asked.

"That sounds like information," Lucy said. "Are you going to give me something for it?"

"You're British. Did Chamberlain send you? 'Cause I told him, I don't know nothing about no missing gin. I don't need his fancy-ass drinks with their botanicals and their glowing bottles."

"I don't know who you're talking about. And I don't have any gin."

She stepped off onto the platform occupied by the gnome, one level up from the base of the silo. He took two steps back and stood staring suspiciously at her.

The place smelled of smoke, ethanol, and spent magic. Two other gnomes and an Ashgrog dwarf sat on a large, stained sofa whose stuffing was escaping from its frayed covering, and they all stared at her. The Dwarf had a pipe lit, and Lucy was sure that what she smelled was too sweet for tobacco. All four magicals were drinking clear liquid from jam jars.

"I know you," the dwarf said. "How do I know you?"

Lucy shrugged. As she did, crockery *clicked* in her bag. The gnome who had watched her descent licked his lips. The sleeves of his overalls slipped back as he rubbed his hands together.

"You said you brought Pickard?" he asked.

"Are you Grast?"

"You can call me Willum."

He walked across the room, and fragments of broken crockery crunched beneath his boots. On a shelf along one wall was a row of commemorative plates from the 1990s *Flintstones* movie, half of them intact, the others in pieces. One of Willum's guests raised a finger, pointed at one of the plates, and let out a bolt of magic. The plate exploded, and the gnomes howled in laughter. The dwarf kept staring at Lucy.

A still filled the far side of the room. It was a complex arrangement of glass and metal, with bubbles running up spiraling pipes and clear liquid dripping into a clear tub at one end. Willum turned a tap at the bottom of the tub and let a couple of fingers of clear liquid run into another jar. Then he held the drink out to Lucy.

"My finest brew so far this year." He clinked his jar against hers. "Cheers."

Lucy took a sip. The stuff tasted like banana-flavored battery acid, and her eyes watered just from having it nearby. Despite the horror of the liquid, Willum knocked back a good swig, then refilled his jar before stumbling a couple of feet and collapsing into a patched recliner.

"Show me, then." He held out one hand while setting his jar down on a grimy coffee table to his right-hand side.

Lucy set her backpack down on the floor beside him, opened the top, and took out a plate. It was white with a black border, simple yet elegant. The gnome weighed it in his hand, then put it down carefully on the coffee table.

"Nice," he said. "Bauer's good if you like color, and for stoneware you can't beat Bennington these days, but Pickard, they understand tradition."

Lucy handed him the other plates one at a time, then a set of matching bowls. Willum handled them like a pirate counting treasure, but for all his care, there was a tremble in his hands as he set each piece down.

"So, what are you after, witch?" Willum raised an eyebrow. "What do you think is worth these here fine pieces?"

"Information," Lucy said. "I want to know—"

"Griffin!" The dwarf shouted the word like it was a curse. He leapt to his feet, pointing the stem of his pipe at her. "I know where I saw her—she's a damn Silver Griffin."

Still crouching by Willum's seat, Lucy slid a hand into her back pocket and wrapped her fingers around the handle of her wand. She watched the other magicals, waiting to see how they would respond to the accusation.

"Is that a problem?" she asked.

Willum took a sip of his drink, then shook his head.

"I'll make me a deal with anyone," he said, "so long as they're good for the bill."

"But the Griffins—"

"Can it, Kradak. The lady's a guest, so act like a goddamn gentleman, sit back down, and pass that pipe around."

The dwarf scowled, then flung himself back down on the sofa, which expelled spurts of dust from its seams. He took a long puff on his pipe, then passed it to the gnome next to him.

"You said you was after information." Willum watched Lucy through narrowed eyes. "What sort of information?"

"I'm looking for some witches."

Willum gave her a disdainful look. "Seems like something you should be asking yourself about, not me. Ain't you the top authority for all witches on this here lump of rock?"

"These are ancient witches, lost witches, ones that no one has heard from for centuries. They might still be out there, living in hiding, and I want to find them."

"So, you come to me, the source of all that's hidden and safe, huh?"

Lucy glanced at the shattered dinner plates. She wasn't sure that anything could be considered safe in the hands of Willum and his friends, but things were certainly hidden down here.

"Can you help?" she asked.

"Depends. You ain't given me a lot to go on. You got more?"

"These witches were associated with the forests." She glanced at Kradak, who had stiffened and was staring at her, his jar of acrid drink an inch from his lips. "They used this symbol." She held up a sheet of paper on which she'd sketched the woodland witches' mortar and pestle symbol. "Do you know it?"

"The Tolderai!" Kradak leapt out of his seat and pointed an accusing finger at Lucy. "She's talking about the Tolderai!"

"You idiot!" One of the other guests sprang to his feet and slapped Kradak across the back of the head. "Why'd you say that name?"

The guests ran to the ladder and scrambled madly up it, their feet clanging against the worn metal steps. Kradak was the last to disappear from view, a pair of scuffed steel toecaps disappearing up the missile silo to an accompanying chorus of curses and complaints.

Willum snatched the sheet of paper from Lucy's hands and tore it to shreds.

"What did you do that for?" he snarled, waving the scraps in her face. "You done wrecked my party, chased off my guests, and probably brought a damn curse down on us."

"All I did was ask about—"

"Don't say it! Don't even think it! Just get the hell out of my home."

His face twisted in fury as he shoved Lucy hard, pushing her toward the ladder.

"At least let me grab my bag," she said.

But as she tried to move back across the room, Willum raised his hand and fired off a bolt of sizzling blue magic, like the ones that had smashed the Flintstones plates. Lucy ducked, the spell skimmed her shoulder, and her Silver

Griffin amulet flashed as its defensive magic dispersed the hit.

"That's it." She whipped out her wand and turned to face Willum. "No more Mrs. Nice Witch."

She chanted a spell, and rope sprang from the end of her wand, rushing toward Willum. It spiraled around him and closed in, a tightening tangle of loops.

Willum stretched his hands out, palms down, and a pair of kitchen knives leapt out of a drawer beneath the still. They slashed at the rope, slicing it to pieces with their wickedly gleaming blades. Chunks of diced hemp fell to the floor, frayed ends unraveling. Then Willum waved his hands again, and the knives flew at Lucy.

She got off a heat spell, melting the first knife, which spattered in molten droplets across the floor. However, the blades were moving too fast for her to get them both. She flung herself to the floor, and the second knife flew through the space where she had been. There was a crash, dampness splashed her back, and the room filled with a chemical stink.

"My still!" Willum cried out, sinking to his knees. Tears rolled down his face as he looked at the jagged remains of shattered glass protruding from the copper parts of the contraption. "You smashed my beautiful still!"

While the gnome knelt sobbing and staring, Lucy raised her wand and cast another binding spell. This time she went for a chain instead of a rope. Links *clinked* as they wrapped around Willum, pinning his arms to his sides. Realizing what had happened, he wriggled around, trying to break free, but only succeeded in falling on his side.

Lucy peeled herself off the floor and went to stand over him, wand pointing at his face.

"What was that all about?" she asked.

"It's about you ruining my still. You know how long I've worked to perfect that thing? How much time and money it took to—"

"I don't mean your wailing and gnashing of teeth. I mean, why did you attack me, and why did all your friends run off in such a hurry?"

"Because of..." Willum looked around fearfully, then lowered his voice to a whisper. "Because of them."

"Them who? The witches I'm looking for? The ones Kradak called the Tolderai?"

"Shhhhh! Don't say that name!" Willum writhed on the floor, making his chains rattle.

"Why not? It's only a name."

"I thought Griffins was supposed to understand how the magic world works. You say that name, and they'll hear it. You even talk about them too much, name or no name, they'll pick up the whispers. They don't like it when folks talk about them. They'll creep out and kill you when you're not looking, and no one will even know it was them." He looked around, eyes wide. "They'll probably kill me for listening to you."

"If their victims don't know that they're the killers, then how does anyone know about this?"

Willum's mouth opened, shut, opened, shut again. At last, he seemed to reach a coherent thought.

"So maybe it ain't them. There's different stories anyway. Some say it's the folks who killed them, still looking to finish the job, preying on anyone who keeps their memory alive. Or maybe it's ghosts, coming back for vengeance from an ancient war. All I know for certain is what any smart person knows—you don't talk about them."

"You just talked about them."

Willum shivered. "Now I know I'm gonna get killed, all 'cause of you and your fancy dinner plates."

Lucy took the remaining plates out of her bag. Willum's eyes widened, and he licked his lips as though he was staring at the tastiest meal he'd ever seen.

"I still have some of those plates," Lucy said. "I should probably take them all away, given that you attacked me, but I feel as though you've been punished enough for that." She nodded at the broken still, then set the plates down on Willum's empty chair. "So, all these can be yours if you can tell me some way to find these Tol—"

"Don't say it!"

"To find these wood witches."

Willum's face crumpled in consternation. He wanted those plates to have some source of comfort to cope with the ruin of his still. Still, he'd already put himself in terrible danger with what he had said so far. Did he dare to say more?

"There's this wizard," he said. "Goes by the name of Nathaniel Oakmantle. Word is, he's been looking for the people I ain't going to talk about. You find him, and maybe he'll have some clues you don't."

"Do you know any more about him, like where I can find him?"

Willum shook his head. "Only that he's earned some heavy debts chasing his dream. You wanna catch him while he's still around to be caught."

"Well, thank you." Lucy pocketed her wand and picked up her bag. "See, that wasn't so hard. Maybe next time we can talk, instead of making all this mess."

She started climbing the ladder, its rungs cold under her hands.

"Hey, wait!" Willum's chains *clinked* as he rolled over. "Ain't you gonna let me out of this?"

"You're a smart chap. You'll find a way to wriggle free. If it takes a while, well, think of that as time to absorb today's lesson—don't mess with a Silver Griffin."

CHAPTER SEVENTEEN

Ashley sat in her treehouse in the back yard of the Heron family home. As treehouses went, it was the best one she had ever been in. She had designed it to make sure of that and built it with help from her parents.

Her dad should have been the most useful one on that project. He worked with technology. However, Ashley had learned over her eight years that sometimes Mom was more reliable with hands-on work. So, while her dad had dealt with the wiring, the wireless booster, the monitor brackets, and all that IT work he was familiar with, Mom had helped Ashley most with the sawing, hammering, and general construction work to build a solid house up in the branches of an old but sturdy oak.

It was after school, and most kids Ashley knew would be running around in the garden, riding their bikes up and down the street, maybe watching cartoons. Those weren't activities that interested her. The world was full of things to tinker with, to build and mend and improve. Dylan and

Eddie could have all the cartoons they wanted. She was happier here, working on her latest project.

She rolled half a dozen gleaming silvery marbles around in her hand. They made a satisfying *clunk* as they struck each other, a sound that helped her think. Today, she was debating a modification to the treehouse, adding a raised platform on the roof that could hold a telescope. That way, she could take astronomical readings and use them to check the accuracy of astronomical tables on the internet. It was important to check the accuracy of things on the internet, as most people made far too many mistakes. Then again, she assumed that people were in a rush to share the things they were excited about. Rushing was understandable when you'd found something cool.

Carefully, she placed the marbles on top of others piled up on the floor in the shape of her treehouse. The magnetic fields the marbles generated held them in place, letting her construct models for works in progress. The added marbles formed the platform and the telescope, helping her envision what it would look like in reality, with the telescope stretching out through the branches into the night sky.

Yes, that would work. She smiled to herself, used her tablet to take a few quick photos of the model, and turned to her main computer.

A reminder flashed on the screen. She was due to post a new video to her YouTube channel, and she hadn't finished it yet. First, the telescope platform.

She brought the model's photos up on screen and used them to assemble a 3D render in her favorite design software. From that, she pulled out measurements for the platform's components and worked out in her head how many planks of what width and length she would need, as well as the fixings and tools involved. All that went into a list, which went into an email that she shot across to her dad. An eight-year-old girl couldn't go out buying hammers and nails by herself, but fortunately, her parents were happy to pay for projects like this. They were pretty cool, for Ashley's engineer-like definition of cool.

Time for the video. She closed the design software, fired up an editing suite, and switched on her camera. Then she dragged a box out of the corner of the room, took out two machines, and placed them just out of shot.

She had already done most of the hard work for this video, and the second, smaller device was proof of that. She liked to shoot the intro and outro for each video last so that she could take account of what she'd made and how she'd explained it. This was her chance to shape a narrative, reinforce lessons using the rule of three, and make sure that her viewers had the smoothest experience she could provide. Just the basic things that any kid would do for a video, she assumed.

She pressed record and smiled at the camera.

"Hi there, tech geniuses of the future. Ashley here with my latest rebuilding video. Today, I'm going to show you how you can take a Nintendo 64—" she held up the console for her viewers to see "—and turn it into something more compact." She put the Nintendo down and held up her handheld version. "This portable prototype does everything the 64 can, but in a box you can carry around with you, and using its own power source. If you joined in with last week's build, the solar charger backpack, you can use it to charge this device as you walk around for cleaner, greener gaming on the go.

"So, let's get started…"

She stopped the recording and played it back to make sure that everything looked good. She could usually tell when she'd made a mess of a take and would need to re-record. This didn't feel like one of those days, but it was always worth checking.

As the image of herself holding up a console filled the monitor, an alert popped up, not a calendar entry this time, but a message from one of her pieces of monitoring software. It was flashing amber rather than red, so it wasn't urgent, but the title caught her eye: "Potential Misinformation."

Ashley frowned and bit her lip. On the one hand, this video was due to go out today. Thousands of eager viewers would be waiting on her. On the other hand, misinformation was like a germ. It could easily spread if it wasn't dealt with. People's mistakes could lead to confusion, which led to poor decisions and building things in inferior ways. Better to deal with it straight away.

She glanced at the time. Still a couple of hours until the video was due to go up. She could look at this first.

She hunched forward over her keyboard and clicked on the link in the alert. A browser window opened and a Wiki page loaded, with her private monitoring script running down one side, a running commentary on the contents of the page, and an analysis of its edits, color-coded to draw her attention to problems. That was something that adults often overlooked but that, as an elementary school pupil, she kept being reminded about: how great colors were.

Ashley frowned and stuck the tip of her finger into her mouth, sucking on it as she considered what she was looking at. Of the thousand or more Wiki pages that she edited and monitored, both on mundane Wikipedia and in the magical world's hidden Wiki, this seemed like one of the least interesting. It was a page for an engineering company based in Maine, one that had been running for over a hundred years, quietly ticking along without making any groundbreaking innovations, but also without going bust or being taken over by someone larger. Ashley was interested in them because they had developed some minor but necessary components for both the space race and the early days of the internet. It was nice to keep a record out there of a company like that and keep an eye on what they did next, as it might be useful.

The changes her software had alerted her to were near the bottom of the page, in a section about the company's investors and relationships with other businesses. This was a section that Ashley had written herself after painstaking research, and she was very proud of it. She'd carefully phrased everything to avoid bias or exaggeration and diligently sourced it.

Someone had added a new paragraph, only a couple of lines, about how a company called NTS holdings had financed the engineering firm in the early nineties. That was surprising. Ashley had gone over the company's historical financial records and didn't remember anything like that. She clicked the link for the source and headed down through a series of apparently separate pages that eventually circled back on themselves, a sure sign that someone hadn't done their research properly. Either it was a mistake, or someone was deliberately sneaking something into her page. Either way, it had to go.

She saved a copy of the page for future reference, then edited out the offending paragraph. It felt good to know that she was stopping the spread of disinformation.

With the page corrected, she closed the browser and got back to her video. Then another alert popped up, and a third one, both similar to the first.

Ashley frowned deeply. If there was one thing she had learned from reading about her favorite scientists, it was that patterns mattered. When those patterns showed someone up to no good, there was one person she knew to call on.

"Mom!" she shouted.

She clicked on an alert and followed its link to a page about microchips, this one edited to include the influence of a company she had never heard of before. The third alert was about an investment firm, with a suspicious addition to its Wiki page that implied a key role in developing drones.

"Mom!" Ashley shouted again, but there was still no response.

She called up an app and hit the "Launch" button. A swarm of mechanical fireflies took flight from a beam in the tree house's ceiling, tiny lightbulb bodies glowing and hair-thin wings fluttering. They hovered expectantly in the air in front of Ashley.

"Go fetch Mom," she ordered.

The fireflies bobbed down for a moment in acknowledgment of the order. Then there was a buzzing of wings as they flew out the window and away.

Lucy and Charlie were in the kitchen, making dinner together while Dylan did his homework on the breakfast bar.

"What are you working on today, sweetheart?" Lucy looked up with a smile from the potatoes she was peeling.

"Biology," Dylan said. "All about how plants grow."

"Well, that seems fitting."

Dylan blushed and huddled closer over his book as if he was trying to disappear into the page.

Eddie walked in from the next room, where he had been watching cartoons. "Want a cookie," he announced, holding out his hand.

"What you want and what you need are very different things," Lucy said. "Besides, it won't be long until dinner."

"But I'm hungry." A gleam of inspiration shone in Eddie's eyes as he settled on a bright idea. Rules around when he could have cookies could be pretty strict, but his parents were also firm on not wanting him to use his abilities. "Too hungry to not change."

He held out his hands and let his power into them. His fingers shimmered and tingled, then started to grow fur.

"Eddie Heron," Lucy said sternly, "you stop that this moment. I know full well that your powers have nothing to do with how hungry you are."

Disappointed that his ruse had failed, and now fearing the loss of future cookie privileges, Eddie let his hands return to their normal form.

There was a tap at the window, then a buzzing as

mechanical fireflies swarmed in. They gathered around Lucy and hung glowing in the air.

"Looks like Ashley wants me in the treehouse," she said.

"Most kids would come in to find you," Charlie observed.

"Most kids don't rebuild the microwave on their fifth birthday."

"That kid is going to build a new world some day."

"Then immediately take it over."

"Nah, she'll be too busy working on the next invention. Now Dylan..."

"What?" Dylan looked up from his homework. "I'm not doing anything wrong!"

"I know, sweetheart." Lucy ruffled his hair and kissed the top of his head. "Your dad's only teasing. Now, I should go out and see what Ashley wants..."

CHAPTER EIGHTEEN

Lucy stepped out the back door and crossed the garden. It was a warm, bright day, with birds singing in the trees and real insects buzzing around alongside the mechanical ones. A bird darted from a tree and caught one of Ashley's fireflies, only to find that it was chewing on something far harder and less tasty than it had imagined. The bird opened its beak, and the firefly emerged, one wing bent, then followed the swarm as they accompanied Lucy back to the foot of the oak tree.

"Hey, Ashley!" Lucy called from the ground. "Is it all right if I come in?"

"Of course, Mom. I sent the bright bugs for you."

Lucy smiled and climbed the rope ladder. While she knew that Ashley expected her, she also felt that it was important to respect her daughter's private space. She couldn't knock on the treehouse door, at least not until she was already up the ladder and practically inside, but calling a greeting would do.

The fireflies buzzed ahead of Lucy, settled on the door

handle, and used their combined mass to push it open. By the time Lucy reached the top of the ladder, the mechanical insects had settled on their home beam.

She climbed into her daughter's private lair and closed the door behind her. Even having helped to build this place, Lucy was amazed by it. It was like a whole tech lab up a tree, with living branches twining between cables and boxes of spare circuit boards. Creations studded with microchips, dangling wires, sensors, and antennae filled the shelves, and also devices that Lucy couldn't have named, never mind built. Thanks to meeting Charlie and having kids, she had chosen not to finish her undergraduate degree, and she stood open-mouthed in amazement at the fruits of her daughter's incredible mind.

"Did you want to ask me something?" She kissed Ashley on the top of her head, then sat on the stool next to her.

"I want to show you." Ashley sucked on the tip of one finger while her other hand deftly operated the tracker ball of the mouse, closing and rearranging windows on the bank of monitors across one wall. "Look at it."

Lucy looked. The windows were open to web pages, most of them on Wikipedia. Each page had a section of text highlighted. The pages seemed to be for various topics relating to technology—some of them about devices, some about companies, one about a computing theory. Beyond that, she didn't know what they had in common although the highlighted sections repeated the same company names several times.

"Is this to do with something you want to build?" she asked. "I'm sure it will be amazing, but we can't spend so much on microchips this month. We promised Dylan a new trumpet."

"This isn't my project," Ashley said. "It's somebody else's. It's a project made up of lies."

Lucy looked at her daughter, whose brow was furrowed, her expression rearranging itself around a deep and disapproving frown. "What do you mean, sweetheart?"

On a separate screen, Ashley brought up a spreadsheet. It contained a list of the pages they had been looking at, and next to each one was a name, a date, and a time. Lucy didn't recognize the names. The dates and times were all within the past twenty-four hours.

"Somebody changed these pages to fit a story," Ashley explained. "On their own, they're small things, easily ignored. Together, they add up to a big fat lie, one that most people wouldn't notice."

"Explain it to me," Lucy urged. "Remember I don't have the same big old brain as you."

Ashley sucked on her fingertip for a moment, then pointed at the spreadsheet.

"You see these names here? These are the people who made these edits. See anything about them?"

"They don't repeat very much, so it's a lot of different people doing it. Ooh, or one person using several names."

"Exactly. And here, the geolocation information shows that they're spread around the world. So, either someone hired people from all over, or they're spoofing that data well enough to hide the truth from me."

"So how do you know that these changes are connected?"

"Because of what they say and when they were made.

They were all made recently, and they're all about a small number of companies."

"This looks like a lot of different companies."

"Shell corporations, and shells within shells." A flick of the mouse wheel and a string of legal documents appeared on another screen. "I don't know who the big owner is or the person these companies have hired to make them look good, but all this work is one thing. The pattern is there."

"What are they doing?" Lucy read a few of the highlighted passages, trying to piece it all together. "These seem like very small lies. Who cares if a company invested in microchips in 1974, or that this other one built a component for Wi-Fi routers?"

"Hundreds of little changes like this, put together, make a company look like a big deal. They make the person running it look smart and powerful and important."

"Why use Wikipedia for that?"

"Because they're not showing off what they can do now. They're rewriting history, telling a false story to show how they've always been smart, always been useful. They're making... What's a word for looking like you know what you're doing?"

"Competent? Credible?"

"Yeah, that. They're giving it credible."

"Credibility," Lucy corrected, knowing her bright daughter was instantly storing away all these new words for future use. Lucy could bring out all the ten-dollar words she wanted, and Ashley would keep absorbing them, able to talk in ways that would leave some adults reaching for the dictionary.

"It's..." Ashley hesitated. "Subtle? Is that the word for

when you do something in an um, way that people might not notice?"

"That's right, sweetheart. Well done."

Ashley beamed. "It's subtle." She rolled the word around and paused a moment before moving on. "That's why they've used all these different people to hide it. But it's there, and it could be important."

Lucy sat back, absorbing what her daughter had told her. She wasn't going to start doubting any of it. Ashley was too smart and too insightful to be wrong about something like this. Still, she might have misunderstood its importance. For all her intelligence, she was only eight years old, and there was a lot about the world that she didn't understand. The importance of the things she cared about sometimes got exaggerated in her mind.

"Does this really matter?" Lucy asked. "It looks like marketing to me."

"Not marketing, misinformation."

"Who's going to notice or care?"

Ashley stared at her mother. How could an adult miss this point?

"It's never been easier to spread false information," she said. "Whoever can get people to believe their story holds the steering wheel for the world. With that kind of power, you can launch invasions, change the outcome of elections, or turn a company into your private kingdom. Someone has put information out onto the web from computer networks placed around the world. They're using it to change what reality people believe in, to make the companies around them more powerful. Someone who does that must be bad, right?"

"Someone like this NTS Holdings?" Lucy pointed at a name on the screen.

"Yes, just like them."

"You're right. We should tell someone about this, the police perhaps, or the FCC."

"Or the Silver Griffins." Ashley looked expectantly at her mom. "You can fix this, right?"

"If it's not about magic, it's not our business."

Ashley brought up a fresh batch of pages on the magical side of the net. Once again, NTS Holdings appeared, and another name.

"Looks like this is our business." Lucy's eyes narrowed as she saw a new target coming into view. "Who on earth is this Mister Zero?"

Zero sat in a chair in the center of a room in the back caves of his private kemana. Computer screens covered the walls, and gnomes sat in front of them, busily typing away at their keyboards. More gnomes sat on benches sticking out from high up the walls to maximize use of the space, row upon row of them.

Some of the gnomes shifted uncomfortably under his gaze.

"I miss the old days of empires," he finally said, sounding wistful. "Not the British. They were too hung up on their confused image of civilization, but the rough and tumble ones, practical, down and dirty empires like the Romans."

Gruffbar shrugged. "Before my time."

Zero ignored him. "Or the Portuguese, building their string of forts along those sunbaked foreign coasts, like our own little fortresses of information. Those forts had an influence far outside their size and the number of men in them. Now we're going to do the same, but with data."

"I'm a lawyer, not a historian," Gruffbar said, "but I wouldn't mind living somewhere I could clap my stupider clients in chains."

Zero tilted his head and looked at the dwarf, evaluating him. Was he at risk of losing his right-hand man?

"Do you ever consider crossing back over?" he asked. "Stepping through a portal and back to a world where you don't need to live in secret?"

Gruffbar shook his head. "I might bitch about the idiots from time to time, but I love it here. Oriceran's too clean. It doesn't have the plastic, the smog, all those little touches that show industry at work. What dwarf wouldn't love that?"

In Zero's experience, the answer was most dwarves, but he wasn't going to try to persuade Gruffbar to leave.

"If you ever change your mind, let me know. I can arrange a portal for you, at a discounted fee for a loyal employee."

Not to mention a hit squad on the far side. No one was walking away from Zero's operation with all the knowledge that Gruffbar had in his head.

Gruffbar started to say something but quickly stopped when he saw the dark swarm creeping up over Zero's shoulders. The inky black throng of shadow mites gathered neatly around Zero's neck, creating a lacey pattern up near his ears.

They whispered to Zero about the ancient tribe of witches they had found and warned him that the coven was already on the move again. A necessary habit they had developed over the years. The coven had once been much larger but was decimated a long time ago by endless battles they wanted nothing to do with. The remaining witches had spread out far and wide, at least that was the legend, whispered the mites, buzzing around Zero's fleshy orange ears.

Zero cocked his head to the other side, arching a brow and considering the information. "Not much there," he muttered.

The buzz intensified, and the shadow mites circled in a clockwise direction. No witches had been seen near Los Angeles in all this time. Until now, the mites hummed. They're meeting again. Something has changed.

Zero smiled and coughed at the same time, letting out a gaseous burp even the mites were reluctant to withstand. They drew back, disappearing into the background until the buzzing disappeared altogether.

Gruffbar shook his head in disbelief even though he had seen the miniscule magicals operate many times before. "Tiny assassins are the worst," he muttered, making his way out of the chamber.

A pair of gnomes suddenly hurried in, catching Zero's attention. They carried a dirt-stained wooden chest between them. It was damp in the deep, abiding way that came from years in the ground or hidden in some forgotten cellar. The iron of the lock and hinges was thoroughly rusted, orange stains seeping from there across the planks. The gnomes set it down on a low table in front of Zero, then bowed respectfully.

"We found it at last, your worship," one of the gnomes said.

"Three of us were killed stealing the map to the hiding place," his companion added. "The decoding magic drove Wuthershuff mad. Grimbletack lost a leg going down into the caverns, but we—"

"Enough," Zero said. "I don't care about your sob stories. I have something far better to enjoy."

As the bruised and mud-smeared gnomes scurried away, Zero leaned eagerly forward, his chair creaking under him. He took hold of the lock on the front of the chest, channeled magical power into his hand, and squeezed with unnatural strength. The hasp crumbled into fragments of rust.

His heart racing with excitement, Zero tipped back the lid. "Perfect," he whispered as a green glow illuminated his face.

Gruffbar peered over his boss' shoulder. There was a statue in the box, a foot high and carved from green crystal. It showed two people, simply rendered so that they could be almost any species. They were joined at the hip but pulling apart, one becoming two. Runes glowed around the base of the statue, radiating powerful magic.

"That's the cloner?" Gruffbar asked.

"The Splitting Stone." Zero touched the cold crystal with a single finger. Immediately, his skin started to peel back, flesh parting to divide him in two. He jerked away and clutched his hand as blood ran from the wound and gnomes ran up with bandages and salves to treat him.

"That could tear a being apart as easily as it could make a copy. The elf was right. I'll need all my power to make this work." Zero looked up at Gruffbar, and despite his injury, he grinned. "It's going to be worth it."

Gruffbar stared at the Splitting Stone. Something about it turned his stomach. Not the fact that his boss' blood stained it. That sort of thing had never worried him. The thought of being duplicated, of being split in two, of more than one of him out there. How would he know that he was the real Gruffbar? No, he was much happier remaining unique.

Zero, on the other hand, had grand ambitions.

There was some muttering among the gnomes working at the computers. Gruffbar strode over, knocked two of their heads together, and turned them to face him.

"What's the problem?" he asked.

"No problem." One gnome laughed unconvincingly. "Please, we can fix it. We just need time."

"Don't lie to him." The other gnome said in an angry hiss. "The boss will know. The boss will always know."

"Will know what?" Zero appeared behind Gruffbar. His finger was bandaged, and a magical salve was knitting the torn flesh back together. The tickling, writhing sensation of new-grown flesh annoyed him, undermining the triumphant feeling of a moment before. "Out with it, before I pull it out of you."

"Someone's undoing our work," the second gnome said. "All the good work we've been doing for you, master."

"What?" Zero flung the gnomes aside and heaved himself into a seat in front of the screens. The legs of the bench squealed and strained but didn't break.

On the screen in front of Zero was a Wikipedia page. Only an hour before, one of his gnomes had inserted a reference to one of his companies, "proving" that it had played a part in DVD technology development. Around the room, other gnomes were doing similar work, building up the profile of Zero's NTS Holdings or the clients who paid him to improve their profile. Their careful entries had vanished, and when he looked at the nearby screens, he saw the same thing. Someone was wiping out his work.

With a roar of frustration, Zero smashed the keyboard in front of him. Plastic caps and other small parts flew across the room and clattered on the floor. The gnomes typed faster than ever.

"All of you!" Zero bellowed. "Hands up if this has happened to your work!"

Two-thirds of the gnomes raised their hands. All of them were shaking with fear.

"I need you to get this done!" Zero rose to his feet and paced back and forth, flip-flops flapping against the hardened tar floor. "Without these edits, the companies I've created will have no credibility, no standing in the cities where I've built them. My clones will be starting from scratch, building an empire from nothing. You know who builds an empire from nothing?"

The gnomes were too smart or too scared to answer.

"Nobody!" Zero bellowed. "Every empire ever created stole from those who came before, built on the foundations of what they found. I need you to lay those foundations, to build my network. Then, once the Splitting Stone has done its work, some of you will be sent with each of me to occupy those foundations, spread this empire, and create an enterprise that stretches from coast to coast, hidden in the cracks behind mundane reality. You understand?"

This time, the gnomes were smart enough to nod frantically.

"Who's done this to us? Who is this...this..." Zero stared at the Wikipedia editor's handle on the screen. "This TreeHouseGenius? Who is finding so many changes so fast in so many places and unraveling all my hard work?"

The only sound was the echo of Zero's words. None of the gnomes knew the answer, and none of them would ever mention that they were the ones doing all the hard work.

"Find out," Zero ordered. "We need to stop them." He turned to Gruffbar. "That goes for you, too."

"I'm a lawyer, not a programmer," Gruffbar pointed out, a moment before he realized he should keep his mouth shut.

"Then use your lawyering," Zero snapped, teeth bared as he loomed over him, hands stretched out like claws with magical power buzzing along his fingers. "Because someone is going to suffer for this, and if it's not Tree-HouseGenius, someone else will have to take their place."

CHAPTER NINETEEN

Reidar Haugensen waved his wand, illuminating the wards around the inside of his new pawnshop. It had taken every trick he had to escape from Ringo Fuller, and if the bounty hunter hadn't been distracted by engine trouble with his van, all of those tricks might not have been enough. Reidar wasn't going to take any chances with the spells designed to keep the likes of Fuller away.

Reidar looked around at his wares. The new shop was still pretty empty since he hadn't opened yet, and hadn't had new clients bringing in their goods. All he had were a few prize pieces he'd lifted from the old shop when the Silver Griffins weren't looking. That had been risky, too risky in normal circumstances, but he needed some resources to get him started in a new city. Atlanta wouldn't give him money for nothing. Then there were the items he didn't want falling into anybody else's hands, at least not until the dust had settled and everybody forgot there was a price on his head.

He waved his wand again, and the wards reverted to

invisibility. Other gnomes mocked his wand as an affectation, a piece of posturing to make him look like a wizard, but he wouldn't give it up for the world. It helped him to focus his magic, and that made it easier to get things done while he was distracted by other issues. Issues like the store's security cameras, which were newly installed and already seemed to be malfunctioning.

His laptop sat on the counter with the video feeds showing on the screen. Black dots were drifting across the view like soot blowing on the breeze—some sort of static, perhaps. Reidar knew nothing about computers beyond what he needed to price one for secondhand sale. Could this be something in the cables, or maybe a software thing? Did he need to get the cameras themselves replaced? That wasn't the sort of money he wanted to part with right now, but he really didn't want to be caught by surprise if the Silver Griffins found him again.

An alert popped up at the bottom right corner of the screen, accompanied by a recurring chime. Someone was trying to reach him with a video call. Reidar frowned. He'd had to re-establish all of his online presences from scratch, as the Silver Griffins might be watching his old profiles. Who had he given his new contact details to that might call him now? What kind of emo loser chose Nothingness as their screen name? It was probably some sort of spam. Reidar rejected the call and started searching the web for information about security camera glitches.

The video call alert chimed again, and again Reidar rejected it. The third time, he gave in and answered. When he saw who was on the other end of the call, he almost screamed at himself for being an idiot. There were certain people it was always profitable to talk to.

"Zero." He put on his salesman's grin. "It's good to see you looking as radiant as ever. How did you find me?"

"I can find anyone if I need to." Zero's eyes bulged through the folds of his orange flesh. The distortion of the call added to the sputtering sound of his voice. "I have some business for you, Haugensen."

"Always happy to work with you, Zero," Reidar said. "Just don't expect any discounts. I'm going through a period of rebuilding after a small setback."

"We all heard about your setback. I'd hardly call getting raided by the Griffins and carted off by a bounty hunter 'small.'"

Reidar gritted his teeth. "As you can see, I've moved past that. New shop, new location, same business. Though I'm not in LA anymore, so you might want to talk with a local broker."

He didn't want to turn down an opportunity, but after that start, he didn't feel like doing Zero many favors. The orange toad had stiffed Reidar on deals in the past, and he was determined to work his way from now on.

"I'm trying to track someone down," Zero said.

"You seem to have succeeded," Reidar replied.

"Someone more difficult. Someone who can cover their tracks against opponents bigger than a two-bit bounty hunter."

"Some people might take offense at a comment like that."

"Smart people don't let offense stand in the way of profits."

"True. So how can I help?"

"You once offered me a Hostem Inveniet device. It didn't show up in the inventory the Griffins made of your store. That leaves me thinking that you still have it."

Reidar glanced at the warded safe at the back of his store, where he had stashed the Hostem Inveniet device, along with other trinkets he didn't want to let go. He didn't know how Zero had seen the Griffins' inventory, but he wasn't going to insult the creature's intelligence by claiming he was wrong.

"Even if I had that, it wouldn't be for sale," he said. "I'm keeping a low profile right now, and I don't want certain people walking around with a magical compass for tracking people. Not that I'm saying you'd sell it to my enemies, but maybe you'd sell it to someone who sells it to someone who hires it out to a bounty hunter, and this time they fasten the handcuffs tighter on me."

"I want that artifact." Zero leaned closer to the camera, making the tar visible as it seeped from his pores. "I'm going to have it. So cut the crap and give me a price."

"Sorry, no deal. Is there anything else I can help you with?"

"You don't say no to me," Zero hissed. "I've been failed by enough gnomes today, and I know that none of you have a backbone worth using. Set aside that magic twig you're so proud of, come back to cold financial reality, and tell me what you want."

To his surprise, Reidar laughed out loud. He'd been intimidated by Zero for years, but the orange blob was far less intimidating when the tar pits were hundreds of miles away and Reidar lived in a city far from Zero's influence. He felt liberated. Maybe this fresh start wouldn't be so bad.

"Later, loser." He hung up the call.

For a moment, Reidar felt giddy. He had just told one of the most powerful figures in the LA underworld where to get off. Yes, he knew that he would eventually go crawling back and maybe pay a higher price than he had wanted to on some deal. For now, he was in Atlanta, Zero was in LA, and there was no business between them. He didn't have to take the other creature's insults.

Smiling and whistling, he glanced at the security feeds with their traces of black static, then picked up his keys and set about securing the store. He closed the shutters from the inside, locked the front door, and returned to the counter. He was about to turn the alarms on when he noticed something on his computer screen. The black dots had gone from the security feeds, leaving the images perfectly clear.

"This evening just gets better and better." He grinned. He twirled his wand, the stick Zero had been so dismissive of, then set it aside and reached under the counter for a bottle of tequila he had stowed there for special occasions. He deserved a drink to celebrate his courage and his good fortune.

As he unscrewed the lid of the bottle, he ambled around the store, looking over the shelves and imagining the goods that would soon fill them. Computers, televisions, and consoles; necklaces, watches, and rings; electric guitars and amplifiers; all those precious luxuries that people pawned to help them pay the bills, and that they had to abandon with him when they never quite got their finances back in order. It was a hard life, and someone had to profit off it.

"Here's to a new start." He raised the bottle to the room.

He took a swig and swirled the tequila around his mouth, enjoying that strange, startling taste.

Across the room, a shadow filled the doorway, seeming to ooze up the corridor from the back door. Reidar glanced up, but the light above the corridor was still on, and it should have expelled that darkness. He frowned as a buzzing rose around him and stared down at the bottle.

"Have I accidentally bought the special stuff?" he asked the cartoon Mexican on the label.

Past the bottle, on the floor at his feet, another shadow was spreading. Reidar stared at it for a moment in alarm, then jerked away. He staggered to the middle of the room and looked around. The shadows were approaching from both doorways, spreading out to surround him, pools of darkness that rose from the floor. The buzzing grew louder, like a swarm of angry insects.

Reidar dropped the bottle and reached into his pocket, but his wand wasn't there. It lay beside his laptop on the counter, and now a pool of shadow swept over, engulfing it.

"I'm not scared of you." Reidar shook as he raised his hands and tried to think of a suitable defensive spell. It was hard to concentrate with all that buzzing and the first numbing hit of tequila to the brain. If only he had his wand to help him focus, this would be easier.

The shadows rolled forward, their outer edges covering his feet and creeping up his legs.

"I'm not scared," he muttered, tears welling in the

corners of his eyes. "I faced down Zero. I can deal with you."

Tiny black bodies tickled his flesh, then tingled, then gnawed. They rose past his knees and across his thighs before staining the bright edge of his shirt.

"I'm not scared," he whimpered. Then it came to him, the perfect spell to fend off the darkness. He spread his hands wide and called forth all the power he had. "Illumi—"

The shadow mites poured into Reidar's mouth, cutting off the words of the spell. They raced down his throat, choking him as they chewed him up from the inside out. He thrashed around for a moment, then collapsed and went still.

Slowly, over the next ten minutes, the shadowy body that had been Reidar Haugensen diminished. At last, the mites peeled away, their absolute blackness leaving behind only a heap of white bones.

While some mites soaked up the tequila, a dizzying sensation that filled the swarm with an excited buzz, others swarmed across the shop, over the counter, to the safe at the back. They slid up its sides, through the nearly invisible gap at the edge of the door, and into the lock's seams. There was another, longer period of stillness before the hinges creaked, then broke, and the safe door fell to the floor with a *clang*.

A cloud of mites emerged from the safe. Between them, they carried a compass made from a red metal, with blue runes stamped into its sides. Instead of the letters for north, south, east, and west, the dial showed flickering images of people. The needle spun constantly, never settling on one symbol.

Giddy with triumph and alcohol, the shadow mites gnawed through the hinges of the pawnshop's back door. It crashed to the ground, startling a homeless woman who was crouched behind a nearby dumpster. She yelped in fright, then ran off as a black cloud emerged with a compass floating in its middle and flew away.

Zero sat back in his seat. The gnomes who had held the laptop during his video call backed away, bowed, and hurried out of the room.

"You didn't feel like haggling some more?" Gruffbar asked. "I could have ridden over to Atlanta, had a word with him. Everybody has their price."

Zero shrugged, sending a ripple through his orange flesh. "I try to play nice, but they won't always let me. Haugensen, he wouldn't let me. So now he can be a warning."

"Will anyone know that's what he was?" Gruffbar asked. "He was a long way away."

Zero looked up at one of the sets of screens on the wall, where gnomes were frantically updating Wiki entries for a company based in Georgia, trying to make updates faster than their unknown opponents could wipe them away.

"Oh, people will know. When there's another one of me offering services to the people of Atlanta, everyone will know better than to cross me on a deal."

CHAPTER TWENTY

Lucy finished checking the magical inventory in the garage and closed the secret panel in the wall. This time, she had kept the door closed, even though Buddy kept running over and barking to be let out. She wasn't going to risk exposing her secrets to a neighbor again.

"Here, boy." She bounced a ball off the wall and across the open space in the middle of the garage. Buddy leapt excitedly after it, his little legs racing and his tail wagging back and forth. He grabbed the ball between his teeth, set it down in front of Lucy, and looked up expectantly.

"One more." She held up a finger. "Then we have to go in for dinner."

Buddy's bark might have meant agreement or simply excitement at the prospect of a game. Lucy lobbed the ball, bouncing it off the door and the sidewall, and Buddy darted after it again, bounding around in delight. When she opened the side door into the house, he eagerly followed her through, proudly carrying the ball with him.

"The noble hunter returns," Lucy announced. "He has

slain the monstrous Ball Demon and now offers up its carcass for our feast."

Buddy ran into the kitchen and dropped the ball at Charlie's feet, then looked up at him expectantly.

"Sorry, Buddy." Charlie nudged the ball away with his foot. "I'm kind of in the middle of something here."

He opened the oven and removed a large dish, its contents topped with mashed potato that had crisped to a golden brown. A delicious smell made Lucy's mouth water, and Buddy drooled as he yapped and danced around Charlie's feet.

"Seriously, pal, I need to get past." Charlie smiled down at the dog.

"Allow me." Lucy opened a cupboard and took out a sack of dog biscuits, as well as a can of Buddy's favorite food. That got his attention, as did the rattle of the biscuits falling into his bowl. Lucy had to nudge him aside to get at the other bowl and tip in the tinned food.

"Good boy." She patted his head.

For the first time in an hour, Buddy had nothing to say. He was too busy eating.

Lucy followed Charlie through to the dining room, where he had put their dinner out on the table.

"Kids!" he called. "Dinner time!"

There was a thunder of footfalls, and the rest of the Heron family rushed into the room.

"I'm starving!" Ashley announced.

"Glad to hear it." Charlie dug into the dish of mash, revealing a layer of minced beef and vegetables underneath. "Pass me your plate."

"What is that?" Ashley peered curiously at the dish.

"Cottage pie. Or as your dad calls it, shepherd's pie." Lucy rubbed her stomach. "I've been looking forward to it for ages."

"Is this a British thing?" Dylan eyed the food with suspicion.

"I guess so." Lucy put on her most exaggeratedly upper-class English accent. "It's jolly good, old chap."

"It looks like you tried to make a burger and fries, only they fell apart, so you smushed them up together in a dish."

"I suppose that's one way of looking at it."

Dylan shrugged and passed Charlie his plate. "I guess I like burgers and fries, so this should be okay."

"Where does the name come from?" Ashley asked as she examined her food.

"I don't know, sweetheart. Perhaps they used to make it with lamb? You could always look it up."

Ashley reached for her tablet.

"I meant after dinner," Lucy said. "This is family time."

"Family time, family time," Eddie sang, hitting his plate with a spoon.

"Is that the tune from one of your shows?" Charlie asked.

Eddie shook his head. "It's mine."

"Maybe there's a future for you as a composer," Lucy said. "You'll need to eat your dinner first so you can grow big and strong."

Eddie flexed the muscles of his little arms, then set about devouring his dinner with wild abandon. Within seconds, there was mince and potato on the table, on his t-shirt, and dribbling down his chin.

"You eat like a pig." Dylan shook his head at his brother.

"A big pig!" Eddie agreed, oblivious to the fact that it might be an insult. He dropped his spoon, then there was a shimmering in the air, and he transformed into a pig. He shoved his snout into his food, chomping and licking the sides of the plate, and filling the room with snorting noises.

Dylan and Ashley laughed. Lucy fought to keep from joining them. Sometimes it was hard to draw boundaries with Eddie, given the entertainment value of his antics and the good-natured enthusiasm with which they always started.

"Eddie," Charlie forced himself to look stern, "you know you're not supposed to change at the table."

"Maybe this isn't a change," Dylan said. "He's revealing his real self."

Eddie looked up, his snout smeared with mash, and snorted his agreement.

"Do you think that's helping, Dylan?" Charlie asked.

Dylan shrugged. "It's helping keep me entertained."

"I think you've made your point, Eddie." Lucy struggled to stay serious. "Now please turn back."

Eddie tilted his head and looked at her with dark, beady eyes.

"Now," she said firmly.

The air around the pig shimmered, and a moment later, there was a three-year-old boy in its place, his face still filthy with food. Lucy grabbed a napkin and wiped the worst of the mess away, while Eddie squirmed and tried not to be cleaned.

"Now, go and put a slip in the magic jar," she instructed.

"I'm eating." Eddie picked up his spoon and waved it around as if it was the ultimate answer to all arguments.

"No excuses. Magic jar."

With a sigh, Eddie got out of his seat, took a slip of paper from a pile on the sideboard, and scrawled an "E" on it—the only letter he knew how to write—before standing on a stool so he could reach and put the paper in the magic jar. That was one more chore he would have to do as payment for breaking the rules, but he didn't regret it for a moment. Eating like a pig had been a lot of fun.

"What have you been doing today, Ashley?" Charlie asked.

"Helping Mom," Ashley announced proudly.

"Really?" Charlie grinned at Lucy. "Have the Silver Griffins started using child labor now?"

"Ashley found something we might be interested in," Lucy said. "Although she can explain it much better than I can."

Ashley smiled proudly and brushed back the single strand of dark hair that had escaped from her neatly kept ponytail.

"I found some people changing my Wiki pages," she said. "Only it turned out to be part of something larger. They're trying to change the way people see them, or the companies they work for."

"It's marketing?" Charlie asked.

"Not just marketing, disinformation. They created web pages with fake facts, then linked them to each other to make it look real. Then they linked to there from Wiki-pedia or the magical Wiki."

"Magic jar!" Eddie pointed at her with his spoon.

"It's okay to talk about these things at dinner," Lucy said. "Just not to do them."

"Oh." Eddie's face grew thoughtful, and he pushed scraps of food around his plate as he pondered the distinction.

"What were these changes all about?" Charlie asked.

"Fraud!" Ashley spread her hands and set her face in a serious expression, the way she had seen politicians doing on the news when they wanted to seem extra dramatic. "They're trying to make these companies look better and older than they are so that people will put money in them. Some of them were made to look small to start with, then…"

She started explaining the details she had found since first showing the tampered pages to Lucy. There was talk of shell companies, derivative investments, evidential boundaries, search engine optimization, and a jumble of other terms that seemed completely out of place coming from the mouth of an eight-year-old. Lucy and Charlie looked at each other in a mixture of pride and confusion as the conversation drifted far past their ability to follow it. Meanwhile, Eddie was growing restless, and Dylan was staring off into space.

"Why don't you tell your dad about the other thing you've been working on?" Lucy gently interrupted her daughter. "The robot."

That got everybody's attention, even Eddie, who had seen enough cartoon robots to have a clear and exciting image of what they could do. While the others talked, he tried to will his body into the shape of a robot and grew increasingly red-faced as his power refused to take him from organic life to machine.

"It's a robot for seeing things," Ashley explained. "One with cameras and other sensors. I can send it into places I can't get to, or that might be dangerous. So, I can film videos for my channel from up trees or down tunnels."

"I've been going down a lot of tunnels lately," Lucy said. "Maybe I need your robot to save me the effort."

"Why were you down tunnels?" Dylan asked.

"Work things," Lucy said.

"Chasing bad people?"

"Mostly talking to good ones." She needed to include that "mostly" since Willum didn't count as good, given his willingness to attack a Silver Griffin. "Plenty of good people live underground because that's the safest place for them."

"Like moles!" Eddie exclaimed.

There was another shimmer in the air, and he sat waving a pair of clawed paws while peering at them from small, near-blind eyes.

"Jar," Charlie said.

The mole became a boy again and went to put another slip in the jar with his usual confident, no-regrets walk.

"What about you, Dylan?" Lucy asked. "What have you been working on today?"

Dylan hesitated. He knew that what he'd been doing was a good idea, but he wasn't sure whether his parents would see it the same way. Still, it wasn't as if he could keep hiding this forever.

"I've been practicing my magic," he said. "Safe and out

of sight, like you taught me. I want to make sure that I don't have another accident, like at school."

"That's a very sensible attitude," Charlie said. "It's good to practice and get your abilities under control, right honey?"

"Absolutely." Lucy smiled, offering reassurance to her nervous-looking son. "You're at least as gifted with magic as I am, and it took me years to learn how to control my abilities. I'm proud of the fact that you're sensible about it."

Dylan, embarrassed and uncertain of himself, looked down at his plate. He'd braced himself for more trouble after all the fuss at school, but maybe now he had a chance to show off how much he'd achieved.

"I've even managed the same spell, only under control," he said. "Watch." He pulled a seed from his pocket and held it in the palm of his hand. "Crescent plantae."

Almost immediately, a green shoot emerged from the tip of the seed, unfurling into the light. It extended up and out, growing with increasing speed, while a root ran out the other end and trailed down Dylan's wrist. Within moments, the plant's stem thickened and a flower burst from the top, a sunflower that seemed to fill the room with its golden glow. Then the whole plant, unanchored from any soil, tipped over and fell into the shepherd's pie.

"See, that's all I was trying to do at school," Dylan said.

"I think you're missing the point, sweetheart," Lucy said. "You shouldn't have been casting magic at school at all, and definitely not a spell you couldn't control yet."

"I can control it now."

"That's great, but now isn't the problem."

"Well done, though." Charlie fished the sunflower out of the food. "Do you think we can plant this?"

"With the right nutrients," Ashley began, "a common sunflower can—"

"Magic jar!" Eddie declared, pointing his spoon accusingly at Dylan.

"He's right," Charlie said. "That was good magic buddy, but you shouldn't have been casting it at dinner."

Buddy the dog thought they'd called his name, so he bounded in and started yapping as Dylan got out of his seat.

"Doggy!" Eddie yelled and began another transformation while Ashley sculpted a mashed potato model for her robot's legs.

"Geography quiz?" Lucy asked hopefully, looking at the chaos around her.

"Got to be worth a try," Charlie said. "All right, everyone, your starter for one point. What is the capital of Zambia?"

CHAPTER TWENTY-ONE

"All right, everybody." Angela, the running club's leader, stood by the edge of Silver Lake, bouncing from one foot to the other as if she might take off at any minute. "Are you all ready for a great run?"

At the back of the small pack of runners facing her, Lucy and Sarah also started jogging in place, warming up their muscles. Next to them, Jackie was stretching, grunting a little as she eased out her legs and arms.

"I still say this is too early for a Saturday," Jackie groused. "There must be clubs that go later in the day."

"But Angela's so much fun!" Sarah smiled brightly.

"Besides, you need something to haul you into action after one too many tequilas," Lucy added. "Or is it just the time in the morning that's making you look bloodshot and pale?"

"It's the thought of facing you all." Jackie fished a pair of sunglasses from her backpack and covered her eyes. "Somehow, I endure it."

Sarah nudged her. "You love us, really."

"I love you barely, and far less on a morning like this." Jackie started shifting from one foot to the other although with more of a slouch than a bounce. "All right, I'm ready. Let's run."

Seeing that her group was ready, Angela took off at a gentle pace, heading away from the lake and toward the nearest of the brightly painted staircases that were a neighborhood feature. When she emailed the route for that morning's run, she included a description of some of the staircases to look out for, and Lucy was looking forward to it. Any chance to take in more art was a good thing.

Despite her hangover, Jackie was soon ahead of Lucy and Sarah, her blonde bob bouncing with each step. They went up one staircase with steps the bright blue of an imaginary sea in a children's picture book and another with a stenciled wolf howling on one side.

"How do you do it?" Lucy asked as she struggled to catch up with Jackie. "We've been running with you for years, and you still always get ahead."

"Long legs," Jackie said. "A misspent youth running away from mall security guards. And of course, all that time running after escaped trolls and rogue wizards."

One of the other runners gave Jackie a quizzical look.

"She's into *Dungeons and Dragons*," Lucy said, her default excuse to cover up any mention of the magical world.

Jackie fell back, and Lucy and Sarah with her, so that they were alone at the back of the group.

"If word gets around that I spend my Friday nights fighting imaginary monsters, I'm going to blame it all on you," Jackie said.

"What harm can it do?" Lucy started up another set of

steps, the extra effort tugging at her calf muscles. "Perhaps you'll find a nice nerd to drink and roll dice with."

"You settled for a computer geek, but I'm looking for someone a bit more exciting."

"Charlie can be exciting! He took me to Disneyland on our first American date."

"He's lovely, but he's not my type." Jackie picked up the pace again so the rest wouldn't leave them behind. "I'm not after someone with twelve-sided dice."

Lucy thought of Ellis, the out of town wizard who she had met on the train. He would certainly meet Jackie's requirement for someone exciting. On the other hand, she'd seen people face the problems of dating within the workplace, and she didn't want to nudge one of her best friends down that path.

They were halfway up the hill toward Sunset Boulevard when a commotion broke out ahead. Angela and the leading runners had stopped halfway up a street to look at something in the bushes.

"It looked like it had claws," Angela said. "It was so bright, I swear, it was almost like it was flashing as it ran across the street."

Lucy stopped and bent over, hands on her thighs, using the chance to catch her breath while she tried to work out what had drawn the other runners' attention. A slender trail of smoke was drifting from under the bush, and something in the greenery was rasping.

Lucy didn't know a lot about the animals living around there, but she was willing to bet that whatever went scavenging in people's trash didn't normally start fires or flash with light. She glanced at Jackie and Sarah, who looked back at her with raised eyebrows, but none of them said anything. This wasn't a problem to label out loud while mundane folks were around.

Careful not to move too fast in case she drew the joggers' attention or alarmed what was under the bush, Lucy reached around to her back, where her wand hid in a specially designed holster under her shirt. It was one of the many useful little creations Jenkins had provided from his armory.

"What's that moving over there?" Jackie pointed toward another bush farther up the street.

The runners turned to look.

"I don't see anything," Angela said.

"I do!" Sarah moved that way. "It was like there was a flash, then a movement."

The others instinctively followed her, leaving Lucy behind. She pulled out her wand, making sure to keep it down by her side and out of sight, and approached the bush where Angela had initially stopped. The wand was a reassuring presence in her hand, its smooth grip fitting neatly in her palm, the throbbing of power clearly felt within it.

"All right," she whispered. "What are you doing in there?"

A scaly snout poked out from under the bush, fire flaring around its nostrils with each breath. A pair of narrowed eyes looked up at Lucy from the face of a lizard with a body a foot long and a curled-up tail that could stretch to twice that length.

"Are you lost?" Lucy asked. "Who brought you here?"

The firedrake snorted, and there was a bright flash of

fire. Lucy jumped back, then glanced around in case the others had seen what was happening. Jackie and Sarah had them distracted, following a trail of imaginary sightings along the bushes up the street and around the corner.

"Fine." Lucy leveled her wand. "If you want to play with fire, I can play with ice. Stat glacies."

Streamers of icy magic spiraled from her wand toward the drake. It snorted fire again, trying to melt those frozen strands, but they withstood the blast. Its scales flashing as if with an inner light, the drake darted away so the spell missed it and froze the patch of ground where it had stood.

The drake scurried downhill, rustling bushes as it went, tail flickering in its wake. At least it was moving away from the rest of the runners. Lucy dashed after it, glad that she had her running shoes on. The drake was surprisingly fast for such a small creature. She needed to get ahead of it before it ran into more humans, but she wasn't catching up with it fast enough.

"Stat glacies!" Lucy snapped off the spell again, a faster and more forceful version now that she wasn't worried about alarming her target. It overshot the creature and created a patch of black ice three feet in front of its frantically scrabbling claws.

The drake stopped in its tracks, turned its neck, and breathed fire at Lucy. She flung herself aside, and the fire ignited a sapling, reducing the small tree to ashes. Then the drake seemed to see something of interest, as an open doorway caught its attention.

"Oh no, you don't." Lucy launched a string of magical chains, meaning to stop the drake before it could reach the doorway and alarm the house's inhabitants. Instead, the lizard proved its agility again, running fast enough to dodge the chains and reach the entrance with Lucy hurrying after it.

She followed the drake through the doorway. The house's inhabitants were clearly at home, or the door wouldn't have been open. She would have to deal with this as quickly as she could and wipe their memories. Better that than to leave them to have their house burned down.

She followed the patter of the drake's paws and the smoky smell that trailed behind it, down a hallway and toward the kitchen door.

"Well, look at you!" someone said.

"Be careful," Lucy shouted ahead. "That lizard is dangerous. You should step back and…"

Her words trailed off as she entered the kitchen. Instead of the mundane scene of domestic life that she'd expected, she saw a row of cages filling the far wall, each of them holding a firedrake. The bottom row was open, the drakes from there wandering the kitchen floor, eating dog food from large, soot-stained bowls, rubbing their heads against each other, and cleaning their scales with their tongues. In the middle of them stood a man in a bathrobe and a pair of fuzzy slippers. He had slightly more belly than the average elf, but his silver hair and pointed ears gave him away. The drake Lucy had chased was curling itself around his feet.

"What are you doing in my house?" the man asked.

"What are these firedrakes doing in your house?" Lucy asked. "Your house in the middle of residential LA?"

"I don't see why I should answer your questions. What gives you the right to barge in here anyway?"

"I'm a Silver Griffin."

"Do you have any ID?"

Lucy hadn't come out prepared for work, but there were some things that you couldn't leave behind. She flicked her wand, and the distinctive symbol of the Silver Griffins appeared in the air, with her badge number and portrait next to it. The version of her in the picture was a lot less hot and sweaty and wasn't trying to catch her breath after a long jog and a frantic chase, but they were undeniably the same woman.

"Hm." The elf scrutinized the magical ID. "I suppose that seems real. That doesn't give you the right to come barging into my house for no reason at all."

"No reason? One of your firedrakes was out there, roaming the streets. I'm only here because I followed it back to you."

"Oh. Well, sorry about that. It won't happen again."

"It certainly won't. You're not allowed to keep magical pets in the center of a mundane city like this, not in such large numbers, and certainly not without a license."

"My babies need a home! Look at them. Could you reject a face like that?" The elf held up a drake with big, sad eyes and a trickle of burning oil running from its nose. "Some of them are too sickly to survive in the wild."

"There are options other than keeping them here or letting them run wild." As her professional instincts took over, Lucy pulled out her phone to gather evidence. She took a photo of the cages along the wall, another of the drakes roaming the floor, and one of the elf himself, still clutching a sickly drake. "You could return them to a habitat in Oriceran, keep them on an isolated farm where they won't burn houses down, even pass them on to people who know what they're doing."

"I know what I'm doing!"

"The drake I just chased down the street tells me otherwise. I'm going to send these photos to our supernatural animal services division, along with your address. You'd better keep your pets in their cages until they come around."

"But it's so cramped in there, and the little darlings need to run free."

"You should have thought of that before you brought them to LA."

Lucy hit send on a message with the photos, then put her phone and her wand away. If she moved quickly, maybe she could catch up with the running club.

The elf looked so sad that she almost wanted to reach out and pat him on the shoulder and tell him that it would all be okay. However, it nearly hadn't been, and it was his fault. If she had kept Buddy in a home that wasn't suitable for a dog, she wouldn't have deserved to keep him, and the same was true here.

As she walked out, she closed the door firmly behind her. No point in risking another escape.

Lucy ran uphill again, faster than she had down before, hoping to catch up. At the very least, today was going to be good exercise. After a few turns of the road, she saw the running club ahead, with Sarah and Jackie bringing up the rear. Her legs ached with the effort as she put on a burst of speed to reach them.

"All sorted?" Jackie asked once they were together again.

Lucy nodded. "Firedrake. Out of the way for now."

"And for later?"

"Supernatural animals department are on their way."

"This city's so lucky to have you guys," Sarah said.

"This city's lucky not to have evaporated in a magical fireball years ago." Jackie rolled her eyes. "Give it another year or two…"

CHAPTER TWENTY-TWO

From the end of the running group meeting, Lucy, Sarah, and Jackie kept on jogging together, back to their neighborhood. Despite Jackie's best efforts, the other two kept the pace slow, a gentle finish while they caught up with each other. Along the way, Lucy explained about the ancient witches she was trying to hunt down. Although she didn't believe that the witches would know that she was talking about them, she kept from uttering the name "Tolderai" just in case.

"What makes you think they're out there?" Jackie asked. "It sounds like a load of legends."

"It feels real," Lucy said. "I can't explain it more than that, but I've learned to trust my gut."

"What if they don't want to be found?" Sarah asked.

"They clearly don't," Jackie said, "or they would have shown up by now."

"I don't know," Lucy admitted, "but finding them is enough of a challenge for now. I can work out the consequences later."

They reached her house and paused for a moment to say goodbye.

"Take care." Sarah gave Lucy a sweaty hug. "See you on Tuesday for yoga?"

"See you then. Bye!"

The girls ran off, leaving Lucy alone to get her breath back.

Rather than hurry into the house, she stood on the driveway, admiring their patch of front lawn and the roses that she had planted near the house. The flowers bloomed in reds, yellows, and pinks, a joyful riot of color. In between them, a few weeds had started to take hold.

"Hey there!" Al called from his driveway.

"Hey you!" Lucy waved. "What are you up to today?"

"Heading out fishing." Al opened the trunk of his car, put his tackle box in, and slid his rods between the seats.

"Looks like a nice day for it." Wiping the sweat from her brow, Lucy walked over and crouched at the edge of the flower bed.

"Looks like you've been enjoying the day already," Al said with a chuckle. "Me, I could never get the point of running. All that hurry to go nowhere."

"I never got the point of fishing. All that time sitting there with nothing going on, just waiting."

"Ah, but that is the point. I enjoy a good spot of nothing."

Lucy laughed and tugged a couple of weeds from the soil. "I guess there are worse ways to spend the time."

"You should try it sometime. You could bring the kids along. They say stillness is good for young minds."

Lucy pulled up a third weed, one with thick, dark

leaves. Only this time, the weed kept coming, a seemingly endless ribbon of green coming out of the ground.

"Finally tidying up that flower bed, huh?" Al chuckled. "Good for you."

Lucy hastily hid the strange weed, leaning in to conceal the spot from which it still sprouted. Something here wasn't right, like the firedrake in the bushes.

"I figured it was about time," she said.

"You should fetch a bucket for those weeds before you carry on. That way you won't have to waste time finding them all again to clear away after."

"Good thinking. I'll get one in a minute." With one hand, Lucy kept tugging at the weed, and it kept coming, pouring out onto the lawn like a thick green thread.

"Don't let me slow you down," Al said.

"Oh, I'm thinking about something first," Lucy said. "Trying to work out, um, where I've put the bucket."

"A place for everything and everything in its place." Al showed no sign of leaving. "That's how you save yourself from moments like this."

"True. I'll do that in the future. Now you go enjoy your fishing, don't let me keep you."

"Will do." Al waved, climbed into his car, and drove away.

Lucy sighed in relief, checked that no one else was around, and set to pulling the plant up again, going at it with both hands. She realized as she went along that it wasn't all coming out of this one spot; the plant ran off under the flowerbed, hidden beneath a layer of soil. She followed its trail, pulling it up as she went along, around the side of the house, squeezing through a densely grown bush and onto a patch of dirt hidden between the house wall and the fence. There, the weed seemed to reach its end although it remained remarkably resistant to being unearthed. At last, she gave it a tug with both hands. There was a *popping* sound as something gave way. She fell back against the fence, and a section of dirt burst open, a hidden manhole cover springing up to reveal a tunnel into the ground.

Lucy peered down. Rows of LEDs cast a faint illumination down the tunnel's length, which was lined with rows of neatly joined planks. At the bottom, the tunnel bent and disappeared under the house.

Her curiosity growing, Lucy piled the weed carefully next to the hole, then pushed her way back out through the bushes and went into the house. Charlie was sitting on the sofa, playing around with a piece of code on his laptop.

"Where are the kids?" Lucy asked.

"Playing in their rooms, I assume," Charlie said. "Why, what's up?"

"I have something to show you."

Together, they went back around the house to the hidden opening.

"Wow." Charlie stared down the tunnel. "You've been busy."

"Not me. Someone dug this under our house."

"Who? And why?"

Lucy shrugged. "Want to find out?"

She checked that her wand was still secure in the hidden holster on her back, then swung her legs over the edge of the hole and started climbing down. There were hand and footholds built into the tunnel's side, closely spaced together so that someone short could make the descent. Lucy went two at a time.

At the bottom of the steps, the tunnel turned into a slope that ran farther down into the ground beneath their house. After a dozen yards, it opened into a manmade cave, with more tunnels splitting off to the right and left.

"It looks like a mad scientist's lair." Lucy examined the charts and diagrams on the walls.

"Pretty casual for a supervillain." Charlie nudged a beanbag with his foot. It was decorated with dinosaurs, while the ones next to it had robots and tall ships.

They continued down one of the tunnels, which seemed to run for miles beneath Echo Park, branching off in every direction. There were more caverns, some apparently natural and others artificial, some of them furnished and others empty.

"This is going to take forever to explore," Lucy said. "We should head back to the kids, then come back down and check this out properly later."

"Are you going to report it to the Griffins?"

"I don't think it was made without magic, do you?"

Charlie ran a hand along a smoothly packed dirt wall. "No. Not a chance."

As they were approaching the first cavern, there were sounds from up ahead. Someone was walking back and forth, rustling sheets of paper. Lucy pressed a finger to her lips and drew her wand. Charlie pulled his wand from his back pocket, and they crept along the tunnel until they were close enough to peer into the cave.

Ashley stood at one side of the cave, a pencil in her

hand, scribbling on a sheet of paper that she had stuck up above one of the beanbags.

"Ashley?" Lucy stepped out of the tunnel and lowered her wand. "What are you doing here?"

The girl spun and stared at her parents. Her fingers went white as she squeezed the pencil tight. "I never lied about it."

"Okay, that's good." Lucy paced toward her daughter. "Lied about what?"

"I didn't tell you because it was our secret, you know?"

"What was your secret, sweetheart?"

"All this." Ashley waved her arms. "I built it. Or at least, I planned it, and we built it together."

Lucy's mouth hung open in amazement. Her daughter had impressed her since the bright, alert way she had looked around at the world minutes after she was born. This was at a whole new level. It wasn't simply writing a piece of code or building a treehouse. This was practically a hidden town.

"Who's this 'we'?" Charlie asked although like Lucy, he already had a suspicion.

At that moment, there was a sound of footsteps climbing down the entrance ladder, and a voice echoed along the tunnel.

"Hey Ashley, you left the hatch open," Dylan called. "You should be careful in case someone… Oh."

He stood in the mouth of the cave, looking at the three of them. Eddie stood behind him, peering around his older brother's leg.

"I'm not here," Eddie said, and in a shimmer of magic turned into a worm that wriggled toward the nearest dirt.

"Too late, Eddie." Lucy crossed her arms. "Time to face the music."

The air shimmered again, and Eddie returned to his small boy body.

"How did you make all this?" Lucy asked.

"Robots," Ashley said.

"And magic," Dylan added. "Although I was really careful about it."

"I was a mole," Eddie added, waving his hands like he was clawing his way through the dirt.

"Why?" Lucy asked. "I mean, it's very impressive, but what's it all for?"

Ashley took one of the sheets of paper down off the wall and handed it to her mother.

"It's for this," she said.

Lucy read the title at the top of the sheet: "Goals of the Mini Griffins." Underneath was a list, written in different colored felt tips by different childish hands:

"Fight crime.

"Help people.

"Make our town nice.

"Money for the den."

"The Mini Griffins?" Charlie raised his eyebrows.

"We know we can't become Silver Griffins until we're older," Dylan said, "but we wanted to do good things like mom does. So, we started the Mini Griffins."

"Is it just you guys?"

"Some of our friends too."

"What have the Mini Griffins done so far?"

Ashley lifted one of the beanbags and grabbed a notebook from underneath. The big glittery letters on the cover proclaimed, "Chronicles of the Mini Griffins."

"We solved the mystery of who stole the parcel off Miss Tompkin's porch," Ashley read from the first page of the book. "We cleaned and fed a stray dog, then helped him find a home. When Mister Rodriguez lost his job, we helped feed his family, though they don't know it was us."

"That's part of how we work," Dylan added, pointing to another sheet of paper, this one labeled "Operating Procedures." "We work in secret, like the real Griffins."

"Or Batman," Eddie added.

Lucy rubbed her eyes and looked around her in bewilderment. Her kids had been doing all this right under her nose. Not only under her nose but under her feet, digging tunnels under the house, holding secret meetings, running around their neighborhood fighting crime, and providing dinners. She was stunned that it was happening at all, and even more so that they had gotten away with it.

"How do you pay for all this?" Charlie asked. "The materials for the tunnels, the furniture, the computers we saw in one of the other caves. I know this hasn't come out of your pocket money, or even the treehouse budget."

"If you'd let me finish," Ashley said, holding up the book. "We also provide tutor services and do odd jobs."

"That can't be right." Lucy shook her head. "Do people really pay an eight-year-old tutor?"

"I'm twelve," Dylan said. "That's old enough for some people to listen to what I know."

"Nobody has to know how old you are if you're tutoring on the internet," Ashley added. "Or care about it.

As long as you know what you're talking about, that's all that matters."

"I..." Lucy struggled to find the words. "I don't... I can't..."

Charlie put an arm around her waist and squeezed. He was fighting to hold back a massive grin. Everything he'd seen was amazing, and he was proud of what the kids had done, but he was also aware that they'd done it in secret, and that there were risks in trying to imitate what the Silver Griffins did. He and Lucy would have to talk about this, to work out a united front on it all. For now, she was too stunned, and he wasn't quite ready for the telling off part of the conversation.

"Everybody up to the house." He forced a serious face. "We'll talk about this later."

Ashley and Dylan headed up the tunnel that would take them out. Both of them were trying to stay calm while bursting with pride. They had finally shown Mom and Dad what they were doing. It made it all seem more real, more grown-up.

Eddie instead approached his parents and reached up to tug on his mom's hand. "Are we in trouble?" he asked, eyes wide.

"No, sweetheart." Lucy scooped him up into a big hug. "You've tried to do something good, and that will never get you into trouble. Your dad and I just need some time to think about it, okay?"

"Okay." Eddie hugged her back, then wriggled free and ran after his siblings.

Once they were alone, Lucy turned to bury her face in

Charlie's chest, letting his shirt muffle the sounds of her laughter.

"What are we going to do with them?" she asked at last.

"I don't know," Charlie admitted. "But I'll say one thing. Our kids secretly built a Batcave under the house and used it to help neighbors in trouble. That has to be a sign of good parenting."

CHAPTER TWENTY-THREE

Lucy stood in the back room of a Sunset Boulevard book-shop, talking to the gnome who managed the stock.

"You understand why you can't put a grimoire out on the displays though, right?" she asked.

The gnome snorted and flipped her dyed pink hair.

"These are stupid rules," she said. "Sooner or later, the humans are going to realize that there's magic in their world. Wouldn't it be better to teach them about that?"

"Not everyone is safe to use magic. You know that."

"They're not kids. At least most of them aren't. We shouldn't be infantilizing them due to some outmoded, patriarchal idea of how a good society is run."

Lucy thought about her kids and their amazing hidden lair that she had discovered the day before. After seeing what they had achieved and hearing all the good they were doing with it, she didn't feel like age was really the issue. The problem was that not everyone wielded their power for good or with restraint. Giving most people magic was like giving a toddler a flamethrower and hoping that he wouldn't burn the house down. Maybe you would get lucky, but on balance, it was probably best not to risk an inferno.

"Maybe more people can be trusted with these secrets." Lucy held up the magical books that she'd taken off a shelf in the front of the store. "Maybe they can't. Still, the law is clear. You don't get to take that risk for everyone else. So, you keep everything relating to Oriceran or magic back here, and you only show it to other magicals. Otherwise, I'll be back to arrest you and to pass these books on to someone who can be trusted with them. Understand?"

"I understand."

The gnome's expression made clear that understanding wasn't the same as agreeing, but Lucy didn't think that she was likely to keep breaking the law. This was a woman who loved selling books to people and who had merely gotten carried away with it.

"I suppose I'll have to hide the books of card tricks, too," the gnome snipped. "And the fantasy novels, of course, those relate to magic. Then there's the David Blaine biography…"

Lucy stopped in the doorway and turned. Now she felt like she was dealing with her kids, someone taking what she had said and interpreting it in the most literal way possible, just to protest their unhappiness.

"Remember what you said about not infantilizing people?" Lucy asked. "I'm not going to patronize you by answering a question you know the answer to. You're not a kid. You know where to draw the line. That's why I'm trusting you with these."

She put the books down, then walked out through the store to the street.

As she approached her car, her phone buzzed. It was a message from work, saying that Roger Applegate wanted to see her in his office as soon as possible.

Lucy groaned. Applegate, the regional manager and her immediate superior, wasn't a bad guy, but being called to his office wasn't a good sign. He was a hands-off manager, an approach that partly came from trusting his subordinates and partly from his desire to minimize his workload. If he was calling her in on short notice, something was the matter.

She got into her SUV and headed a short distance down the Boulevard to the nearest Starbucks. A barista smiled in recognition as she walked in, and Lucy nodded in greeting as she joined the queue. Sure, Roger had said that he wanted to see her soon, but it was important to maintain the impression that the Silver Griffins were regular coffee shop customers. If that meant she could put the meeting off by five minutes while also getting a caffeine hit, all the better.

"Tea, please," she requested when she reached the counter and handed over her travel cup.

"What happened to your usual Batman?" the barista asked as she saw the Wonder Woman logo on the side of the cup.

"He's busy fighting a set of Joker plates."

The barista laughed and poured hot water in on top of the teabag.

"That's the sort of hero this city needs, one who cares about the washing up."

Lucy took her cup to the end of the counter, stirred it, then fished out the teabag and added milk. Ready at last to face the inevitable, she stepped through the chocolate scent outside the bathrooms at the back of the store, touched her wand to the wall, and stepped through.

She walked down the spiral stairs to the platform below and jumped aboard a train to Silver Griffins HQ. Two more witches were on board, and between them sat a cage of frantically twitching koala bears.

"What happened to them?" Lucy stared at the koalas. One of the bears turned to her, its eyes glowing, and belched a cloud of magical sparks that floated into the shape of a eucalyptus leaf.

"They were being used in an illegal magical testing lab," one of the witches said. "The owner's on his way to Trevilsom, but now we need to disenchant these poor guys."

The koala stretched out for the shimmering illusion of a leaf, then made a sad face as it evaporated under his paw. Lucy was glad that Eddie wasn't there to see this, or she would have had a koala for a kid for days to come, and a disappointed three-year-old wondering why he couldn't burp magic.

When Lucy got off at the HQ station, Normandy was in his usual place, polishing a griffin ornament that normally lived above the station clock.

"No cakes today, I'm afraid," Lucy said. "I didn't even know that I'd be coming in."

"I'm still finishing off those cookies you made me," Normandy said with a smile. "I knew there would be dangers working for the Silver Griffins, but I never thought that the main threat would be to my waistline."

By the time Lucy made it to Roger Applegate's office, she had drunk most of her tea and felt far more ready to face the meeting. She walked in with a bright smile, which only faltered a little when she spotted Kelly Petrie sitting at one side of the room. Lucy glanced down at her jeans and crumpled t-shirt, comparing them unfavorably with Kelly's impeccably pressed pantsuit and blouse. Lucy had no idea how anyone managed to turn up for work like that when they were also managing kids and chasing down rogue magic, but although she felt a little envious, she wasn't going to commit the effort it would take to look so smart. There were better ways to spend her energy.

"Take a seat, Lucy." Roger waved from behind a pile of papers. He was somewhat portly and a little red-cheeked but made up for it with a three-piece suit that threw even Kelly's efforts into the shade. Bright eyes shone from a face that was just starting to wrinkle. "I hope that you don't mind Kelly being here. She's shadowing me as part of the management development program, seeing what my job involves and how I do it."

"Sounds like a great idea." Lucy shot a sideways look at Kelly. "Really looks good on the CV for promotions."

"I suppose it does." Roger chuckled. "Kelly, could you close the door, please?"

Lucy sank a little lower in her seat. Roger liked to be seen as approachable, and if his door wasn't open, something was almost certainly amiss.

"I've had a report about a school in your area," Roger said. "As I understand it, one of your sons goes there."

He turned his monitor so they could all see a series of photographs, one coming up after another, all capturing the playground that Dylan had turned into a jungle. There were towering trees, lower clusters of ferns and exotic flowers, chunks of broken concrete, and overturned benches. Then there was the cleanup: tree surgeons taking the forest down piece by piece, trucks being loaded up with hardwood logs, volunteers pulling up plants, all of it supervised by someone Lucy recognized as a Silver Griffin.

"That's Dylan's school, yes," Lucy said. "The forest is his handiwork too."

"So I understand." Roger glanced at Kelly, then back to Lucy. "This has turned into a serious incident. We were too late on the scene for a 'never was, never will be,' and this was probably too big to handle like that anyway. The PR department has been tying themselves in knots keeping it out of the press, and we've had to spend some serious money on the cleanup so that nobody asks why the city paid for a logging operation at a middle school."

"I'm really sorry," Lucy said. "I got there as soon as I could and tried to reassure the principal."

"Yes, well, that was a start, but this should never have been an issue in the first place. We expect better from the children of Silver Griffins."

"Don't I know it! I've told Dylan over and over that he shouldn't use his magic in public, and normally he's really good about that. Well, as good as any kid his age can be. I wish that the one time he broke the rules hadn't gone so wild."

"He chose to turn his school into a chunk of Amazon rainforest. That goes beyond childish misbehavior."

"It was an accident. He was trying to grow a single plant to show off to someone, but the spell was more powerful than he realized. His magic got away from him, but he would never do anything like this on purpose."

Roger looked at the screen and nodded seriously. "It's certainly an impressive display of power. That makes the incident even more worrying. If young Dylan's magic is this strong, and he's prone to using it in an irresponsible manner, the Griffins may need to intervene."

Lucy's blood ran cold. The last thing she wanted for her son was to spend his time being constantly watched by the Griffins, or worse. She knew there had been cases where they used artifacts to prevent magic users from wielding their power, and Dylan was so proud of his magic, something like that would make him miserable. Or what if they decided to send him to Oriceran, where his magic wouldn't be so disruptive? She didn't want him torn away from her, from Charlie, from all his friends.

"I really think that he's learned a lesson," she said. "His power is greater than he realized, but this put a fright into him. He's promised that he'll never do anything like it again."

"The problem is, you already told me that he didn't mean to do this." Roger frowned as he looked at Lucy. "It doesn't matter what he promises if he could do something so unmissable by accident. It's about actions, not intentions."

Lucy clenched her hands around her cup of tea and drew a long, deep breath. She dealt with deadly magic on a nearly daily basis, but somehow this conversation was scarier than any of that. It didn't help that Kelly sat so close, barely even trying to hide her smug smile at Lucy's discomfort.

"I have a plan in place," Lucy said. "Charlie and I are arranging extra tuition for Dylan in how to control his magic, and we've laid down the law on when and where he can practice with his powers. We even have a magic jar at home to reinforce the rules, like a swear jar for spells."

"A magic jar." Roger chuckled, to Lucy's immense relief. "I like that."

He turned the monitor back toward him, and Lucy relaxed a little as the jungle image disappeared from view.

"What does your boy want to do when he grows up?" Roger asked.

"He wants to be a Silver Griffin." Lucy decided not to explain how far he'd gone with that already, building a secret base and finding missions around the neighborhood. That wouldn't reflect well on how much she had Dylan under control.

"Excellent news. We could do with more Griffins who have his level of raw power." Roger typed something into his computer, then nodded to himself. "Obviously, we'll keep an eye on Dylan's progress from now on. If there are other incidents like this, I expect to hear about them directly from you, not through third parties."

Again, he glanced at Kelly. So that was who had drawn this to his attention. Lucy started dreaming up revenge schemes, then set that thought aside for later.

"Are you going to punish Dylan?" Lucy asked.

"It sounds like you have that in hand. While it doesn't reflect well on you that this happened, it sounds as though you're managing it all. Honestly, I don't know if I could cope with a kid that powerful, or if any of us could. Right, Kelly?"

"Of course, Roger." Kelly laughed.

"Well, that's that then." Roger smiled at Lucy. "You can leave the door open on your way out."

Still clutching her cup, and in it the last cold dregs of her tea, Lucy got out of her seat and left the room. She nodded to friends and colleagues as she strode down the corridors and out along the tunnel to the station but didn't stop to say hello. She was too preoccupied thinking about how they could keep a closer eye on Dylan without stopping him from doing good work with the Mini Griffins. It was a difficult balance to strike, but with Charlie's help, she was sure she could do it.

"Everything all right?" Normandy asked as she passed his booth at the entrance to the station.

"It will be." Lucy flashed him a smile. "Just facing the challenges of raising a super-powered kid."

CHAPTER TWENTY-FOUR

The whole way back to the Starbucks and from there to the nursery to pick up Eddie, Lucy was lost in thought. She wanted to trust her kids to do good things, to use their gifts as Mini Griffins. However, she also needed to keep a close eye on Dylan's magic, and those two aims didn't go well together.

She pulled up in front of the nursery and jumped out. Eddie was already waiting for her in the doorway, his little backpack at the ready and a happy grin on his face.

"Mommy!" he called.

"Hi, sweetheart." She swept him up in a hug, then set him down so they could walk to the SUV together. "What have you been doing today?"

"I built a robot, and he fought another robot, and there was cookies and juice, and we sang a song, then it was sand time, and you came."

"What did you like best?"

Eddie pursed his lips and gazed thoughtfully into the distance.

"I liked the sand. I mixed it like we were making cakes."

"Would you like to make some cakes for real when we get home?"

Eddie grinned. "Yay!"

Lucy strapped him into his seat and headed out through the traffic. Along the way, they sang a song about a cat, then one that was teaching Eddie about different types of weather. Lucy's spirits lifted although she was still in need of some stress relief.

Buddy met them at the front door of their home, yapping excitedly.

"Buddy dog!" Eddie wrapped his arms around the dachshund. "Best dog."

Buddy licked Eddie's face, making him giggle.

"Come on, both of you." Lucy led them into the kitchen. "It's time to bake buns. You can help if you want, Buddy, or you can have this treat."

She pulled a bone-shaped biscuit from a box on the counter and handed it to the dog. He grabbed it between his teeth and hurried off to a basket in the hallway, where he sat gnawing contentedly on the tasty treasure.

"Now, Eddie…" Lucy pushed a pair of wooden steps in front of the sink and turned on the faucet. "If you want to bake, you have to clean your hands first."

Eddie clambered up the steps and stuck his hands into the running water, then grabbed the soap and giggled in delight as he made bubbles fly everywhere.

"An excellent start." Lucy grabbed a couple of aprons off the back of a door, one for her and one child-sized. She washed her hands, helped Eddie down from the sink, and slipped the loop of the apron over his head.

"I'm a fish," Eddie declared while waving his wet hands around. "Splish splash."

The air shimmered, and he flopped to the floor in the shape of a trout. He wiggled and squirmed for a moment, then the shimmer returned, and with it the little boy.

"Not so exciting being a fish?" Lucy asked.

"Can't swim in the kitchen."

"Very true."

Lucy tied both their aprons into place, then took out a small folding table from the corner of the room and set it up next to the end of the counter. It had scratches and stains left behind by Dylan and Ashley when they were younger, a history of their family in furniture form. Now Eddie took his place at the table and clapped his hands eagerly.

"We make cake!"

"I'm thinking sticky buns," Lucy said. "Then we can eat them for breakfast tomorrow. How does that sound?"

"I like buns." Eddie licked his lips. "I like sticky."

"You certainly do." Lucy laughed and rolled her eyes. "You're going to need a bath by the time we finish here, but it'll be worth it. Ready?"

"Steady!"

"Bake!"

Lucy took out a measuring cup and set it in front of Eddie, along with a bowl and a bag of flour.

"Four cups, please," she said.

While Eddie carefully measured out the flour, wearing an expression of intense seriousness of the sort reserved for small children and preachers, Lucy gathered the other ingredients and set them out on the counter.

"Done it." Eddie held up the bowl of flour.

"Thank you, sweetheart." Lucy took the bowl, then put a smaller one down in front of Eddie and added some flour. "Now we add the sugar and salt."

Together, they measured out the new ingredients and stood mixing them together, each of them working in their bowl.

"Now the butter." Lucy chopped up the butter, added some pieces to Eddie's bowl and the rest to hers. Simply going through the motions of baking relaxed her. There were few things as enjoyable as working with her hands like this, especially when she knew that she would get to eat the cinnamon-flavored results.

They both rubbed the butter into the flour, Eddie scattering white dust widely around him.

"Keep going until it's all mixed in," Lucy said.

"Mixed, mixed, mixed!" Eddie banged his hand against the rim of the bowl, almost tipping the contents across the floor.

"Are you having fun there?"

Eddie nodded, then looked up at her. "Wanna change."

Lucy considered the request. It was good that he had asked, or at least talked about it, before taking on a different shape. That should be encouraged. He did need practice to control his power, as Dylan did.

"All right," she agreed. "But if you get fur in your baking, no one else has to eat it."

The moment she said the words, she realized her mistake. Eddie grinned at the thought of having a whole batch of buns to himself, then the air around him shimmered, and he transformed. Instead of a small boy, a capybara perched at the low table next to Lucy, an apron hanging around its broad neck, forepaws poised over the bowl, hooded eye looking up from its strange, flat face.

"That's not the help I expected," Lucy said. "Can you mix the dough like that?"

Eddie pushed himself up on his rear paws and reached down into the bowl. Within seconds, his brown fur was dusted white.

"I guess that will do." Lucy added yeast, eggs, and milk to both bowls, then set to mixing hers, while Eddy did his best to stir the ingredients using paws without thumbs and legs that could only just reach the bottom of the bowl. Half-made dough spattered the table and the floor around him in a joyful mess.

Once her dough was thoroughly mixed, Lucy set it aside to rise while she gathered the ingredients for the filling. Pecans, cinnamon, and more sugar went into a food processor.

"Do you want to do the whirring?" she asked.

Capybara Eddie's head shot up, and he clapped his doughy paws together.

"All right, clean your paws first. I don't want that mess all over the outside of the mixer."

Eddie paused for a moment, looked from his sticky paws to the sink, then down at his step, as if working his way through an elaborate puzzle. Then he jumped down and pushed the steps over to the sink, using his head as a ram. Once they were in place, he leapt up and operated the faucet using his teeth. It was an imprecise way of working, and his head got as covered in soap and water as his paws did, but Lucy was impressed at his efforts.

"You're getting good at using your animals," she said. "Next time, maybe think about turning into something that's good at what you're doing, like maybe a monkey with hands for mixing the dough."

The dripping capybara jumped down off his steps and shook himself, spattering Lucy with fat drops of water. She laughed, then moved the steps over so that he could reach the food processor.

"All ready."

Eddie climbed up the steps and pressed his snout against the button that made the machine work. There was a whir as it started up. Nuts rattled around the container as the blades chopped them into pieces. A vibration ran from his nose, through his head, and down into the rest of his furry body, a ticklish sensation that made him laugh, or as close to a laugh as a capybara could manage.

"All done," Lucy said, seeing that the nuts were finely chopped and the filling well-mixed. "Now we deal with the dishes while we wait for the dough to rise."

Putting measuring spoons and dirty bowls into a dishwasher was the sort of task a capybara could manage, as long as he used his mouth and didn't want to put any of them on the upper rack. Lucy wiped the counter, the table, and the floor while Eddie scuttled back and forth. Even working at the pace of a transformed three-year-old, the dough hadn't finished rising by the time they were cleaned up, so for the first time all week, Lucy sat down to watch cartoons with her son.

"This is one of the advantages of being a parent," she commented as the capybara snuggled up next to her on the sofa. "It's an excuse to watch all the best telly."

For the best part of an hour, superheroes and villains fought each other across brightly animated landscapes. There were moments when Lucy was amazed at the wild imaginings of the cartoons' creators, and others when she thought about things she had seen in real life, magical creatures and events so much stranger than anything on TV.

"Time to finish what we started," she said at last and peeled herself up off the couch. "We need to get the buns cooked before the others get home so there's room in the oven for dinner."

Back in the kitchen, they kneaded and rolled out their dough. Lucy made hers into a neat rectangle while Eddie formed a flat blob that reminded him of the speech bubbles he had seen on an old superhero show. Lucy brushed both dough pieces with melted butter, and together they sprinkled the filling over the top.

"Now press it in." Lucy picked up a full-sized rolling pin and set a smaller one on the table in front of Eddie.

Rolling anything turned out to be difficult for a capybara. After a few failed experiments, Eddie decided that his best option was to push the rolling pin back and forth with his head. That got his fur covered in butter and nutty cinnamon filling, a price he was more than happy to pay.

While Eddie was grappling with the capybara cooking challenge, Lucy coated two baking trays with a mix of butter, sugar, and maple syrup then rolled up her dough, sliced it into buns, and placed them on the larger tray. Eddie's dough, rolled up as well as he could manage without hands, was sliced and placed on the other tray. Even with a capybara's face, his pride was clear as Lucy took the tray and put it into the oven along with hers.

"We're done." She brushed her hands off on her apron, then looked at the sticky, flour-whitened capybara. "Time to turn back into a boy."

The air shimmered, and her son became human again.

"Fun!" He waved his buttery hands in the air. Flour covered his cheeks, his arms greasy to the elbows, and there were chunks of dough in his hair.

"One of us needs a bath," Lucy said.

"But buns…"

"Will have finished cooking by the time we get you clean. Come on."

She took his hand and led him out of the kitchen.

As they left, Buddy the dog woke from a very restful nap. He got up onto his little legs, tottered through to the kitchen, and sniffed at a smear on the floor. Butter and sugar, delicious! He stuck his tongue out and licked up the remains. He loved baking days.

CHAPTER TWENTY-FIVE

Zero sat in front of the vast black crystal at the back of the kemana—his kemana—and felt the magic flowing around him. This was the place of his greatest power, the place where he felt almost invincible. It was the perfect spot for what he was about to try.

He opened the rusty old chest and bathed in the glow of the Splitting Stone. Immediately, the power around him changed. He felt currents of magic swirl and sway, brushing at his mind with tendrils of potential. This was it. This was his moment.

Tar oozed from his pores, ran down his skin, dribbled along the sides of his seat, and dripped onto the floor. Thick, black tar, as dark and irremovable as any of the debts owed to him.

He stretched out a hand, and one of the gnomes handed him a thick towel. Keeping the cloth between his flesh and the statue, Zero lifted the Splitting Stone out of its container, closed the lid, and rested the artifact on the top of the chest. The whole room seemed brighter from its light, but it was a sickly brightness, one that added a sense of something rotten to the gleam of the tar walls.

"At last," Zero whispered. "It's time."

Gruffbar leaned against the wall, arms folded, watching warily. That statue set his teeth on edge. He understood the plan, understood in theory why it would appeal to a creature like Zero, and it was never Gruffbar's way to stand against the plans of an employer. Still, he didn't like this.

"Are you sure about this, Mister Zero?" he asked.

"I've never been more sure of anything." Zero's voice bubbled with excitement, and the light from the Splitting Stone gleamed in his eyes. "You've seen how much I've achieved with only one of me in the world, now imagine what two can do, three, four, a dozen, a hundred. The whole of this miserable, mundane place will be mine to command, and the people who think that they're in charge won't even know what's really happening."

He held his hands out, one on each side of the stone, and let the power flow. Slowly, he moved his hands closer. He felt the power of the stone drag at his flesh, tearing at it, pulling his hands in and yet somehow pulling him apart. His skin touched the stone, and cold magic gripped him.

"Yeeeeesssss!" The word came out on a long, juddering breath as magic rippled through Zero's body. His flesh wobbled, his bones shook, his internal organs writhed around each other. The stone had him in its grasp, and he had its power in his mind. He was controlled, and he was in control. He was two things at once. He was being split.

Gruffbar watched as the magic took hold of his boss. Zero vibrated, then started to spread, his blob-like flesh stretching out to the right and left. Buttons flew off his brightly colored shirt as his body expanded and started to pull apart, splitting from the head down. Even for a dwarf with a strong stomach, it was unpleasant to see his employer's insides exposed for that brief moment before orange skin washed back across them.

Zero had split almost halfway down before he realized that anything was wrong. Skin was growing back over the gaps, but it wasn't doing everything it should. Each half of him was supposed to form a new whole, duplicating eyes, ears, and teeth, absent bones and missing organs. While parts of this substitute flesh appeared, they were stunted and incomplete. He blinked out through a tiny eye in the side of his head, felt rows of teeth as small and pointed as those on the edge of a saw, looked down, and saw new ribs start growing, then falter, stop, and retreat.

Not enough power, that was the problem. He was more than halfway there, but anything short of the whole way would be useless. He concentrated on the kemana crystal, sucking in all the magic he could, then channeling it through the stone. So much power that the air around him sizzled and tar evaporated as it poured from his skin, leaving a blackened and crumbling crust.

"Come on, come on, come on!" He gripped the statue tight until the tips of his fingers ached where they pressed against the stone. It was no use. He had to stop now while he still had something left, or give in to the stone's will and risk tearing himself apart.

He pushed the magic back out in a great rush. As it went, the two halves of his body slammed together. There was a slap of wobbly skin and a squelch as organs rearranged themselves, returning to their old positions. He let go of the statue and slumped in his seat, his failure so clear that he could feel it as a pain in his flesh.

Gruffbar pushed off the wall and paced toward his boss. He'd seen Zero tired before, along with lazy or half-asleep, but he'd never seen him look as utterly drained as he did now. Lids peeled back revealing bloodshot eyes, and Zero let out a low, frustrated moan.

"I was this close." He held a finger and thumb half an inch apart. "This close!"

He kicked the chest with one tiny foot, and it rocked back. The Splitting Stone fell to the floor, and Gruffbar jumped clear rather than let it touch him for even a moment.

"You'll come up with another plan," the dwarf said. "Hire some assistants to run those other companies, maybe, or summon some demons."

"No, this is the plan!" Zero pounded his fists against the sides of his seat. "Me, me, and more of me, me from sea to shining sea. It is the best plan, the only plan, and I am going to make it work."

Don't argue with the boss. It didn't matter if the boss was losing his mind. That was still a rule that Gruffbar lived by.

"So how do we do this?" he asked.

"More power. That's what I need. Enough to complete the magic. Enough to make two of me."

"And then?"

"Then we'll gather the next lot of power twice as fast, and faster again when there are three of me, four, more…"

"You want to call in some debts?"

Gruffbar snapped his fingers, and one of the gnomes

scurried over, clutching a tablet. It handed the device to Gruffbar, then backed away, out of the sickly light emanating from the Splitting Stone.

"Not so fast," Gruffbar said. "Get some gloves on and get that thing back into the chest. We need to keep Mister Zero's prized possession safe."

"Of course, of course." The gnome hurried off in search of protective equipment.

Gruffbar unlocked the tablet, pulled up a spreadsheet, and started scrolling down a list of debtors.

"There are a few that have come due in the last few days, so we can chase those." He looked at the names and considered the power they had to offer. It wouldn't be enough. "Maybe we can call some debts in early or offer to reduce the interest payments for anyone who pays off their principal now."

"I want more payment, not less." Zero narrowed his eyes.

Gruffbar shrugged. He might choose not to disagree with an employer's plans, but that didn't mean that he would hide the hard facts or tough decisions. "You can have it fast, or you can have it all. You taught me that."

Zero rubbed a hand down his tar-slicked chest.

"I was right, of course," he said. "But there are some methods that encourage both swift and total payment."

He reached into a pocket of his shirt, pulled out his whistle, and blew. A pair of gnomes, walking toward them wearing oven gloves and protective overalls, clapped their hands over their ears and buckled over, groaning to themselves.

Deeper darkness coalesced against the blackness of the

ceiling, a shadow that swallowed even the Splitting Stone's sickly green light. It poured down in a stream that spattered the ground in front of Zero, then rose back up, forming a pillar of absolute black.

"Yes, master," the shadow mites buzzed, their bodies vibrating into recognizable words, barely audible.

Gruffbar took a step back and another.

"I have a mission for you." Zero stared into the void. "Debts to collect. Power to carry home. A reckoning for many of my customers. Gruffbar has the list."

Gruffbar swallowed, then straightened and faced the swarm of mites. There was no way to tell where their attention was, whether they were looking at him now or had been staring at him all along. Then he realized that the darkness was creeping toward him.

"Here." He held up the tablet, its screen away from him, displaying the list. "Names, addresses, what they owe. Gather whatever you can."

"If they refuse?" That last word gained a sinister, almost hungry buzz.

"If they're in red on the list, make an example of them. If not, scare them but leave them intact. These are Mister Zero's golden geese. No point killing them while they could still lay."

The shadow mites drifted out across the city. They didn't have to talk to share the decisions they would make. They were a swarm. Understanding simply emerged, became a splitting of the dark cloud, then another, and another, each separation a gathering of mites heading toward a different debtor.

Kradak sat on a battered sofa, his phone in one hand and a pipe in the other, smoke curling from its bowl. Across the room, an old TV showed old episodes of a game show where contestants charged around an obstacle course, crashing into barriers and slipping in pools of mud.

"I know you're not dead, Willum," the dwarf croaked into the phone. "If you'd been arrested, it would've been announced on the magical web. Give me a call when you get this. I'm almost out of pipe weed, and I need you to fix me up with your guy."

As he set down the phone, a shadow crept across the TV screen.

"Rocks be cursed, not this again." Kradak strode across the room and banged on the top of the TV set. The picture wobbled, but the blackness didn't recede. In fact, part of it came away on his hand. "What the…"

He stepped back, but a black swarm was spinning through the air around him, forming a circle around his head.

"Zero wants his payment." The words seemed to come from every direction at once, buzzing like a saw blade that scratched at Kradak's brain.

"I thought I had more time," Kradak said.

"Your name is in red," the cloud of shadow mites said. "We can make you an example."

"No, no, no, no, no!" Kradak flung up his hands. "No need for that. Just look in that box."

He pointed at a shoebox sitting in the corner of the room. A trail of mites broke off from the cloud, went over to the box, and lifted the lid. Inside were three fat rolls of used banknotes and a small pyramid of stones, each with a dwarven rune engraved in its center.

"Twelve for the principal, four for interest," Kradak said. "Just like we agreed."

"Five for interest. You were late."

"Just by a day!"

"We can make an example."

"No examples, no examples! Just take them all, and, and thank Zero for his kindness, for letting me off. I promise I'll pay promptly next time."

"Yes," the cloud buzzed, its tendrils lifting the stones and leaving the cash behind. "You will."

Grishgash the Willen flicked his tail back and forth in time to the music emerging from the radio. He loved country and western, with its songs about debt and disaster, its strange combination of cheery tunes and miserable subject matter. He would miss it when he was back on Oriceran, but it was time to get out of town. He'd had too many close calls now, whether with people he'd stolen from or people he had debts to. It was time to find a nice, quiet town full of gullible magicals where nobody knew his name.

He flung a couple more vests into his suitcase and

looked around for his solar-powered battery charger. He would need that to keep the radio running.

The song got fuzzy for a moment, then descended into pure static. Where the radio had been, there was now a dark and shifting cloud, like a hole in the world.

"Who cast that?" Grishgash called.

While keeping his eyes on the cloud, he slid toward his bedside table and the knife he always kept there.

"No one cast us," the cloud of shadow mites buzzed. "Or perhaps we cast ourselves."

The blackness of the mites reminded Grishgash of those caves beneath the tar pits where he had negotiated a loan from Zero. When had that one come due, a week ago, two, a month maybe? It didn't matter. He had moved around the city twice since then, never leaving a forwarding address. Zero was one more sucker he would leave in the dust.

"What do you want?" he asked.

"You were hard to find, but you have a scent we remember. You owe Zero. Now it's time to pay."

"Sure, just give me another day."

"No more days. Pay now."

"You want to give me one more day," Grishgash said, and his pupils started to spin. A little hypnotism to buy him time, and he would be out of town before this supernatural flunky could do anything about it. Easy as picking an old man's pockets.

"No more days. Pay now or be an example."

"I guess you're immune to hypnotism, then?" Grishgash shrugged. "How about persuasion instead? I don't have all the debt here right now, it's a lot of raw magic crystals to keep in one place, but I had plans to pick them up tonight. Come back tomorrow, or better yet, let me bring them in. I can maybe give you two as a sign of good faith."

"Not paying," the shadow mites said. "Example."

They surged forward, like a storm wave breaking across the room. Grishgash grabbed the knife and flicked it through the air. Against a dwarf or a gnome, that move would have left his enemy trailing guts and wishing they had never been born. Against the shadow mites, it was as useless as his eyes had been.

"Example," the swarm buzzed as they swamped Grishgash, knocking him back onto his bed, completely covering him. He kicked and squirmed as long as his strength held, then gave one last twitch and fell still.

A trail of shadow mites emerged from under the bed, carrying a bag of glowing crystals. Others drew a box of artifacts from the creaking wardrobe and an antique grimoire from the bedside table. Then the whole swarm floated away out the window, leaving Grishgash's bones and his useless knife.

Three cats watched Lucy as she knocked on the door of the ground floor apartment. One of them was missing a leg, and another had scars on their face, but all of them seemed well-fed and peaceful. Even the birds perching on a feeder above them didn't seem to get the cats over-excited. They just sat and swished their tails while a gentle evening breeze stirred the potted plants around them.

The door opened a crack, and a man peered out. He

was in his mid-twenties, with a blond ponytail and an underdeveloped goatee.

"Hey there," he said. "Can I help you with something?"

"Are you Nathaniel Oakmantle?" Lucy asked.

"Yep, that's me. Who are you?"

"Lucy Heron, Silver Griffin field agent 485. I heard that you were an expert in a topic I'm learning about, and I hoped to pick your brain on it."

"An expert, huh?" Nathaniel smiled. "I don't get called that very often, even with a doctorate and advanced magical certification."

"Well, today you're the expert I need. Is it all right if I come in?"

Nathaniel looked at the cats. "What do you think, ladies? Does she seem trustworthy?"

The cats prowled over, sniffed Lucy, and started rubbing around her legs.

"Looks like a yes." Nathaniel took the chain off the latch and opened the door. "Come on in."

Accompanied by the cats, Lucy followed the wizard into his home. The apartment wasn't big, but he had made the most of it, fitting potted plants into every space he could find. Small trees stood in the corners, flowers bloomed on the windowsill, and creepers dangled down the fronts of the kitchen cupboards.

Nathaniel flung himself down on a sofa covered with tie-dyed sheets. One of the cats leapt up into his lap. The other two stood by the other end of the sofa, watching Lucy expectantly.

"I'm trying to learn more about a tribe of ancient witches and wizards," Lucy said. "They lived in the forests, including the ones around here. Their symbol was a mortar and pestle."

Nathaniel froze in the middle of tickling under the cat's chin. The cat tipped her head and nosed at his fingers, trying to nudge him back into action.

"Why do you think that I would know about them?"

"Because you've been investigating them yourself, apparently even running up debts in the process." Rather than join Nathaniel on the sofa, Lucy pulled out a chair from under the small kitchen table and sat on it so that she could watch him as they talked. Undeterred by this small act of dissent, the three-legged cat leapt into her lap. "You must be really determined to go to all that effort."

Outside the window, there was a flutter of wings, followed by a low buzzing sound. A shadow fell across the room.

"That's odd." Nathaniel got up, leaving the cat on the sofa, and went to the window. "Must be a storm moving in."

A streamer of absolute blackness snaked through a gap at the corner of the window. It reared up in front of Nathaniel, like a cobra preparing to strike.

He stumbled back, fumbling in his pocket for a wand.

"What is it?" he asked, his voice rising in alarm.

"Shadow mites." Lucy had seen them in textbooks but never in real life. She leapt up and whipped out her wand.

All three cats hissed and backed away, spines arched, tails rising.

"You owe power to Zero," the mites said, their voice emerging from somewhere in the cloud. "You must pay."

"It's not due yet," Nathaniel said. "I still need time. If the spell he gave me had worked, I might have got help to pay you back, but as it is—"

"You owe Zero." The swarm swirled around Nathaniel. "You must pay."

"Please, this wasn't the deal." Terror gripped Nathaniel. Only desperation had driven him to this point, but now a different sort of desperation gripped him. He wanted to live, and a cloud this dark could surely only mean death.

"Lux penetrabilior," Lucy chanted. A bright beam of light shot from the tip of her wand and cut through the mites. Some of them fell like dust on the ground. The rest swirled away from Nathaniel with an angry buzzing sound.

"You hurt," the mites said. "You kill. Now we kill."

The mites swarmed at Lucy, a cloud of terrible darkness sweeping over her. She cast the spell again and swung her wand, creating a blade of light that sliced through the blackness. More mites tumbled to the ground, but most of them were still on her, and now she couldn't see. There was only darkness and the tingle as the mites landed on her skin.

"Lux penetrabilior." She ran the light beam down her arm, sweeping some of the mites away. "Lux penetrabilior." She shone it into her face, and for a moment, blinding light replaced impenetrable darkness. "Lux penetrabilior."

The cloud of mites shifted, clumping together on Lucy's arm, weighing it down. Although she couldn't see through the darkness, she could feel the mites dragging the wand from her hand while others swarmed across her arm. There was tingling as tiny teeth latched onto her flesh.

The three-legged cat leapt up, hissing and clawing,

trying to savage the mites. The swarm parted as the cat reached it, then reformed. Part of it covered the cat's head, while the rest still swarmed around Lucy's arm. The cat clawed and hissed but couldn't tear herself free.

"Lux penetrabilior." Lucy cast the spell again. A beam of light shot out through the mites, casting a few more to the ground, but they had hold of her wrist, and she couldn't bring the wand around to aim it back up her arm. Her skin tingled, painful now as the mites dug in.

"Do something!" she shouted.

Nathaniel grabbed a lamp from the side of the room and switched it on, then thrust it in among the mites. The light shone brightly, an imitation of summer sunlight meant to nurture his plants through the winter. The mites curled back from it, dropped away from Lucy's arm, and formed a dark puddle that swept across the floor to the door.

"You owe Zero," the mites said as they started to slip out under the door. "You will pay Zero, or Zero will come for you."

The last of the mites slid under the door, and the whole cloud scattered, then vanished into the air.

Lucy clutched her arm. Tiny bites covered it, like the stings of a colony of insects. None of them had broken the skin yet, and the redness was starting to recede, but her arm still tingled painfully.

Dead mites crunched under Nathaniel's feet as he walked over to the three-legged cat and picked her up. She pressed her head against his chest.

"It's okay." He stroked her head, soothing her. "You're safe now."

"Thanks for the assist," Lucy said to the cat and scratched her under the chin. Then she turned her attention to Nathaniel. "Care to tell me what I got attacked for?"

Nathaniel sighed and sank onto the sofa. The other cats joined him, curling in close for comfort.

"I'm descended from those witches you're looking for," Nathaniel said. "I've spent years trying to find any that are still alive, even to bring back the ones lost years ago. They cared about plants and keeping the earth in balance. I think that they could make the world a better place.

"The problem is that I didn't have the power I needed to revive them, so I went to a loan shark, a dude called Zero who lives under the tar pits. I promised him a year's worth of my magic in return for some resources. I thought that I would have the Tolderai back by then, that they would be able to use their magic to defeat Zero as they did once before, and that would keep me free. But the spell didn't work. I've been running around like crazy, trying to find other options before my time ran out, but apparently I was too late. He's calling my debt in early."

"I've heard of this Zero," Lucy said. "I think he's part of a disinformation campaign, trying to make some companies look powerful so that they can jump past their competitors."

"Sounds like him. He's greedy and ruthless, the sort of dude no one should get involved with, but when you're desperate…" Nathaniel shrugged sadly.

"I have access to resources you don't." Lucy thought of the Silver Griffins and Ashley's incredible online search skills. If she could accidentally uncover this shifty Zero, maybe she could find the hidden witches. Or perhaps the

Griffins would have tools that could help. "If we team up, we might have a better chance of finding the Tolderai or of contacting their spirits if that's all that's left."

"That would be amazing." Nathaniel brightened, but only briefly, as his reality sank in again. "Zero will still be after me."

"Based on what I've seen so far, the Griffins should be going after Zero, so maybe you can help us with that too. First, I need time to come up with a plan..."

CHAPTER TWENTY-SIX

"No talking about work," Charlie said as he and Lucy settled into their seats in the corner of Ostrich Farm.

The restaurant was bustling, waitstaff hurrying back and forth with menus, cocktails, and plates of delicious-looking food. Lucy felt hungry just looking around.

"I didn't even mention work," she said.

"No, but you were thinking about it." Charlie winked. "Remember, date night rules mean no shop talk."

"I can live with that. I need to stop the mental plates spinning anyway. I've been trying to work out how—" Lucy stopped herself and laughed. "I guess I did need that warning."

"Don't get me wrong." Charlie reached across the table to squeeze her hand. "It's wonderful that you want to be out there saving the world every minute of every day. It's one of the things I love about you. It's also nice, just occasionally, to have you to myself."

"It would be a shame to waste the opportunity while Emily's at our place looking after the kids." She looked down at the cocktail menu. "Seeing as we're not in charge of any children right now, what do you say to tangerine mimosas?"

"Are we celebrating something?"

"Each other." She leaned in to kiss him. "Isn't that enough?"

Charlie grinned and turned to the approaching waiter. "Two tangerine mimosas, please. And we'll need a few minutes to think about food."

Lucy sat back and looked around the room. It was simple but elegant with its wooden tables and green leather sofas. People chattered and laughed, filling the area with a joyful spirit.

"Nice place," Charlie said. "What made you think of it?"

"Jackie came here on a date and came back raving about the chicken liver mousse."

"Not about the date?"

"Not so much."

"Good to see that she's still looking for Mister Right."

"Or Miss Right. What's the phrase she used? 'Why limit myself to the entrees when I could be sampling the whole menu?'"

They both laughed.

"Well, I'm happy with the dish I picked." Charlie smiled warmly at her.

"I should think so too. You weren't going to do any better, hiding away in your computer cave."

"Like you were out wildly partying. I met you in a museum, remember?"

"A gallery. That's far more sophisticated." Lucy picked

up her glass and struck a pose, little finger sticking out, her gaze one of intense thoughtfulness.

"Um, is something the matter?" a waiter asked, looking in confusion at the spot on the wall Lucy seemed to be inspecting.

"She's eying up the portraits," Charlie said.

"The what now?"

"They're all in my head." Lucy tapped her temple. "Don't worry. The crazy lady isn't going to scare off your customers. At least not yet."

The waiter laughed, set the mimosas down on the table, and pulled out a notepad. "Are you ready to order?"

"Not yet," Charlie admitted. "Could you give us a few more minutes?"

"Of course."

The waiter headed off to another table while Lucy and Charlie turned to their menus.

"This happens every time," Charlie said. "We get distracted, and we take forever to order, we come home late…"

"Emily has to spend the evening catching Eddie because he's turned into a rabbit. I remember."

"Do you think this happens to everyone?"

"It's a British thing. We can never make up our minds."

"Really?"

"No, don't be daft. I thought it might soothe your poor colonial soul."

"Hey, less of the C-word, or I'll go tip all your tea in the harbor."

"Barbarian!"

"Only when I'm playing *Dungeons and Dragons*."

Lucy laughed and set her menu down.

"I'd better try that chicken liver, see what all the fuss was about. Have you made up your mind?"

"Yeah, but I reserve the right to change it at the last minute. I spend my days surrounded by people eating Doritos and slurping soda. It's hard to pick between this sort of food when that's your baseline."

"You like Doritos and soda."

"True, but I don't think they serve that here."

Lucy picked up her glass. "I'm glad you found me in that museum."

"It's a gallery, remember? Far more civilized."

"Then here's to us, in a civilized way." They clinked their glasses together. "And to one calm, delightful night without the kids."

"I thought I'd find you down here," Dylan said as he walked into the first cave of the Mini Griffins' underground network.

"Mrs. Sanders wasn't paying attention." Ashley looked up from her laptop. "I thought I'd get out while I could."

"Mom and Dad said we should stop doing Griffins things."

"They didn't say we couldn't sit here though."

"True." Dylan flung himself down on the beanbag next to her, his dark hair flopping around his face.

"How did you get out?" Ashley asked. "Last time I looked, Mrs. Sanders was helping you practice your spells."

"Eddie turned into a parrot, and she tired herself out

chasing him around the house. Now they're both asleep on the couch."

Dylan smiled. His little brother had looked cute for once, curled up next to the exhausted babysitter. Ashley seemed more interested in her screen than in anything that had happened in the house.

"What are you working on?" Dylan asked. "Another video?"

"It's those people I was telling Mom about," Ashley said. "The ones who keep messing with my Wiki pages. I'm trying to find out more about them."

"What did you find?"

She turned the screen so that he could see, but it didn't help much. The problem with having a genius for a kid sister was that she sometimes forgot that not everybody viewed the world as she did. The map of anagrams and images, joined together by colored lines, seemed like nonsense to Dylan.

"Are those connections between people?" he asked. "Or places?"

"Companies are in blue. Magicals in green, and the red ones are pawnshops."

"Pawnshops?"

"I've been looking at the bank accounts of those shell corporations—"

"You can do that?"

"Can't you?"

Dylan shook his head. "Not unless there's a spell for it I could learn."

"This was just social engineering and a bit of code I wrote when I was bored. Anyway, it turns out that those companies all have links in LA and to a few magicals here. A dwarf lawyer, some gnomes, and their employer, I don't know what he is, but he calls himself Zero. Between them, they do a lot of business with pawnshops. I don't get that bit."

"I do." Dylan leaned forward. He could sort of make sense of the diagram now, and he felt a rush of excitement. "It's because they have a lot of things they want to sell without explaining where they came from, so they do it through the shops. Things they've been given instead of money for debts, and maybe things they stole too."

"That explains the bikes."

"What bikes?"

"Lots of bikes have gone missing around Echo Park. They've been turning up in these pawnshops, mostly the same pawnshop each time. The thieves could be disguising them so they can sell them."

"This sounds like a job for the Mini Griffins."

Ashley frowned. "We're not supposed to do Griffins stuff, remember?"

"That was before we found out about this. Don't you think it's important to stop crime?"

A gleam appeared in Ashley's eye. "What Mom and Dad don't know can't hurt them."

"Exactly. Where's our nearest tunnel entrance to this pawnshop?"

"Number seventeen."

"Then let's go check it out."

Ashley set down her laptop, put on her backpack, and pulled a remote control from her pocket. There was a whir of gears and her information gathering robot emerging from the next cave. It was half as high as she was, with a body like a thick textbook covered in sensors, held up on eight folding legs.

"All right, I'm ready," she said.

They ran down the tunnels, the robot following them. As they ran, Dylan cast a speed spell, and soon they were racing along. They reached the steps up to entrance seventeen in a cloud of magical sparks, dust, and laughter.

"Okay," Dylan said. "Up we go."

The tunnel entrance emerged under a pile of old wooden pallets in the alleyway behind a row of small stores.

"It's that one," Ashley whispered, pointing at the scuffed door at the back of one of the stores. It had a metal security door of iron bars attached outside the ordinary door, but that extra security measure was hanging open.

"Let's go look inside." Dylan eagerly started to climb out of the tunnel.

"Wait," Ashley whispered. "Let's send Octo in first."

"Octo?"

"The robot. Octo because it's got eight legs."

Ashley pushed the robot out into the alley, then started working the remote control. A row of small screens showed her images from Octo's assorted cameras.

Crouching low to the ground, Octo scuttled to the doorway, then stretched out one long leg to reach the handle. To Ashley's surprise, the door was already open, hanging slightly ajar. Octo pulled it out a few more inches, then tipped onto its side and squeezed through the gap.

Its feet made the lightest of tapping noises against the bare floor as Octo made its way down a short hallway to the store's main room. The place was closed for the evening, but some illumination seeped in through cracks between shutters, casting stripes of light and dark across shelves full of jewelry and electronics, racks of instruments, and most importantly a row of bikes.

Two teenage magicals, an Arpak with a crippled wing and a witch with glowing eyes, stood by a counter in the middle of the shop. They didn't notice the robot peering at them from the doorway, too intent on looking at the jewelry in the case.

"Are you sure this is the one?" the witch whispered.

"Positive," the Arpak growled, glaring through the glass. "We should take some of the others too, see if we can return them to their owners."

"We don't know they've all been stolen."

The Arpak snorted. "We know who runs this place. That's enough. If we can't find the owners, wouldn't it be better if we sold these to feed the other kids, instead of going into the pockets of you know who?"

Back in the tunnel, Ashley and Dylan looked at each other.

"They know about the criminals too," Dylan said. "They're here to steal things back."

"Maybe we could work with them?" Ashley asked. "More Mini Griffins."

"Let's find out."

Dylan climbed out of the hole and led the way down the alley to the pawnshop. He and Ashley walked in as quietly as they could, but the teenagers still looked around as they approached. The Arpak spread out the one stable wing, the other emerging more slowly and dipping toward the floor.

He even puffed out his chest, but the witch only tipped her head to one side, looking with curiosity at the two children and their robot.

"Who are you?" Dylan looked up at the older kids.

"Who are you?" the Arpak responded.

"I asked first."

"So?"

"Don't be an ass." The witch laid a hand on the Arpak's arm. "Look at them. There's no way they're on his side." She smiled and raised a hand in greeting. "I'm Twylan. This is Leontine."

Dylan hesitated for a moment, but he would have to try and trust these two if he hoped to work with them.

"I'm Dylan Heron," he said. "This is my sister Ashley."

"Heron?" The Arpak raised an eyebrow. "Like that Silver Griffin agent, Lucy?"

"You know our mom?"

"If you're her kids, I guess you must be on the right side. What are you doing here?"

"We came for those." Dylan pointed at the row of bikes.

Ashley had taken a tablet from her bag and was comparing descriptions of the stolen bikes with the ones in front of her. They matched.

"It's them," she said. "The bikes stolen around Echo Park."

"These guys stole from someone we know as well," Twylan said. "Jewelry belonging to a lady who runs a shelter near us, and things from people in the neighborhood above where we live."

"Above?" Dylan asked. "You live underground?"

A noise made them all look around. A van had pulled up behind the store, and a large black motorbike next to it.

"Quick," Dylan hissed. "Everybody down behind the corner display."

"That won't hide us," the Arpak said.

"Trust me."

They followed Dylan to the corner and crouched behind its display counter. He pulled out his wand and started chanting a spell as two gnomes got out of the van and followed the motorbike's owner, a dwarf in bikers' leathers, into the store. With one last twitch of the wand, the four kids and the robot became invisible.

"I don't care if it's a bike-friendly neighborhood," Gruffbar said as he strode down the hallway. "You can't keep selling all the bikes through the same store. Someone's going to notice." He stopped at the entrance to the main room and looked around for the light switch. "You're getting those bikes out of here, you're repainting them or switching bits around or whatever you do, and you're shipping them out to our other stores."

"That's more work," one of the gnomes protested, flicking the switch. Overhead, light strips buzzed into life, illuminating the store and all its contents.

"I'm a lawyer, not your union rep," Gruffbar said. "If you have a problem with working conditions, take it up with Mister Zero."

"No, no, no," the gnome said hastily. "No problem. No need to say anything to Mister Zero."

"That's what I figured."

Hidden beneath Dylan's spell, Ashley pulled another, smaller robot out of her bag. She tapped it against the remote control to connect them, then set it down on the floor. It rolled away on three little wheels, heading for the back door.

"A dozen of them." Gruffbar shook his head. "Do you think that everyone in LA is an idiot, that they won't think to look for their bike in a pawnshop with a reputation for bikes?"

Outside the back door, the little robot opened its speakers and started a stream of noise—jumbled voices, hurried footfalls, clangs, and bumps.

"What the hell's that?" Gruffbar pulled a revolver from inside his jacket and led the gnomes out into the alley.

"This is it," Leontine said. "Grab what you came for and let's get out of here."

"No, wait!" Twylan grabbed his arm. "They'll see us getting away. They've got guns as well as magic."

"I have a better plan." Dylan waved his wand and chanted the words of the invisibility spell again. This time, the bikes disappeared from view.

After a minute, there was a gunshot, and the noises stopped outside. A moment later, Gruffbar came back in, leading the gnomes. The dwarf held up the broken pieces of the small robot.

"Whoever owns this piece of crap, they'd better—" He froze, staring at the space where the bikes had been. "By my beard, it was a distraction. Someone's stolen the bikes."

"I know," one of the gnomes said. "How else did you think we got them?"

"No, you idiot, someone's stolen them off us." Gruffbar tossed aside the broken robot and ran for the back door. "Come on. They can't have got far. We'll drive around the neighborhood until we spot someone with a bunch of bikes, and we'll show them how hard it is to cycle with broken knees."

The gnomes exchanged a resigned look and hurried out after him. There was a roar of engines, and the motorbike and van raced away.

Dylan dropped his spells, making both the kids and the bikes visible again.

"That should give us enough time," he said. "But which bikes do we take?"

"All of them." Leontine grinned fiercely.

"There are only four of us, and there's a dozen bikes."

Leontine gave a sharp whistle, then walked over to the bikes. By the time he reached them, more teenage magicals were surging in through the back door of the store.

"Resigno," Twylan said, and her eyes flared as she waved her wand. The locks holding the bikes fell open, and the chains around them unraveled.

"Everybody take a bike," Leontine said, "and get them down out of sight fast as you can. We'll worry about returning them to their owners later."

As the teenagers grabbed the cycles and wheeled them out the door, Twylan went to the jewelry case.

"Per pervenire," she said and touched the glass. It rippled and parted, letting her fingers through. She took a necklace and two matching bracelets, then drew her hand back out, leaving the glass intact. "Let's go."

They all hurried out of the building, and Dylan pulled the door into place behind them. In the alley, the teenagers were gathered at a large, open manhole cover, where they passed the bikes down into darkness, then followed them.

"You guys want to come with us?" Leontine asked. "We have a place you can hide out until this blows over."

"No thanks," Dylan said, despite his immense curiosity about these older kids, who they were, and where they lived. "We should get back before Mom and Dad come home."

"Well, it was good working with you." Leontine started climbing down the conduit.

"Wait." Ashley held out two silver pin badges the size of a dime, each stamped with an image of a claw. "These are communication badges I made. You can use them to call us if we can help you again."

"Thanks." Twylan took one badge and handed the other to Leontine. She pinned hers to her shirt and gave it a quick polish. "I'll wear it with pride."

"Don't I get one?" Dylan asked.

"Later," Ashley said. "We need to get home, remember?"

CHAPTER TWENTY-SEVEN

The sun was rising as Lucy met Nathaniel at the edge of Elysian Park. She was dressed in sports clothes so that anybody they passed would assume she was a jogger out getting some early exercise. Nathaniel's idea of dressing to blend in was very different, with camouflage trousers and shirt.

"You know that we're not hiding from snipers or wild animals, right?" Lucy asked. "I mean, I know this country has plenty of both, but we're in LA."

"You said to be inconspicuous, and we're going to be in the trees, so I thought..."

"There's nothing inconspicuous about the lone survivalist look. You might as well wear a sign saying, 'I have a gun, and I feel like shooting.'"

"I don't even own a gun! Why would I own a gun?"

"Isn't that what Americans do?"

"We're not all... Wait, are you making fun of me?"

"It's hard to resist when you look like a rejected extra from a war movie."

"I guess. Don't we have better things to do?"

They walked into the park, Nathaniel leading the way. Lucy was familiar with the area from romantic walks with Charlie when she'd first followed him out to LA, and from family days out, taking the kids to run around among the trees. Nathaniel knew this place far better. Some deep part of him sensed what it had been like when everything for miles around was woodland, before houses and roads and smog, before the park became an isolated island of greenery amid a vast concrete sprawl. He sensed what this place had meant to his ancestors, not exactly remembering their presence here but feeling the longing for it in his bones.

"This way." He led her uphill.

They walked away from the roads, leaving behind the early morning traffic as the first commuters tried to get ahead of the day. Soon they were in among a cluster of trees, leaving human civilization as a background noise somewhere out of sight.

"This is it." Nathaniel stopped and leaned against one of the trees. "The plants that were here in the old days of the Tolderai are gone, like the Tolderai themselves. But their descendants live on like I do, and their roots reach down into the memories of the earth. If we're going to summon them without heading out into the wild, we'll do it here."

Lucy set down her backpack, opened it, and took out the mortar and pestle she'd retrieved from Haugensen's store. She unwrapped it from the evidence bag that had held it in a Silver Griffin strongroom. As she set it on the ground, blades of grass turned like compass needles in the presence of a magnet until they all pointed at the artifact. The treetops rustled and their branches leaned in.

"Do you think this will help?" Lucy asked.

"Oh, yes." Nathaniel crouched beside her, gazing at the large mortar and pestle with a look of almost religious awe. Tentatively, he reached out a hand to touch it, feeling the green-veined stone, its edges worn smooth by long generations of witches. "This was their most prized and powerful magical focus. If we can't summon them with this, nothing will do."

He opened his backpack and took out a chicken. Still unable to bring himself to kill, he'd gone to the organic butcher again, but this time he'd managed to get a bird that still had its feathers. He laid it in the mortar, then took a step back and pulled out his wand.

"I brought you an offering," he said and pointed his wand. "Inferno."

Flames engulfed the chicken, filling the air with a smell of roasting meat that made Lucy wish she had eaten breakfast. Faces flared for a moment in the air above the mortar, staring intently at Nathaniel and Lucy, then vanished as the last remnants of the chicken's bones crumbled to dust. Ashes swirled on a breeze neither of them could feel, then hit both Lucy and Nathaniel in the face.

Suddenly, Lucy wasn't in Elysian Park anymore. She was in her own home, and shadow mites were swirling around her, sweeping in to attack her family. She shouted and blasted the creatures with beams of light, but they kept coming, a vast throng of them, far more than she had seen at Nathaniel's apartment. She screamed at her kids to run while she and Charlie desperately fought the mites. And then…

…Then she was in a forest, vast and ancient trees reaching like skyscrapers into the air. She was dressed in furs, painted with ashes, and the wand in her hand was thicker than she was used to. Even her skin was darker than usual. She was standing with other people like herself, witches and wizards dressed in hides and painted for battle, wands, bows, and spears at the ready. Others were closing in on them, an army emerging from the forest, and she knew with terrible certainty that she was about to die. She raised her hand and chanted an unfamiliar spell. Thorns emerged from her skin, an armor of deadly spines, one that would make anyone regret attacking her up close. The enemy stepped out from beneath the trees, a cry of anger and grief and determination rose from the throats of her people, and then…

…Then she was back in Elysian Park, in her synthetic jogging clothes, wiping ashes from her eyes.

"That was more than before," she said. "Not just a glimpse of my future, but somebody else's past."

"Unmoored in time," Nathaniel said, wiping his own face. "The most powerful possibility of the artifact. That will help, I think."

"Did you see something too?"

Nathaniel nodded.

"What did you see?" Lucy asked.

"It's personal."

Nathaniel pulled out a notebook and, following its instructions, scratched a circle in the dirt around them. He marked twelve points around its circumference with symbols.

"Did you bring the power crystals?" he asked.

"Courtesy of the Silver Griffins armory." Lucy took a dozen glowing crystals from her bag and laid one on each of the symbols.

"Cool. I couldn't afford to buy anymore, and I'm already in way more debt than I can deal with."

Something was shifting in the air around them, a presence that seemed uncannily familiar to Lucy. It was like she was being watched, but almost like she was the one watching.

Nathaniel tapped each crystal in turn with his wand. They cracked, and their power emerged, filling the air in the circle. Together, he and Lucy chanted the spell written in the book.

The words were strange, ugly, twisted, but their power was undeniable. Lucy felt as though her mind was tugging at a chain, dragging something out of a pit toward them.

The air spun in spirals that sucked dust and leaves from the ground, which settled into pillars, rippling and twisting. The faces of witches and wizards appeared on them, like those that had stood around Lucy in her visions, facing their foes as a single tribe, ready to die so that something might live, something they had sent away.

The mortar. The mortar and their children. The witches had sent them out into the world, hope for the future. Now that future had arrived, but was it the one they had hoped for?

The bark of the nearest tree bulged, then burst open. A

witch stepped out, dressed in a plaid shirt, faded jeans, and sturdy boots. Her footsteps left a trail of sap.

Another tree spasmed and shook. A wizard dropped from its branches, lean and wiry, with a weather-worn face and a braided gray beard. He crouched and stared at them, one hand clutching his t-shirt, the other resting on the handle of a knife on his belt.

Next came another witch, short and dark-haired, dressed in a green velvet skirt and a loose blouse. Then another wizard, spectacled and squinting, a textbook in one hand and a blue flower in the other. Then another, and another, until a dozen witches and wizards stood at the points of the circle.

"Cousin," the first witch said, looking at Nathaniel. "You just couldn't let go, could you? For centuries we stayed hidden, dispersed, safe. Now you want to force us into the open."

"I didn't know," Nathaniel said. "I thought I was alone. Why didn't you tell me that you were still out there?"

"We might have, in time. But trust is earned." The witch scowled and drew her wand. "Instead of showing the patience needed, you have done this." She made stabbing motions at the cracked crystals. "Why?"

"Because I didn't want to be alone." Nathaniel sank to the ground, his hands lying limp in his lap. "I didn't mean to hurt anyone. I just wanted to be part of something."

The witch's expression softened.

"Maybe you can be," she said. "How did you find the mortar?"

"I did that," Lucy said. "Lucy Heron, Silver Griffins."

"I am Heather Fields, chief of the Tolderai." The witch's voice hardened. "How do you have what should be ours?"

"I confiscated it from someone who was trying to sell it. This artifact is too dangerous to be out there in the world."

"That we can agree on," Heather said. "You will return it to us."

"I can't just give it to you. The Silver Griffins locked it up for a reason."

"It was hidden from us, and we're grateful that you've let us find it again. But if you don't give it back, we will take it back, over your body if we have to."

"It's not a good idea to threaten a Silver Griffin."

"We've gone for centuries without caring about worldly authorities. What makes you think we'll change now?"

"The world is growing smaller. It's full of satellites, drones, security cameras, phones everywhere. If you want to stay hidden, you'll need help."

"She's right," said the gray-bearded Tolderai. "There are eyes everywhere, watching you, recording you. Even with my warding spells and my foil vest, they see me sometimes. With their shifty lenses and their lists and their—"

"We get it, Mackam," Heather said, then narrowed her eyes as she looked at Lucy. "So how can you help? And why would you?"

"Do you know a magical named Zero?" Lucy asked.

Heather's face crumpled into a scowl, and she spat in the dirt. "We know him. Filthy creature. There's nothing of nature about him."

"Nathaniel said that you have magic that can cancel Zero's power, that he was going to use it to get out of Zero's debt once he got you back."

"Nathaniel is smarter than he looks. He's right. Our people countered Zero's power once before, the trees drinking up his tar and his magic, leaving nothing but a wailing heap of flesh. He had us hunted after that, almost destroyed. It's not something we would do again."

Lucy bit her lip. She'd counted on getting the support of these witches, ready to take down Zero and his grasping schemes. She needed to persuade them.

"This time you wouldn't be doing it alone," she said. "You'd be working alongside the Silver Griffins, and—"

"No," Mackam snapped. "No Griffins. They've the biggest eyes."

Lucy took a deep breath. "All right, no other Silver Griffins. But I have other friends who can help. If we take down Zero together, we can do it for good this time, make the world safe from his schemes."

Heather snorted. "That world you're talking about is the human one. And the world of magicals. None of that matters to us. These days, humans are more dangerous to the trees than Zero ever was."

"In return for your secret, then. From inside the Silver Griffins, I can make sure they don't find you. I know someone who can delete the electronic trail you leave. Those traces the electronic eyes capture. If you help me do what I have to, I'll help keep you safe."

The Tolderai looked at each other. Each one held up their left hand, some flat, others forming fists. It took Lucy a moment to realize that they were voting and that she had no idea what each symbol meant. She could only hope that it went her way and keep a tight grip on her wand in case.

"We agree," Heather said. "On one more condition." She

pointed at the mortar and pestle. "You let us take what should be ours."

Lucy hesitated. It would be hard enough to justify why she had taken the artifact out of stores if she wasn't telling anyone about the Tolderai. Explaining how she had lost it and why no one needed to hunt it down again would be even more difficult. Still, that was just bureaucracy. Zero was a real threat to the world.

"All right," she said. "We have a deal. I need time to plan my move against Zero. How can I contact you when the time comes?"

Heather took hold of Lucy's hand between both of hers. The leaves above them parted, and a beam of sunlight fell on their hands. Something bulged between them, small and hard. When Heather let go, she left Lucy clutching the most perfect acorn she had ever seen, its shell a glorious gleaming green.

"Hold it and speak my name," Heather said. "I will come."

"You couldn't just give me a phone number?"

"Where would the wonder be in that?" Heather touched Nathaniel on the shoulder. "Come with me, cousin. It's time to teach you your place in the world."

Mackam picked up the mortar and pestle, then the Tolderai stepped back into their trees, leaving Lucy alone with only the branches above and the whisper of the wind.

CHAPTER TWENTY-EIGHT

It was dark in the kemana and no clients were around. The gnomes cowered around the edges of the chamber, watching nervously as Zero sat in front of the central crystal, glaring into its black surface.

Gruffbar walked into the cavern and crossed to his master, clutching a tablet.

"Things have become unacceptable," Zero said, his voice low with menace. "The Splitting Stone won't work. Our online efforts are being undone. Some witch stopped my mites collecting my debts. Now someone is robbing my pawnshops." His words became a deep, angry splutter. "It. Is. Unacceptable."

Gruffbar held out the tablet. On the screen was a picture of a witch, along with her name, address, and Silver Griffin badge number. It was Lucy Heron.

"I found the witch who protected Oakmantle," he said quietly, standing as far from his employer as he could while still making the information readable.

"A Silver Griffin." Zero said the words like they were a

curse. "Of course she would be. Well, her badge won't protect her now."

"There's more. This TreeHouseGenius who's been undoing our Wiki edits, her IP address matches Heron's house."

"Really..." Zero's eyes bulged, and his scowl finally shifted into a malevolent grin. He took the tablet and stared at the picture, leaving a trail of tar down the image of Lucy as his finger ran down the screen. "I don't know what I did to draw your attention, little Griffin, but I'm going to make you regret it."

Zero pulled the whistle from his pocket and blew. The gnomes clutched their ears. Was it Gruffbar's imagination, or did he hear something this time, the faintest hint of something shrill?

The blackness of the ceiling shifted, and the mites descended to hover around their master. They saw the picture in his hands, and a ripple ran through the swarm. The mites weren't sophisticated. They didn't feel love or satisfaction or melancholy. But they could feel anger and pain, and they could remember the parts of the swarm that Lucy had killed. A furious buzzing spread through them until it sounded like someone had kicked a wasps' nest.

"Find her," Zero said. "Kill her."

Their buzz rising in tone and volume, the shadow mites swirled away out of the cave.

"So, geography quiz," Charlie said as he scooped spaghetti onto his plate. "What sort of questions do you want today?"

"Maybe not geography?" Dylan said as he skewered a meatball with his fork. "We've been learning a lot of capital cities. It's getting kind of boring."

"But geography is what I know!"

Lucy laughed and took the pasta dish. "All the more reason to change the topic. Dinner shouldn't always be your chance to show off."

Charlie gaped in mock shock. "*Moi*, showing off?"

"It's me, not *moi*," Eddie said through a mouthful of spaghetti.

"Actually, *moi* is the French for… You know what, never mind. What sort of quiz shall we have?"

"History," Dylan said.

"Science," Ashley declared.

"Animals," Eddie shouted, spattering himself with tomato sauce as he waved his fork around.

"Lots of good options there." Charlie stroked his chin thoughtfully. "But no consensus. Maybe Mom should have the deciding vote?"

They all looked expectantly at Lucy as she considered her options. If she picked a subject that one of the kids was good at, they would be the one with all the answers, and the others would get bored. If she picked a subject none of them knew about, there was a big risk the quiz would end in frustration. Still, maybe it was time to put them in charge.

"How about if you take it in turns to ask questions on your subject," she said, "and the rest of us get to answer, even me and your dad?"

"I like that," Ashley said.

"Me too," Dylan said.

"Me, me, me!" Eddie banged his fork on the plate.

"Okay then, how about if Dylan starts?"

As she looked at her eldest son, something else caught Lucy's eye. A shadow was growing across the ceiling, stretching from the window into the room. She hadn't seen it at first, as some magic had hidden it from view. Now that she knew to look, she couldn't miss it. The shadow was blacker than any night, a thing so dark that all the light around it seemed to vanish.

She kept herself calm. Panicking wouldn't help, but nor would letting the shadow mites know that she'd seen them. She had to create an opportunity before they could do whatever they had come here for.

Heart beating hard, she got up out of her seat.

"Who'd like some lemonade?"

"Me, me, me!" all the children exclaimed. Lemonade with dinner was a rare treat, and none of them was going to say no. Charlie, confused, caught Lucy's eye. The tiny shake of her head told him to stay where he was, not to make a fuss, just to keep things normal.

"Come on, Dylan," Charlie said as Lucy headed into the kitchen. "You're supposed to be quizzing us."

Lucy opened a cupboard and crouched as if looking inside for a soda bottle. Out of sight of the mites, she drew her wand. Then she drew a deep breath and rose.

"Lux penetrabilior," she shouted while pointing her wand at the center of the cloud of mites.

Bright light blasted across the room, killing some of the mites and scattering the rest. Lucy shot the spell again, sending the mites into complete disorder. However, there were far more of them than she had faced before, and more coming in with every moment. She had to get the children to safety.

"Into the tunnels," she ordered. "Quick."

Dylan grabbed hold of Eddie and dashed for the door, Ashley running after him. Some of the mites tried to follow, but Lucy cut them off with another blast of light.

Charlie had his wand out now and joined her in firing spells at the mites, but he wasn't as well-practiced with the light spell as she was, and the mites soon closed on him, swirling arcs of them that spiraled in, looking for a chance to grab hold.

"You get to the tunnels too," Lucy said.

"Not without you."

Together they dashed to the front door, fired one last volley of light, and ran out around the house. They couldn't use their magic here where neighbors could see them, but once they were in the tunnels, it would be another matter.

The hatch beside the house stood open. Charlie scrambled down the tunnel, and Lucy climbed in after him, then hung for a moment in the entrance, long enough to grab the hatch and pull it down.

She wasn't quite quick enough. Some of the mites got in before it slammed into place. They immediately started swarming over it, tugging at the handle, gnawing at the hinges.

Lucy reached the bottom of the entrance shaft and hurried into the first cave. Charlie and the kids stood there, lined up and facing the entrance. Dylan had his wand out, Ashley was guiding Octo the robot around with torches strapped to its forelegs, and even Eddie had prepared himself for action, turning into a mole with big flat paws that could squash the mites. Still, there were only five of them against a whole swarm of the dark creatures.

"We need help," Charlie said. "Can you call the Griffins?"

Lucy patted her pocket, then shook her head. "I left my phone in the house. You?"

"Same."

"I can get help." Ashley tapped a pin badge on her chest and spoke into it. "This is Ashley. If you can hear this, we need your help. Come to this signal as fast as you can and bring light magic."

"Who was that?" Lucy asked.

"Some friends. I hope they get here in time."

The buzzing of mites in the tunnel was growing, setting Lucy's teeth on edge as surely as the sound of a dentist's drill. The swarm was working its way inside.

"We can use the tunnels to our advantage," Lucy said. "Use narrow spaces to contain them and take out as many as possible, then fall back when they get to us."

Together, they stood in the narrow entrance to the cave, tensed and ready. Blackness swarmed toward them.

Lucy, Charlie, and Dylan let fly with their magic, beams of bright light cutting through the swarm. Ashley's robot swung its legs around, waving torches. Those beams weren't bright enough to kill the mites, but they confused and disoriented them, slowing the swarm's advance.

"Back!" Lucy shouted as the first of the mites reached her hand.

The family dashed across the cave, along the next tunnel, and into the room beyond, their way lit by the low glow from rows of LEDs that illuminated the passageways the kids had built. Again, they gathered in the tunnel entrance, wands raised.

"I have an idea," Ashley said.

She opened a panel in the wall covered with dials and switches, then started changing the wiring behind it. Wire cutters, pliers, and a tiny soldering iron appeared from her pockets as she worked.

The mites had paused in the first cave, regrouping and waiting for more of them to get past the hatch. Now they surged forward again, a wave of midnight black that swallowed up the light.

Then those LEDs brightened and flickered as Ashley finished her work. She turned a dial back and forth, light levels rising and falling in fast, irregular patterns, some lights shining brightly while others dimmed. The chaotic flashes broke the creatures' formation, as parts of the swarm veered away from one patch of brightness only to run into another. The whole cloud swirled and twisted in broken curves.

While Ashley slowed the shadow mites, Lucy, Charlie, and Dylan opened fire with their wands again. Light blasted the creatures, hundreds of them tumbling broken on the floor, but there were thousands more spinning around each other in the confused and flickering light of the tunnel.

Some of the mites found the wiring in the wall. They burrowed in and dragged it out. It was harder to chew through a wire or its plastic covering than it was to chew through a body, but the lights were making them angry, which made them determined. They bit their way through until they reached metal, then bit down again. A dozen mites died in a flash of sparks, and the LED lights in the tunnel went out.

"Back again!" Lucy shouted.

The family ran across the cave and down another tunnel to the room beyond, where Dylan and Ashley had set up a small library. As the mites shook off their disorientation, they followed, buzzing down the tunnel again, straight into the deadly light spells.

Ashley went to a control panel in the wall, but before she could brighten the lights in the tunnel, the leading mites slammed into them, shattering the LEDs one by one, creating safe darkness for the rest of the swarm to come through.

Again, the family cast spells down the tunnel while Octo waved its torches and Eddie stood ready, paws raised in case the mites broke through. Tiny black bodies tumbled to the ground, diminishing the swarm, but it kept coming, tendrils reaching from the tunnel.

"Back again," Lucy said.

As the family ran across the library cave, the mites swarmed after them. The first ones got ahead, blocking the way into the next tunnel, then swirled around the Herons, a vortex of blackness closing in on them.

As the cloud drew closer, Lucy sent out blast after blast of magic, but she was getting tired, her power starting to fade, her body and mind getting slower. Her family fought bravely around her. Charlie and Dylan used light to kill mites and magical gusts of wind to repel them. Eddie and the robot swatted at the tiny black creatures, and Ashley waved torches around to disorient the swarm.

Several mites reached Lucy's hand and clung on, biting her flesh like insects. She brushed them off, but more came, crawling over her. The same was happening to the others, Eddie slapping at his body in a desperate attempt to get them off, Dylan blasting light down his front as shadow mites landed on his back.

A black cloud closed in on the Heron family.

Suddenly, there was a burst of light. Twylan strode into the room, hands raised, lightning crackling from her eyes and her fingertips. Her magic tore through the cloud of mites, scattering them, forcing them into smaller clumps to escape the bright trails of electricity that danced around the room. Behind her came Leontine, waving a pair of high-beam torches that sent the mites cowering back against the walls. Other tunnel teens, armed with magic or lights, followed them.

"We got your message," Leontine shouted over the furious buzzing of the mites. "What's the plan?"

Lucy looked around the room. There were fewer mites now, and they were in smaller clumps, many of them trying to reach the tunnels and get away.

"Use the lights to keep them in isolated groups," she said. "Stop them escaping. Then we can use magic to finish them off."

The torch beams drove the mites away from the tunnel entrances, herding them into clumps between the book-shelves. Eddie joined in, turning into an oversized firefly and chasing back any lone mites that tried to make a getaway. With the mites surrounded, it was easy to aim at them, using beams of bright, magical light or flares of lightning to finish off one clump at a time. At last, the buzzing died away, and all that remained was a layer of tiny black bodies, like soot strewn across the floor.

Finally, Lucy had a chance to catch her breath and deal with her surprise.

"What are you doing here?" she asked Twylan.

The teenage witch smiled, and the magic flared in her eyes, leaving lines of shadow across her face.

"We met your kids the other day and decided to team up." She tapped a silver pin badge on the lapel of her long brown coat. "We're practically Mini Griffins now."

"The Mini Griffins are still a thing?" Lucy sighed. "This is going to lead to trouble later, isn't it?"

Charlie wrapped an arm around her shoulders. "I'm okay with the kind of trouble that saves our lives."

"Even when our kids are involved?"

Charlie looked proudly at their children, who had fought against the mites with such courage and determination, now talking excitedly about their adventure with the tunnel-dwelling teens.

"Especially when our kids are involved," he said.

CHAPTER TWENTY-NINE

"These are your tunnels, huh?" Leontine looked around the library. "They're cleaner than ours."

"We dug them ourselves," Dylan said proudly. "I used magic and Ashley built tunneling robots."

"I dug too." Eddie tugged on his brother's shirt. "I was a mole."

The air around him shimmered, and he became a mole again, waving his paws at Leontine. The Arpak looked down at him and laughed. It was the first time that Dylan had seen him not looking serious, and it didn't last.

"Have we beaten them all?" Leontine crouched so he could scoop up a handful of dead mites. Now that they had stopped moving, it was possible to see the creatures better. Each one had a rounded body like a swollen tick, tensed legs like a flea, and rows of tiny, pointed teeth like something out of a dentist's nightmares.

"I think so," Dylan said although he looked around warily, nervous about anything faintly like a shadow.

"They worked for the same magical who runs the

pawnshop gnomes." Ashley held up a tablet with her diagram of interconnected businesses and people on it. "The one called Zero."

"Then I'm doubly glad we came." Leontine's voice hardened to match his face. "That guy preys on good people. He needs to be stopped."

"Can't we take a bit of time to celebrate first?" Twylan asked. She had been talking with Lucy and Charlie, but now she came to join the conversation. "We've just had our first big victory."

"Your magic was amazing!" Dylan looked up at the power that flashed from her eyes. "What else can you do?"

"Lots of things," Twylan said. "I keep learning more spells when I get the chance."

"Do you know the light one, like we were using?"

Twylan took out her wand, chanted the incantation, and shot a beam of light down the nearest tunnel.

"That one?" she asked.

"That was cool." Dylan looked thoughtful. "Why didn't you use it against the mites?"

"I thought the lightning would be more useful against so many of them. It spreads out better, though it's hard to control."

"I have trouble controlling my magic sometimes."

"Maybe I could help you learn?"

"Thanks, I'd like that. Say, can you make plants grow?"

"A bit, but there aren't many plants where we live…"

While the magic users talked about spells, Eddie shifted back into his human form and gazed up at Leontine's wings, one feathered and shapely, the other stunted and curled in along one side.

"Can you fly?" Eddie asked.

"Eddie," Ashley hissed, nudging her brother. "You shouldn't ask that."

"Why not?" Leontine asked fiercely. "I'm not going to ignore this. Why should other people?" He stretched out his wings, making the difference between them even more obvious. "Yes, I can fly, but not fast and not for long. This wing gets tired very easily, and it doesn't lift me much. It takes a lot of effort to fly straight."

He stared at Ashley, daring her to show the least sign of pity.

"Cool," she said. "I wish I could fly."

"I can!" Eddie shimmered, then turned into a pigeon, which flapped up and landed on Leontine's shoulder.

"Careful," Dylan said. "If the Silver Griffins mistake you for a messenger pigeon, you'll be stuck carrying letters and eating worms."

Eddie landed on the floor and turned into a boy again.

"I might like worms," he said thoughtfully. "Mom, can we have worms for dinner tomorrow?"

"If you really want," Lucy said. "How about spaghetti instead? It's like worms, but it won't crawl off your plate."

Ashley tugged at Twylan's sleeve. "Want to see the rest of the lair?"

"Yes, please!"

Ashley headed off through the underground base, a trail of curious teenage magicals following behind her.

"Should we leave them to it?" Charlie asked. "It's good that they're making new friends."

"I want the tour, too." Lucy took his hand and followed

the small crowd. "I still haven't seen everything our brilliant children made."

"We made those children, so does that mean we've made something brilliant too?"

"Sure, I think we deserve a little credit. Although we look much less brilliant when you remember that we missed them building all this."

"So, you've seen the library." Ashley turned her head to talk over her shoulder as she walked. "It's still a small collection, but we want to get more books on science and spells."

"And animals!" Eddie shouted.

"And animals."

"Those spell books..." Twylan hesitated, suddenly nervous and embarrassed despite being older than her host. "Might I be able to look at them? I don't have a magic teacher, and I'd love to learn more."

"Of course," Ashley said. "You can come and use the base whenever you want."

They walked into another artificial cave. This one had workbenches along the walls and a few tools hanging from hooks. A set of shelves held boxes of nails, screws, hinges, wires, microchips, and other components.

"This is the workshop," Ashley explained. "It's where I built Octo."

The robot pressed against her knee and she patted its sensor-laden head.

"This is amazing," Leontine said. "All we've got is some rusty hammers and saws to build our shelters with."

"I could maybe help with that." Ashley looked uncomfortably from her perfectly maintained rows of tools to the eager expression on the Arpak's face. "But I don't like lending out my tools. I like to have them handy and to look after them."

"Sorry, I didn't mean…"

"It's okay." Lucy put a hand on Leontine's shoulder. "I'm sure we can find ways to help you out like you helped us out today. Right, Charlie?"

"Of course! I bet we've got tools in the garage we never use, and it doesn't look like I'll need to do DIY ever again in my life. After all, my daughter's far better at it."

"That's true," Ashley said without the least hint of embarrassment. "I've been fixing dad's handiwork since I was five."

"Really?" Charlie looked shocked. "I always thought I was quite good at putting up shelves."

"Things aren't supposed to roll off of them, sweetheart," Lucy said. "To put it in installation wizard terms, that's a bug, not a feature."

"It was only the once!"

"Yes, because I started fixing them." Ashley pointed down another tunnel. "Moving on…"

The next cave had monitors on its walls and a couple of computer desks, currently empty. Eddie scampered into the room in the shape of a raccoon, leapt onto a swivel chair, and spun delightedly.

"This is going to be the computing hub," Ashley explained. "Once Octo's run a proper data connection down from the house. I usually do computer work in the treehouse, but now mom and dad know about this place, I might move things down here. Did you know I have a YouTube channel?"

"I'm not surprised." Twylan looked around in admiration. "I'll have to check that out."

"Don't forget to like and subscribe," Ashley said earnestly.

A ripple of laughter ran through the room.

"What? Subscribers are important!"

"What else is there to see, sweetheart?" Lucy asked. She was almost afraid of the answer. Were they about to find the shark tank, the orbital death ray controls, or merely the ball pit? Anything seemed possible. She had to count on the fact that she had good kids who would never do anything out of greed or spite.

"This is the last one, for now." Ashley led them down another tunnel. "And the most important. Ladies and gentlemen, I present the den..."

She stepped aside to let them into the largest cave so far. The walls were painted in bright colors, with pictures of animals in a graffiti style. Around the room's edges were sofas, beanbags, and big padded chairs, some of them with drink holders in the arms. There was a table tennis table near the middle of the room and a big TV with a PlayStation, four controllers, and a heap of games. Books and magazines were scattered around one of the chairs.

"Those should be in the library." Ashley frowned.

"Sorry." Dylan went to gather up the books. "It's nicer to read in here."

The teenagers walked into the room, gaping open-mouthed at their surroundings. Compared with their home in the tunnels, this was a place of unimaginable luxury. The cozy seats, the games system, the fact that it was warm and bright and dry...

"Wanna play *Mario Kart?*" Eddie tugged on Leontine's hand.

Leontine, whose expression had settled into a scowl, shook his head and extracted his hand from Eddie's, then folded his arms across his chest. "I don't play games."

"Weird." Eddie turned to Twylan. "You wanna play?"

"I don't know how."

"That's his favorite sort of opponent," Dylan said. "Come on. We'll teach you."

As they headed for the PlayStation, Lucy turned to Leontine.

"Are you all right?" she asked.

"Am I…" Leontine tossed his head as if he was trying to shake off a cloud of insects. "Your kids are great. This is great. But it's absurd. We live in a dirty tunnel, while these guys have made tunnel living into a game, and theirs is already better than ours. It's not…"

"Not fair?"

"That's not what I said! Life doesn't work like that. You don't get fair. That doesn't mean I want reminders of it."

"I'm sorry. Your lives are tough, and ours must seem so comfortable by comparison. I mean, it is, apart from the mite attack, and Zero, and the danger that puts my kids in, and…" Lucy stopped and rubbed her eyes. "Sorry, I'm totally undermining my point. I was trying to say that I understand, but given that we have all of this, I'm sure the kids will be happy to share. Then you'll be more comfortable, have access to spellbooks and computers and—"

"And live off charity?"

"Don't you do that already, sometimes?"

"Yes, but…" Now it was Leontine's turn to run a hand

over his weary face. "You're right. This will be great for the others, and even for me when I get over my pride."

"If it helps, we might need more of your assistance first. Zero is still out there, and after today, we need to stop him more than ever. Not only to stop him attacking us again, but to help all the magicals he's robbed or trapped in terrible deals."

Leontine smiled grimly and rubbed his hands together. "Another fight. That's part of your life I can get on board with."

One last shadow mite, half its legs blasted away by burning light, tumbled down a tunnel and into the kemana cave beneath the tar pits. It crawled across the floor, then climbed up Zero's leg, fighting its way through a stream of tar. At last, it reached his knee, and Zero, looking down, spotted the tiny, midnight black messenger.

From the side of the cave, Gruffbar watched as his employer picked up the tiny creature on the end of his finger. The dwarf tensed for an explosion of anger. The return of this lone, battered mite was a terrible sign.

"What happened to you?" Zero asked and held the mite up to his ear.

From where he stood, Gruffbar could only hear one side of the conversation, but he listened to it with unbending attention.

"Oh, they did, did they?" Zero said. "Yes, I know the kids you mean, the ones living in the old tunnels... Well, they clearly aren't as smart as they think... Lightning?

Good to know. Good to know... You rest now. You've done well." Zero lowered his hand, then raised his voice. "Gruffbar!"

The dwarf strode over, ready for orders. The mites had failed, and he was expecting to see Zero erupt in fury.

Instead, his employer was icy calm.

"Here." Zero handed Gruffbar the dead mite. "Find somewhere to bury it."

"Is that all?" Gruffbar asked.

"Some people have crossed me, and those people are going to regret it. For now, not maintaining the mites gives me some power back. Enough to try the Splitting Stone once more. Every cloud has a silver lining, and when my plan is complete, I'll be so many clouds that all my enemies will see is darkness.

"Now call the Shadow Men and tell them that I'll cancel their debt if they do a job for me. Some sewer rats need stamping out."

CHAPTER THIRTY

Leontine stretched out in the lumpy bed in his shack in the old, abandoned tunnels. He was feeling more content than he had expected. After the victory over the shadow mites, Lucy and Charlie had insisted on feeding all of the teenagers dinner, then packing them some food for the next day's breakfast. It felt weird to have an adult looking after him like that again. He was so used to being independent, to looking after his companions instead of having anyone look after him, that it took some adjusting to. It wasn't a bad feeling to know that somebody cared.

He rolled over and stared out the door of the shack, struggling to get to sleep. His days weren't always quiet, but he couldn't think of one that had ever been as busy in actions, words, and feelings as this one had been. He needed the rest, but his brain wouldn't slow down enough to switch off.

Down the tunnel, something was moving. It was only a shadow at the moment, but a humanoid shadow, with two arms and two legs. Leontine tried to work out who it was.

Everybody had come home after the dinner with the Herons, and he had been the last to go to bed. One of the others must have been equally restless and got up for a walk.

Except that they weren't walking like anyone he knew. Their legs moved in odd ways, folding and unfolding like a length of ribbon, darting across the gap from one shadow to another, then hesitating for a long time before moving on.

Leontine silently pushed off his blanket, pulled on a pair of pants and a shirt, then grabbed a flashlight. He crept out into the dimly lit tunnel, eyes fixed on that shadow as it advanced toward one of the other shacks.

The shadow raised its hands. Leontine saw the shape of a knife, not its metallic glint but its long curve and deadly point, rising against the wall.

"Hey!" He switched the torch on and shone it straight at the intruder.

The torch illuminated a man made of darkness. Not the swarming, shifting darkness of the mites, but flat, unyielding darkness, as if a shadow had been cut from its owner's heels and let loose into the world. It was only in the very center of the blazing torchlight that any features were visible: tiny eyes, a flattened nose, and row upon row of strangely square teeth.

The Shadow Man hissed and reared back against the wall.

"You stay right there." Leontine angrily advanced on him.

Something moved, off to his right. He turned, but it was too late. Another Shadow Man slammed into him, wrapping his arms around Leontine and knocking the torch from his hands.

"Help!" Leontine yelled.

He wrenched his wings free and flapped them hard. The weight of the Shadow Man made it even more difficult than normal to get off the ground, but he lifted himself into the air, straining his wing and shoulder muscles, rotating as he rose thanks to the uneven beat of his mismatched wings. The larger wing buffeted the Shadow Man's face, but he clung on, mouth opening and closing as he tried to bite Leontine.

Other kids were emerging from their beds, rubbing their eyes and looking around, wondering what the fuss was. The smarter ones were switching on lights and starting fires, driving back the darkness so they could see.

A mob of Shadow Men was advancing on them, carrying knives, swords, and clubs that were no less deadly because they were silhouettes. The tallest of them, a Shadow Mage, chanted a string of long, sinister syllables, and the shadows of the shacks shifted, grabbing hold of their inhabitants, trapping some of the kids in place.

Twylan was flinging magic about, blasting the Shadow Men with gusts of wind and arcs of lightning. Other kids mustered their magic, using whatever spells they could remember. Some of the Shadow Men were knocked over or driven back, but others kept advancing.

Leontine's wings were tiring. He couldn't stay up much longer. The Shadow Man clinging to him brought its head around, trying to take a bite out of his side. At last, Leontine got an arm free and punched the Shadow Man in the head. The Shadow Man yelped and let go of him, falling to the ground.

Leontine tapped the pin badge on his shirt.

"If you can hear me, we need your help," he said. "We're under attack. Please, help, now!"

Then his crippled wing gave out on him, and he fell into the mass of Shadow Men.

Lucy was sitting alone in the living room, a book of Jack Vettriano paintings lying forgotten next to her. She cradled her wand with its dark, uneven wood and its narrow gold bands in her hands. There had been a moment during the fighting earlier when she felt as if the wand was trying to redirect her, to reshape her magic. At the time, she had been too busy to think about it, but now, up late and still buzzing from the day's excitement, it was all she could think about.

"Mom?" Ashley crept into the room, dressed in her R2D2 pajamas. "I can't sleep."

"Me neither, sweetheart." Lucy patted the sofa next to her. "Come have a cuddle. Maybe we'll both sleep better after that."

Ashley gratefully climbed onto the sofa and snuggled up next to her mother, who wrapped a protective arm around her.

"I don't suppose there's anything in that big brain of yours about how wands work?" Lucy tapped the top of Ashley's head.

"No, I don't do magic," Ashley said softly, her eyes

sliding shut. "Ask Dylan."

"Maybe I will. I clearly need to listen to you kids more."

There was a crackle of static, then Leontine's voice burst into the room:

"If you can hear me, we need your help. We're under attack. Please, help, now!"

Lucy and Ashley stared for a moment at the badge pinned to the R2D2 pajamas. Then Lucy leapt to her feet.

"I have to go," she said.

"I'll get the others," Ashley said, yawning hugely.

"No, you'll all stay here," Lucy said, putting on her sneakers. "You've been in enough danger today." She kissed Ashley on the forehead. "If you don't hear from me in an hour, wake your dad up."

Then she ran out the door, got into her SUV, and sped into the night.

As she drove through LA, her wand sat in the passenger seat next to her.

"Whatever you were trying to do earlier, I could use your help now," Lucy said. "Those kids need me."

The wand was silent, as wands usually were.

She pulled up in the alley where she'd previously entered the teenagers' tunnels and followed the same route down into darkness, using the torch to light her way. This time she ran down tunnels and jumped down ladders, unwilling to waste even a moment. If Leontine had called for help, then he must really need it.

She sprinted down a final ramp and into the cavernous tunnel where the outcast kids had their shanty-town. The flicker of fires and stark glare of electric bulbs cast uneven light across a scene of frantic action. The kids were at war, desperately fighting against the flat, black shapes of the Shadow Men, a monstrous gang about whom Lucy had heard only rumors before. Shapes shifted back and forth as the Shadow Men grabbed and stabbed, trying to hunt the teenagers down, while those same teens ran, dodged, and fought back when they could. Bit by bit, the kids were being herded back toward their ramshackle shelters, where some of them stood bound in sheets of shadow. Even Twylan, flinging magic out to the left and right, was forced to retreat although she kept herself between the monsters and her more vulnerable friends.

"Oy!" Lucy yelled, her voice echoing around the tunnel.

The Shadow Men turned to look at her.

"Dormeo." She pointed her wand at the nearest Shadow Man, who immediately fell to the ground, fast asleep. "Take that, sunshine."

Some of the Shadow Men were still facing the teenagers, but others advanced on Lucy, their silhouettes of weapons raised.

"Form to contain in bonds of chain," Lucy chanted.

Chains shot from her wand and wrapped themselves around two of the Shadow Men. Another one lunged at Lucy with a knife. She dodged out of the way, then punched him in the side of the head as he went past.

The tallest one emerged from the other Shadow Men, hands raised as he gathered magical power. The light shifted around the Shadow Mage, and he pulled it out of the air, crushing it together into a blazing ball of heat that he flung at Lucy.

"Ire tenebras," she chanted while waving her wand, and

the fiery ball evaporated right before it hit her. "You like to play with fire, huh? Pictura flammae!"

A wall of flames raced from her down the tunnel. Shadow Men leapt back in panic, trying to escape the fire. Some lost their footing and fell. The fire swept over them, and they looked up in confusion as it failed to burn.

"Just an illusion," Lucy said, striding along behind the spell. "Unlike these."

She cast the chains again and again, binding the Shadow Men where they lay on the ground.

A large group of them scattered as the flames approached. In the middle of where they had been, Leontine stood, puffing and panting, his face and his knuckles bruised.

"You made it," he gasped in relief.

"Sorry I took so long."

Together, they strode toward the remaining Shadow Men. The illusory flames had dispersed, leaving the remnants of the gang surrounded by angry teens.

Towering above his companions, the Shadow Mage raised his hands. This time, they were closed into fists instead of open and calling in magic.

"We will leave," he hissed.

"Like hell you will!" Leontine growled.

"Wait." Lucy held the young Arpak back. "Better to let him go. Enough people have been hurt already."

"We will all go," the Shadow Mage added.

"Oh, no." Lucy pointed at the Shadow Men bound on the floor. "There has to be a price for this, and the ones I've captured already will pay it: off to Trevilsom Prison for magical assault."

"If I don't agree?"

"Then we keep fighting. More of us get hurt, and you all end up in jail."

Silence fell. The only movement was the shifting of flames in old oil drums.

"Very well." The Shadow Mage lowered his hands. The Shadow Men gathered around him, and together they walked from the hall, their movements like paper folding and unfolding, flat and unnatural.

"One more thing," Lucy called after them.

The Shadow Mage turned. "What?"

"Who sent you?"

"Zero, the loan shark under the tar pits."

"Why would you admit that so easily?"

The shadows rippled. "Our debt to him is paid. He's nothing to us now."

With that, the Shadow Men disappeared up the ramp.

"That's it," Leontine growled. "We need to go deal with this Zero guy once and for all."

"Tomorrow." Lucy yawned. "I have a plan, but thwarting evil can wait until we've had a good night's sleep."

CHAPTER THIRTY-ONE

Lucy stood at the end of Lake Pit, enjoying a brief moment of quiet before the storm. It was early in the morning with only the occasional jogger passing. The perfect time for business that she didn't want watched. Dawn really was the most magical moment.

She slid her hand into her pocket and touched her wand. A memory of a childhood dream came to her as if from nowhere, a dream in which she had ridden an elephant like the one at the end of the pit. Only hers had been pink, and she had ridden it to school. Today, she would be going somewhere far more dangerous, and she wouldn't have an elephant although she would have some other help.

From her other pocket, she took out a shiny green acorn and held it to her lips. "Heather," she whispered. "It's time."

Farther down the lake, the bark of a tree pulsed, then the chief of the Tolderai stepped out of it, dressed in a flannel shirt and patched jeans. In her hand was a wand. She walked around the pit to where Lucy stood.

"You're sure?" Heather asked.

"I'm sure."

"Then let's do this."

Heather led Lucy away from the lake and into a low concrete structure. She touched a magical sigil hidden in the rough surface of the concrete, and the floor fell away, revealing a staircase into the ground.

"How did you know how to reach him?" Lucy asked.

"My people have always known. He's a scar on our hearts, one that can only be healed with blood. We feel him always. We could always reach him, but this is the first time in centuries that we think we can win."

More Tolderai emerged from nearby trees. Silently, they followed Lucy and Heather down those stairs, into darkness.

The staircase was dirty concrete, illuminated by old electric lights. Lucy felt as though she was walking into somewhere rotten. It would have been dispiriting, except that she was determined to see this through.

At the bottom of the stairs was a cave lined with a thick layer of hardened tar. Electric light gleamed off its surface. At the back of the hall stood a tall black crystal oozing with power, the heart of a kemana.

Gnomes turned as the witches and wizards walked into the cavern. Some of the gnomes ran away when they saw who was coming. Others pulled weapons from their belts. Some stood frozen on the spot, looking from the intruders to the creature who sat in front of the crystal. Tar seeped down the sides of his chair, and a large wooden chest sat in front of him with a smaller one beside it.

Zero looked up, his eyes bulging.

"I'm busy," he gurgled. "Come back later."

"We're not here to do business," Lucy said. "We're here to stop you."

Zero's laughter sounded more like a belch than any sound of amusement Lucy had ever made.

"Stop me?" he asked. "I'd like to see you try."

He raised his hands and magic swirled around them. It was dark and sticky, like tar oozing from the air. The sort of power that clung and stained. "I'll blot you out where you stand. No one defies me in my lair."

"We did." Heather stepped forward, and the rest of the Tolderai fanned out to either side of her. One of the gnomes stalked up to them clutching a mace, but then Mackam lunged forward, his gray beard swinging wildly and his eyes full of madness, a hunter's knife in his hand, and the gnome scurried back in fear.

"You!" Zero exclaimed, his eyes going wider than ever.

"Us."

The Tolderai chanted, their spell becoming a song, swirling music whose words meant nothing to Lucy, but that filled the air around her. Sounds of strength and determination.

The magic around Zero's hands faded away. The tar on his skin dried up and fell into dust. The glistening walls of the cave went dull as the magic of the tar pit was cut off.

"This time, we will finish what we started," Heather said.

"Oh no!" Zero clasped his hands to his mouth. "How

can I survive without the magic I've leached from this land? I'm doomed, doomed I tell you, d—"

His impression of distress collapsed as he burst out laughing.

"I can't do it," he said. "This is too funny to take seriously. You think that, all these centuries later, I'm still that vulnerable? That I haven't prepared for a moment like this? It wasn't my power anyway. I took it from the creature that came before me here, and now I've taken power from those who came after."

He flung back the lid of the larger chest. Inside were heaps of crystals, rune stones, and magical artifacts, a treasure trove of power. Lucy could feel its strength through the kemana's magic, like heat blasting from a furnace. Zero thrust his hands into the heap and grinned.

"I'll use this power to steal your power," he said. "And with that, well..." He flipped back the lid of the other chest, revealing the Splitting Stone. "You don't need to know about that because you'll be dead before it ever matters."

Heather laughed, a fierce, uncompromising sound.

"That sort of magic takes time." She pointed at the gnomes. "You think these can hold us back?"

"No." Zero shook his head. "I've been gathering other debts, other sources of wealth. Enough to buy me some assistance. Gruffbar!"

The dwarf emerged from a side cavern. Behind him came a sizeable mercenary force: elves, dwarves, Arpak, Kilomea, rogue wizards, and witches. Some carried weapons, some held wands, and all looked as hard as the walls of the cave.

Zero placed one hand on the crystal behind him and one on the heap of treasure.

"Deal with them," he ordered. "I have a master plan to complete."

The mercenaries charged, and the Tolderai lunged to meet them. Swords, spears, and axes clashed. Magic sizzled in the air. A shotgun roared.

Lucy fired a length of chain at one of the Kilomea. He dodged, and the chain didn't wrap around him, but it hit him in the leg and knocked him to the ground. An ax fell from his grasp, and Lucy kicked it away.

A blast of cold caught her in the back. Her protective amulet absorbed part of the spell, preventing her from being frozen in place, but the icy tendrils stung as they spread across her flesh. She turned to see a gnome with her hands raised, chanting as she gathered another spell.

"Obliviscatur." Lucy gestured with her wand.

The gnome blinked and looked around in confusion, the magic falling away from her hands. "What was I doing?"

Before the gnome could get her senses back, Lucy hit her with another spell, knocking her out cold.

Something in the air tugged at Lucy. She looked around and realized that it was coming from Zero. Dozens of magical tendrils reached out from him, nearly invisible, sucking the power from the air. He drew on every spell cast, whether it hit, missed, or was countered, using what he had to make himself ever more powerful. His orange body bulged, and his mouth hung open as he soaked up the battle's magic.

She wanted to stop so her power wouldn't feed him

anymore. Then he would win anyway. She had to fight on, had to try to get to him.

At the side of the room, Gruffbar fought Mackam, the dwarf swinging his shotgun with the ax blades on the side, the Tolderai leaping back and forth, darting and jabbing with a wand and a hunting knife.

"I'm going to gut you, little warrior," Mackam said. "Gut you and read the entrails, oh yes."

"I'm not a warrior. I'm just a damn lawyer."

Gruffbar blocked a knife stab, then finally managed to hit the wizard in the side of the head with the flat of his ax. Stunned, Mackam staggered back, and Gruffbar took the chance to run. He hadn't signed up for this.

He was nearly at the foot of the stairs when the sound of footsteps stopped him. Someone was coming. He ducked down behind a pile of boxes and waited to see what came next.

In the middle of the cavern, Heather felt the ancient ways of her people flow through her. She swung and stabbed with the ghost of a spear, a magically summoned memory of a weapon her ancient ancestor had used. The weapon looked like nothing more than a wisp of air, but it was strong as steel. She caught a sword blow on it, then swung the spear up and ran a mercenary through. As he fell, she jerked the spear back and looked for her next opponent. But the spear was starting to fade, its magic sucked away by Zero, and she couldn't reach him through the crowd of his hired guards.

She snatched up a fallen sword and looked around. Her people were outnumbered, surrounded, the mercenaries closing in. Like her ancestors before her, she stood with her tribe, ready to die for their cause. She spat to ward off bad luck, then braced herself as an Arpak charged at her.

By the crystal, Zero throbbed with power. He had never felt like this before, never let himself consume so much of what he'd hoarded. This was it, the moment it had all led to. With trembling hands, he took the Splitting Stone out of its chest and felt it pulling him in two. Everything else in the world faded. This was his moment.

Across the room, Twylan and Charlie ran from the bottom of the stairs, flinging magic out in front of them. A blast of Twylan's lightning left three gnomes twitching on the floor, while Charlie turned the ground to mud beneath a fourth so he sank up to his neck.

Leontine burst out between them, leading the rest of the teenage gang. They charged into the fight using whatever powers they had, some casting spells, others wrestling the mercenaries to the ground. The cavern filled with the cacophony of the ever-growing battle.

Bringing up the rear, Dylan, Ashley, and Eddie reached the bottom of the stairs.

"We have to stay here, remember." Ashley set Octo down. "We promised."

"I know," Dylan said. "I can still do this."

He waved his wand, and a cluster of vines shot from the ground. They wrapped around one of the mercenaries and dragged him down, squirming and yelling.

"I guard." Eddie turned himself into a bulldog.

Ashley hit a string of buttons on Octo's remote control. The robot scuttled up the wall on suckered feet.

Near the far side of the cavern, Heather was advancing. She held her wand in one hand, power radiating from it to form a shield, and with her other, she swung a sword. This wasn't the way her people fought, but it would do. Any weapon was good enough if it meant she could reach Zero.

An Arpak flew over her, wielding a heavy stone club. Heather parried his first attack, then clipped his wing with her sword. With a grunt of pain, he swung his club, and it smashed into her shield, knocking her to the ground. He stood over her, club raised, ready to bring it crashing down.

Magical chains shot out of the air, knocking the weapon from his hands. More chains followed, binding him and flinging him to the floor.

"Here." Lucy held out a hand to help Heather up.

"Look out." Heather lunged, her sword sliding between Lucy's arm and her body, skewering the elf who had been about to stab her from behind.

"We're almost through." Lucy helped the Tolderai chief to her feet.

At last, they emerged from the far side of the fighting to see Zero sitting in front of his heap of loot, the Splitting Stone in his lap. His body was dividing down the middle, skin stretching, muscles splitting, bones duplicating. Two versions of the same face stared at them.

"This is it." Zero laughed wildly. "All I needed was to take your power."

Lucy stepped forward, and it felt like she had walked into a wall. A magical barrier stretched from the floor almost to the ceiling, blocking their way.

"Too late," Zero cackled. "Far too late."

By the bottom of the stairs, Gruffbar emerged from behind the pile of boxes. The only people between him and escape were a couple of kids. This would be easy. He pointed the shotgun at them and put on his most menacing expression, the one he used to shut up stupid clients.

"Get out of my way," he said.

The kids' eyes went wide at the sight of the gun. The girl stepped back, raised hands clutching a controller. The boy stared at Gruffbar, a wand shaking in his hand.

"You think you can cast faster than I can shoot?" Gruffbar said. "I don't want to hurt you, kid, but I will."

There was a growl. Gruffbar looked down to see a bulky bulldog less than a foot from his leg.

"Ah." Gruffbar froze. "Good boy?"

The dog sank its teeth into Gruffbar's shin. He screamed and tried to shake it off, lost his balance, and fell.

"Eddie, get back!" the boy shouted.

The bulldog let go. There was a burst of magic, and a tree burst from the ground under Gruffbar. It thrust him up until he was pressed against the ceiling, trapped by a branch.

"Tree, meet ax." He swung his shotgun. The ax blade sank deep into the branch. There was a crack, a splintering sound, and Gruffbar fell, crashing through several more branches on the way down.

He landed inches from the boy wizard, grabbed the kid's ankle, and pulled him down too. The wand went rolling away across the floor, and the bulldog chased after it. Gruffbar scrambled to his feet, grabbed his shotgun, and ran up the stairs.

At the far end of the room, Heather hammered her fist against the magical barrier while Lucy cast every spell she could think of to break through. The wall held.

"Let me try," Twylan said, appearing beside them with her wand raised. "Diffluo!"

A steam-like spray of power hit the barrier, and it started to waver.

"Too little," Zero said, his two mouths opening in unison. "Far too late."

He still clutched the Splitting Stone, his face and the artifact bathing in the power of the magic gathered in the chest. He imagined how much more he would have with a dozen of him all working together, a hundred even. The world would be his for the taking.

He trembled as the split ran farther through him, down past his belly to his hips. New legs tore away from the old. It was almost done. Any moment now...

Ashley peered past the tree and flicked her remote control. Octo took a few more steps across the ceiling, over the top of the magical barrier. Then its suckers receded, and it fell.

Octo landed in the chest of loot, scattering crystals and rune stones in every direction. Some of them popped through the barrier, riddling it with holes. Others slid away across the floor.

Zero cried out as his power faded. He should still have enough. He must have enough. Only a little longer, that was all he needed, a minute more...

The Splitting Stone tugged at him. He struggled to contain its power, to guide it, to become two without being torn apart.

Then Lucy stepped through the tattered barrier and kicked the chest over, spilling the remnants of Zero's stolen power across the room.

For the briefest moment, both of Zero's mouths hung open. Then there was a rush of power, and a spattering sound as the Splitting Stone tore him apart.

Lucy wiped orange goo from her eyes and looked around. The mercenaries, seeing their employer dead, dropped their weapons and raised their hands. They weren't getting paid this time, but they could at least improve their chances of living. The gnomes did the same.

"That's a lot of prisoners," Twylan said.

"It is," Lucy agreed, then raised her voice. "I'm going to have to call the Silver Griffins to take them all in."

Without any visible signal passing between them, the Tolderai turned and walked over to the tree that Dylan had summoned. Its bark rippled, and one by one, they vanished into it.

Heather was the last to go. She gave Lucy a single, slow nod, then merged with nature and was gone.

CHAPTER THIRTY-TWO

The Silver Griffins' LA headquarters under the Observatory was the busiest that Lucy had ever seen it. Every spare agent had been brought in. Some were processing the mercenaries and gnomes, while others were sifting through the vast heaps of magical artifacts recovered from Zero's lair. A few were already looking at the next steps, making plans to raid the pawnshops and investigate other businesses connected to Zero. Even by the standards of the busy LA office, this was a huge bust.

Lucy stood in a corner of the main office with her family. She felt nervous as well as proud. Today would go down in the history books, and it wouldn't have happened without her and the other Herons. Still, explaining it all was awkward—trying to keep the Tolderai secret without lying to her employers and explaining the part her kids had played in revealing and defeating Zero without sounding like she was exaggerating.

"That's quite a choice you made," Kelly Petrie said.

"Involving your family instead of calling in the rest of the Griffins."

"Kelly raises a good point," Roger Applegate said. "Why did you deal with it like that?"

Lucy glared at Kelly, who was grinning smugly. She clearly thought that this situation would leave Lucy in a lot of trouble and ensure that Kelly got the promotion they were both after. If Kelly could nudge the regional manager's opinion in a particular direction, she was going to do it.

"It wasn't really a choice," Lucy said. "The kids involved themselves. Then they brought in the underground teens when we were attacked. Everything else followed from there."

Eddie, who had been curling around Lucy's ankles in the form of a cat, turned into a crow and fluttered up onto a desk, where he pecked at a pile of papers.

"Your son seems a little agitated." Applegate raised an eyebrow.

"No, this is normal for him." Lucy sighed. "Eddie, stop messing with people's work, please."

Eddie fluttered down off the desk, turned into a snake, and slithered away across the floor.

"Charlie, could you go after him?"

Charlie looked up from one of the computers. "What's that?"

"You know you don't have to fix things here, right?" Lucy smiled at him. "Your support work is in a whole other company."

"I was curious about what software they run and how the network's set up."

"That's lovely, sweetheart, but could you save your curiosity for a minute and go retrieve Eddie? He's just turned into a monkey and is trying to climb the snack machines."

As Charlie hurried away, Jackie appeared, carrying a tray of cups and glasses. Lucy's friend looked less fazed by the busy day than many of the other Silver Griffins.

"I wouldn't normally play waitress," she said, "but you guys look like you need these."

She handed Lucy a cup of tea, set a coffee down where Charlie had been sitting and held a glass of juice out to Dylan, who was playing with a set of magically empowered handcuffs.

"You should probably leave those alone." Jackie took them from him. "Don't want to wind up locked in them."

"I wanted to see what spells they use to open," Dylan said. Then his eye fell on a magical top hat with an evidence tag hanging from its brim. "Ooh, what does that one do?"

While Jackie set about distracting Dylan with gadgets, Ashley took one of the other glasses of juice, then turned to Applegate with a serious expression on her face.

"Excuse me, Mister Applegate," she said. "I have a question."

"Of course, young lady." Applegate thrust his hands into the pockets of his suit and beamed down a patronizing smile. "Fire away."

"Will the mercenaries be charged under Section 237 or Section 419 of the Magical Crimes Code?"

"My, that's an insightful question." Applegate blinked at

her in surprise. "Section 419 seems best, given that they attacked a Silver Griffin agent."

"What if some of them have only recently come to Earth? They could plead immunity to it under the cultural norms clause."

"Well, yes, I suppose so. But that one carries stiffer penalties. Don't you want to see these bad men locked up for as long as we can?"

"You don't need to use short words with me. I'm not Eddie. Will sentencing considerations be more important than consistency of narrative when you get them in front of a judge?"

Applegate laughed uncomfortably and tugged on his collar. "Prosecutions aren't my area of expertise. I'm a manager rather than a lawyer."

"Could I talk to a lawyer?"

"They're a little busy right now," Lucy said. "Why don't you fix the damage to Octo, and we can talk about this later?"

"Okay."

Ashley lifted her dented robot onto an empty desk, pulled out a screwdriver, and started opening Octo's case.

"Sorry about that." Lucy turned back to Applegate. "They're good kids, but they're not used to being in an office. I'll get them out of here, and we can focus on Silver Griffin business."

"Actually, I wanted to talk to you before they go," Applegate said. "While your strategy against Zero was unconventional, it worked. Ashley found the disinformation network, Charlie's and Dylan's magic was crucial in beating the shadow mites, and I'm sure the little chap played his part."

The regional manager smiled at Eddie, who had returned in human form, sitting on Charlie's shoulders.

"I was a mole," Eddie said proudly and waved his hands.

"A very helpful mole, I'm sure. Anyway, the point I'm trying to make is this. You worked very well as a family unit. Your skills complement each other, and your children's gifts proved invaluable in bringing down a substantial crime ring. I wondered if you would consider working for us as a family in a more official role, from time to time."

Lucy stared at him, open-mouthed. That was about as far as things could get from the reprimand she had expected.

"Sir, I'm not sure you've thought this through." Kelly looked aghast. "Becoming a Silver Griffin takes years of training, careful instruction, a willingness to follow the rules..."

"I'm not saying they all become official Griffins," Applegate said. "That's hardly in my power. But we can use contractors, and while that normally means bounty hunters, I don't see why it shouldn't include other assets as they become available."

Dylan glared at Applegate. "Who are you calling an—"

"Asset means resource." Lucy cut him off. "He means that you're very useful."

"Oh. Well, okay then." Dylan picked up a wand off the desk next to him and gave it an experimental wave. "Will we get to use Griffin artifacts?"

"I'm not sure we should be doing this at all." Lucy looked around at her family. "It's a big change to our lives."

"It sounds like a great idea to me," Jackie said. "Look at you all, the IT wizard, the kid genius, the wizard so powerful he summoned a forest by accident, the kid who can disguise himself as any animal he likes. You're going to do great work. You might as well be recognized for it."

"But there are rules," Kelly protested. "Ways things are supposed to be done."

"This is one thing you'll have to learn if you want to be a manager, Kelly," Applegate said. "How to find the rules that suit you. Now, Lucy, what do you think?"

"I think I need to talk to Charlie." She grabbed her husband's hand and dragged him away to a quiet corner of the room. "Well, what do you think?"

"The kids would love it," he said. "Hell, I'd love it, the chance to work with you and do something more than fix broken laptops."

"It could get dangerous."

"Then we ask for a veto over the missions. The family only gets involved when we approve it."

"I don't want the Griffins taking over our lives."

"Again, we use the veto. That way we can do some good while keeping this under parental control."

"It was good knowing that you guys were there to have my back."

"Tell me what's bothering you."

"I suppose I'm used to work and family being separate."

"That was never going to last, not with kids as magically gifted as ours. Sooner or later, they were going to cross paths with the Griffins. At least this way, we're doing it on our terms."

"You're so smart sometimes." Lucy kissed him.

"Only sometimes?"

"All the time." She hesitated. "Still, I don't want to tell Applegate everything, like how much Ashley can do with computers or the extent of the underground network they've built. The kids should have some things they keep for themselves."

"Agreed."

"Okay, we're doing this then?"

Charlie grinned. "You know what they say: the family that fights crime together stays together."

"Who says that?"

"Us, from now on."

They went back across the room to where the kids played with circuit boards and artifacts while Kelly frantically tried to change Applegate's mind. The manager looked up as they approached and raised an eyebrow.

"Well?" he said. "Do I get my shiny recruits?"

"Yes, boss," Lucy said. "From now on, the Herons work for the Silver Griffins."

Three-Ingredient Peanut Butter Cookies (Ashley's favorite)

If you can stir, you can make this recipe. Bonus – it's naturally gluten free and goes over big at the school bake sale. Great for last minute baking when a mission goes overtime.

For a little extra something-something - press a Hershey's Kiss in the center of each cookie before baking.

Set the oven to 350 degrees or 175 degrees Celsius in my kitchen.

- 1 cup sugar
- 1 egg
- 1 cup smooth peanut butter

Stir and spoon round balls onto a baking sheet. Flatten with a fork in two directions to make a criss-cross design. Or do it up Heron style and add that chocolate Kiss in the center.

Bake for 10 minutes and let cool on baking pan.

Get sneak peeks, exclusive giveaways, behind the scenes content, and more. PLUS you'll be notified of special **one day only fan pricing** on new releases.

Sign up today to get free stories.

Visit: https://marthacarr.com/read-free-stories/

AUTHOR NOTES - MARTHA CARR
FEBRUARY 10, 2021

Thanks for checking out Secret Agent Mom, a new Oriceran series! I've always wanted to do a series on the Silver Griffins and love the idea of witches in minivans saving the world.

If you try my fave peanut butter cookie recipe, let me know how it turns out. If you can stir, you can do this recipe. Every book will have a recipe tucked in the back. Most of them will be super simple and all of them will have been tested by me.

Anybody here a homeowner? If you are, you're probably familiar with apps like Nabr or Next Door. A kind of Facebook for just your neighborhood meant to facilitate connections.

Neighbors can post questions about where to find a good lawn guy or a handyman. Others will post that they're selling homemade bread or cookie kits you can do with your kids. Or there's a shout out for a new restaurant nearby or reports of a lost pet.

However, if you've been on any of these sites for longer

than, say, a week, you also know things quickly devolve into bickering or weirdness.

It starts slowly with reports of a suspicious car circling the neighborhood. Did anyone else see it? Then pictures of dog poop left on a sidewalk pop up with comments of mild outrage, or there's vague references to someone's oversized pergola and was that HOA approved?

Then the fun really starts.

My recent favorite was after an airing of 911 Lone Star, a Fox show about firemen set in Austin that always leaves me with the impression they went from the airport to 6th Street but not really anywhere else. The episode was about a fake volcano under a stretch of land in South East Austin that suddenly erupts swallowing a mini golf course and melts the skin off some guy I kind of recognized.

I live in South East Austin and it didn't take long for someone to post that they'd done some research and maybe there was a volcano in Texas right underneath our feet. Was anyone else worried? There was actual back and forth for a while about the possibility of an eruption.

That's the weirdness – and no, there's no forthcoming pools of lava about to spring forth in all of Texas.

The same week there was another post, complaining about all these people posting with things for sale. Couldn't they do that somewhere else? Mind you, these posts are by our neighbors and directed at our neighbors with things like lawn care or selling Girl Scout cookies or someone starting a yoga class in the field by the big road.

Others quickly agreed and for a while the thread was about how to micromanage posts in a stated pursuit to make everyone happy.

Eventually, others complained about the micromanagement and couldn't everyone just sell whatever they want to sell and if you don't want to buy, just keep on scrolling. The thread went off in a different direction after that.

My neighbor, Claire says she likes to get a glass of wine and read these at night for entertainment.

Of course, mixed in between the weird and the wooly are the announcements for a golf cart parade or a band playing at the amenity center or an HOA meeting. That's what keeps me there, for now. But, every now and then I think about leaving and not knowing the inner workings of my neighbors' brains. Going back to being able to wander past them on the street and giving a wave, blissfully ignorant that they're up in arms about a drug store being built just down the road. Of course, I wouldn't get to see all the poop pictures, but I might be willing to let that go.

More adventures to follow.

First, thank you for reading these author notes here at the back of the book!

Second, I have to admit there will be no discussions of poop pictures. I know you will be depressed.

I'm sorry.

Here in Henderson (right outside of Las Vegas), I am working on a set of beats for a Sword and Sorcery series I develop. The Weather app is suggesting it is a nice 73 degrees. I think that's bollocks.

Everything in the desert is cooler than it has a right to be. In the summer, 106 degrees is excellent swimming weather as soon as the next-door neighbors' house blocks the sun.

And I have a shirt, plus a light jacket on top in order to work outside in the shade when it is in the 70s.

Freaking chilly is what it is. The metal outdoor furniture is sucking the heat out of my body. I've placed a small blanket over the metal back to try to retain some of the life-supporting heat my body creates on its own.

It's a fight I am slowly losing.

(*Editor's note: Think of it this way, Michael...for every hour you spend outside, you can probably drink another Mexican Coke without gaining any weight because trying to keep warm burns calories like almost nothing else! There's your pot of gold at the end of the freezing rainbow.*)

What else am I working on?

I mentioned working on a Sword & Sorcery above. But after that, I will be working on a rather crude space-opera story for my Michael Todd pen name. That name does not particularly care about the readers' sensitivities and loves a good cartoon that is tasteless but humorous. Which leads me to...

The Infamous Title

With all the books I work on, titles (and coming up with new ones) are a constant challenge. For the Michael Todd books (*The Unlikely Bounty Hunters* series), the first title is rock-solid and not very inappropriate.

It's called *Code Blue: Alien Jail Break.*

But the second title is causing a bit of consternation with Zen Master Steve™ (for those who don't know, we coined the term Zen Master Steve™ for Steve Campbell, who is the VP of Operations here at LMBPN. He brings a fun and often funny perspective while civilizing the crazy conditions we encounter while publishing so many books a month).

(*Editor's note: who creates those crazy conditions, Michael? Asking for a friend.*)

Anyway, the second book's title is *Anal Probes Suck A$$.* (See, even here, I have to hide the name!) I chuckle every time I see it. Unfortunately, some in the company have a concern the title will put off a few readers.

Probably.

The reason that isn't a bad thing is if the cover title doesn't fit a reader's sense of humor, I guarantee the insides won't. I like to think of it as truth in advertising.

Steve prefers not to think about it at all.

I warned him yesterday that if he keeps giving me too much grief, book 03's title is still open, and I can put his last name, Campbell, into it. I hope he doesn't call my bluff. I wouldn't really do that to him.

(Editor's note: Who are you kidding?)

Until the next book!

Ad Aeternitatem,

Michael

Solve a murder, save her mother, and stop the apocalypse?

What would you do when elves ask you to investigate a prince's murder and you didn't even know elves, or magic, was real?

Meet Leira Berens, Austin homicide detective who's good at what she does – track down the bad guys and lock them away.

Which is why the elves want her to solve this murder – fast. It's not just about tracking down the killer and bringing them to justice. It's about saving the world!

If you're looking for a heroine who prefers fighting to flirting, check out The Leira Chronicles today!

<u>**AVAILABLE ON AMAZON AND IN KINDLE UNLIMITED!**</u>

OTHER SERIES IN THE ORICERAN
UNIVERSE

THE LEIRA CHRONICLES

SOUL STONE MAGE

THE KACY CHRONICLES

MIDWEST MAGIC CHRONICLES

THE FAIRHAVEN CHRONICLES

I FEAR NO EVIL

THE DANIEL CODEX SERIES

SCHOOL OF NECESSARY MAGIC

SCHOOL OF NECESSARY MAGIC: RAINE CAMPBELL

ALISON BROWNSTONE

FEDERAL AGENTS OF MAGIC

SCIONS OF MAGIC

THE UNBELIEVABLE MR. BROWNSTONE

DWARF BOUNTY HUNTER

MAGIC CITY CHRONICLES

ACADEMY OF NECESSARY MAGIC

OTHER BOOKS BY JUDITH BERENS

OTHER BOOKS BY MARTHA CARR

**JOIN THE ORICERAN UNIVERSE FAN GROUP ON
FACEBOOK!**

BOOKS BY MICHAEL ANDERLE

Sign up for the LMBPN email list to be notified of new releases and special deals!

https://lmbpn.com/email/

For a complete list of books by Michael Anderle, please visit:

www.lmbpn.com/ma-books/

CONNECT WITH THE AUTHORS

Martha Carr Social

Website: http://www.marthacarr.com

Facebook: https://www.facebook.com/
groups/MarthaCarrFans/

Michael Anderle Social

Website: http://lmbpn.com

Email List: http://lmbpn.com/email/

Social Media:

https://www.facebook.com/LMBPNPublishing

https://twitter.com/MichaelAnderle

https://www.instagram.com/lmbpn_publishing/

https://www.bookbub.com/authors/michael-anderle